How to Kiss Your Enemy

Center Point
Large Print

Also by Jenny Proctor and available from Center Point Large Print:

Love Redesigned
Love Unexpected
Love Off-Limits
Love in Bloom
How to Kiss Your Best Friend
How to Kiss Your Grumpy Boss

How to Kiss Your Enemy

A SWEET ROMANTIC COMEDY

JENNY PROCTOR

Center Point Large Print
Thorndike, Maine

This Center Point Large Print edition
is published in the year 2024 by arrangement with
Jenny Proctor Creative LLC.

Copyright © 2023 by Jenny Proctor Creative.

All rights reserved.

The text of this Large Print edition is unabridged.
In other aspects, this book may vary
from the original edition.
Printed in the United States of America
on permanent paper sourced using
environmentally responsible foresting methods.
Set in 16-point Times New Roman type.

ISBN: 979-8-89164-301-7

The Library of Congress has cataloged this record
under Library of Congress Control Number: 2024940072

How to Kiss Your Enemy

CHAPTER ONE
Lennox

Tatum *freaking* Elliott. Thousands of chefs in America, and my sister hires *her*.

I'd like to think I've grown up over the years—that since I graduated from culinary school, I've left behind petty rivalries and schoolyard competitions.

But as I watch a black SUV slowly meander down the main drive of Stonebrook Farm, nerves swirling in my gut, I'm beginning to wonder.

I've prepared myself for this moment. I've talked it through with my brothers. I've insisted to my sister, over and over, that, despite my initial freakout when she hired *THE* Tatum Elliott to be the new catering chef at the commercial farm and event center my family owns, I would be fine.

Fine with a capital F. Because I'm totally chill. A fully grown adult who is perfectly capable of leaving my history with Tatum in the past so we can get along like mature, civilized adults.

I reach up and run a hand across my beard, then stick a finger under the neck of my chef's coat, pulling the fabric away from my skin. Has it always felt so tight? So stiff? I might as well be wearing the too-small snowsuit my grandmother gave me for Christmas the year I turned seven. I had nightmares about that thing suffocating me for weeks.

Outside, the black Mercedes S-Class SUV rolls to a stop. It figures she's still driving a Mercedes. She had one back in school, too.

With the winter sun shining down on the windshield, the glare keeps me from actually *seeing* whoever is driving the car, but it has to be Tatum. The U-Haul trailer hitched to the back of her SUV and the California license plate affixed to her front bumper are evidence enough.

I can't believe she's really here.

Not that I have any room to argue. Olivia gave me the chance to sit in on the interviews and offer opinions about who I thought would best fit the Stonebrook Farm culture.

I'm the idiot who was too caught up in my own stuff to bother. But how was I supposed to know the chef who, nine years ago, snarkily signed my graduation card "so happy to never see you again" would apply for a job *here,* of all places?

Whatever her reasons for taking a job far below her pedigree, the farm needs a catering chef, and Tatum is whom my sister hired. Olivia and my oldest brother Perry run Stonebrook together, and they do a good job of it, so I have no choice but to get on board and keep my petty complaints to myself.

"What's cooking, Chef?" Zach, my sous chef,

appears beside me, his gaze following mine to the SUV outside. "Who's that?"

I run a hand across my jaw and give my shoulders a roll, a lame attempt to release the tension building there. "The new catering chef," I finally say. "She's moving in today."

Adding an apartment above the catering kitchen was a strategic decision my parents made twenty years ago, hoping the free housing would lure quality chefs out to Silver Creek.

Bet they never guessed they'd get someone as famous as Tatum Elliott. Or, sort of famous, anyway. I can't imagine what she's going to think of the place after the lifestyle she grew up with.

When I first moved home, the apartment was vacant, so I crashed there for a few months. It isn't a bad place to live by any stretch. It's small, but it's clean and recently updated. I would have happily stayed longer had it not been *on* the family farm. Living at work when work is a family-run business? Let's just say that was a lot of *togetherness*.

Another minute goes by without Tatum getting out of her car, and I half-wonder if I should go out and greet her, but I quickly dismiss the thought. This is Olivia's deal, not mine.

I promised my sister I wouldn't get in the way of Tatum doing her job, but that doesn't mean I have to go out and give her some grand welcome.

That would require me to pretend like I'm happy she's here.

My watch vibrates with a text, and I glance down to read it.

> **Olivia:** Tatum has arrived! On my way to meet her now. Can you make sure her kitchen is ready?

I ignore the request, only because this is Olivia being Olivia, worrying like only she can. Tatum's kitchen is fine. Cleaned yesterday after the sous chef and the rest of the catering staff prepared a farewell breakfast for a group of Asheville yoga instructors who booked the farm for a three-day retreat. There aren't any events today, so Tatum will find her kitchen empty and exactly like her staff left it.

That's one point I can be happy about. Tatum and I won't be sharing a kitchen, even if we are working in the same building. The only overlap between Stonebrook's catering kitchen and my farm-to-table full-service restaurant is an enormous walk-in refrigerator, a little bit of shared pantry space, the loading dock and dumpsters out back, and a staff locker room.

Outside, Tatum finally climbs out of her car. She's wearing street clothes—jeans and a light blue sweater—which immediately strikes me as odd. In my memories, she's always wearing chef's whites. Her hair is down, dark curls wild and cascading over her shoulders, another contrast to the way I remember her. In school, she always had her hair slicked back in a tight, no-nonsense bun.

Zach whistles beside me. "The new catering chef is a smoke show."

I scoff at his reaction, but he's not wrong. She's still the same Tatum, but she looks different somehow. More mature. More *beautiful.* A pulse of attraction flares in my gut, catching me by surprise. If this wasn't Tatum Elliott, and I didn't know better, I'd already be thinking of ways to ask the woman out.

Fortunately, I do know better.

"Maybe on the outside," I mumble under my breath.

Don't get me wrong. I didn't *dislike* Tatum when we were in culinary school. But we were from two different worlds. We still are. And she doesn't belong on Stonebrook Farm.

Zach eyes me curiously. "What's that supposed to mean? Do you know her?" His gaze shifts back to Tatum, almost like it's hard for him to look away.

There's a hunger in his expression that ignites something primal, deep in my gut, and I find myself resisting the urge to bodily move in between Zach and the window to block his view.

The impulse doesn't make any logical sense. I

have no claim on Tatum, nor do I want one. Zach can look all he wants.

"We went to culinary school together," I say, proud of how evenly neutral my words sound.

Olivia pulls up in a Stonebrook Farm Gator, one of the oversized utility vehicles staff use to get around the hundreds of acres of farm property. She climbs out and welcomes Tatum, pulling her into a hug like they're long-lost friends.

They talk for a few moments, then Tatum moves to the back of her SUV and opens the hatch. A giant, black and white dog jumps out, tail wagging. Tatum crouches down and scratches the dog's ears, her smile wide as she says something to Olivia over her shoulder, then they both start to laugh.

"Yeah, I see it now, boss," Zach says, his tone dry. "This woman looks like a real monster."

"I never said she was a *monster*. I just don't—" I bite my tongue. I promised my sister I wouldn't say anything to taint my employees' opinions of Tatum. They won't have to work with her directly, but it's still important they respect her. Which means I've already said too much to Zach. "Anyway." I clear my throat. "She's basically culinary royalty."

"What does that mean?" Zach asks.

Olivia and Tatum move toward the door, the dog falling into step beside her, and I feel a sudden need to flee. To look busy. To be doing something other than gawking at them through the dining room windows when Olivia brings her in to show her around.

"It means Christopher Elliott is her father," I say as I turn and head to my office.

I pass the prep cooks already at work in my kitchen. Griffin and Willow are standing close to the saucier station, clearly arguing about something, but I don't bother to intervene. In another half hour, I'll gather the staff for a pre-dinner service meeting, and I have every confidence they'll bring up their frustrations without me chasing after them.

Zach is quick on my heels. "Hold up. You're telling me you went to culinary school with Christopher Elliott's daughter? Did you meet him? What's he like?"

I refrain from saying any of the words that pop into my head at his question. My feelings about Tatum's father definitely won't help my staff maintain their respect.

I lift my shoulders with feigned indifference. "He's exactly what you might expect of a celebrity chef."

Apparently, Zach's expectations are different than mine, because he's practically beaming with starry-eyed wonder. "Man. *Christopher Elliott.* That guy's amazing."

Sure. *Amazing.* If amazing means entitled, arrogant, and condescending.

Zach follows me to my office, pausing in the doorway while I drop into my chair. "I still don't get it. What's the punchline?" He leans against my door jamb, his arms folded.

I lift my eyebrows.

"Come on," he says, like the question is obvious. "Christopher Elliott's daughter? In the middle of nowhere running a catering kitchen that serves farm-style weddings and family reunions?"

I don't like that Zach so easily landed on the question that's been plaguing me since Olivia hired Tatum in the first place.

"Don't forget the corporate retreats," I say.

Zach shakes his head. "Is she any good?"

"She's good enough to work in her father's flagship restaurant in L.A."

"She worked at Le Vin?" Zach asks.

I nod. "That's where she was before coming here."

That she started her career working with one of America's most famous chefs only highlights how different we are. Tatum was always my biggest competition in culinary school. Every exam. Every evaluation. We might as well have been the only two people in class for how focused we were on beating each other. But it never felt like a fair fight. While she was doing unpaid internships shadowing chefs at the finest restaurants in Atlanta, I was *working* my way through school in chain restaurants—washing dishes, prepping vegetables, doing whatever I could to be in a kitchen. *Any kitchen.*

She didn't just have better knives—which she totally did—she had better *everything*. Better resources. Better opportunities. Extra time with professors. More exposure.

All I had was grit.

My parents helped a little, but I have three brothers and a sister, and back then, the farm was still growing. They didn't have the resources that they have now, so all of us found ways to work our way through school, to fight for what we wanted.

But Tatum Elliott didn't need grit. With her father paving the way in signed cookbooks and celebrity appearances, why would she ever need or want a job like this one?

Zach moves closer, leaning against the edge of my desk. "I still don't get it, but I'm not complaining. It can't be a bad thing to have a woman with those kinds of connections hanging around. Especially not one who looks like *that*." He nudges my shoulder, a grin splitting his face. "Be honest. Did you guys ever hook up? She looks like your type." He lifts his hands and mimes the curves of a woman. "And by type, I mean she—"

"Knock it off," I say, offering him my sternest look. "We don't have that kind of history, and I'd rather you not make other people think we do."

"Um, Chef?" Willow appears in the doorway, her eyes wide.

I'd be happy for the distraction—and the end of Zach's insinuations—if Willow didn't look like she'd swallowed an onion whole.

"Hey. What's up?"

She glances over her shoulder, wringing her hands. "Um, there's a goat in the kitchen."

I stare, dumbly trying to process what she's telling me. "What?"

"A goat. White? Red bandana? It kinda looks like the one your brother-in-law is always putting on TikTok. I guess the back door was left open—the seafood guy was just here—and she just wandered up the loading dock. We tried to shoo her back toward the door, but she doesn't seem like she wants to listen."

I breathe out a sigh. There is a *goat* in my kitchen.

Sometimes I wonder why I ever left Charlotte. The city had nightlife. A foodie culture. And *never* livestock in my cooking space unless it was on the menu.

"I'm sure it's Penelope," I say. "Tyler's out of town. She always wanders when he's gone."

Olivia's husband is a videographer by trade, so his TikTok videos featuring the newborn goat he rescued when her mother rejected her are next level. Penelope has a fan base as big as my little brother, Flint's, and Flint has been nominated for a Golden Globe Award.

Regardless of Penelope's fan base, she doesn't belong inside.

Definitely not inside my restaurant.

I'm halfway down the hallway when I hear the *clop-clop* of Penelope's hooves, followed by a loud bark, then an enormous clatter.

I sprint the remaining distance just in time to see Penelope running a lap around the large silver island in the center of my kitchen, Tatum's dog quick on her heels.

My staff is in disarray. Griffin is holding a tray of what looks like pork chops high over his head, and another cook beside him is pressing an armful of cabbages against his chest. All over the room, food and knives are lifted as the animals bump and jostle their way through the kitchen. My soup chef barely manages to steady a jostled pot when the dog cuts a corner too closely and slams full body into the stove.

I stand frozen, scanning the chaos.

There is a goat in my kitchen. There is also a dog in my kitchen, and right now they're playing what looks like a full-contact game of tag.

I don't even know what my life is anymore.

Whatever it is, it violates all kinds of health codes, so I need to do something *fast*.

Penelope lets out a concerned bleat, then makes a sharp right turn, cutting down the hall and heading for my office.

I motion for Zach to follow the goat, then move

around the outside of the kitchen toward the dining room, hoping I can cut off the dog before he chases them both.

This dog is not slowing down though. His attention is laser-focused on Penelope and nothing or no one is getting in his way.

I'm in front of the dining room door when Tatum comes barreling through, too fast for me to move out of the way before she collides into me with a grunt. Her hands slam into my chest, and I stumble backward before wrapping an arm around her waist to stabilize us both.

Our eyes lock, and for a fraction of a second, all of the chaos around us melts away, and I lose myself in the gray-blue of her eyes.

But then Zach yells from the hallway, and Tatum blinks and steps away from me. She raises her fingers to her lips and lets out an ear-piercing whistle.

The dog immediately skids to a stop, trotting over to Tatum like he doesn't have a care in the world. A door slams down the hall, Zach yells, "I've got the goat!" and just as suddenly as the chaos broke out, all is calm.

Calm . . . and a complete disaster.

A trashcan is on its side, its contents spilled. Utensils litter the floor. A pan of marinating chicken breasts is upside down on the tile, though it looks like most of the marinade hit Willow's chest before it landed at her feet.

Olivia is beside Tatum now, her eyes telling me if I'm not on my best behavior, she'll never let me forget it. She may be younger, but my little sister is a fierce boss.

Tatum steps forward. "Lennox. I'm so sorry. I had no idea—I don't think he's ever even seen a goat before. He's never behaved like this."

Her hand sinks to the dog's head, whose tongue is lolling in a way that makes him look like he's smiling. The image almost makes me laugh, but not in a *hahaha-this-is-funny* kind of way. More in a maniacal *barely-keeping-it-together* way.

The stress of her being here in the first place, mixed with an unexpected tug of attraction is a lot on its own. And now my kitchen is in shambles, and it's too much. I'm feeling too much.

My chef's coat is no longer an ill-fitting snowsuit, it's a straitjacket, and I need to escape.

Olivia clears her throat. "It was an accident," she says to Tatum, her voice smooth. "I'm sure Lennox sees that as well as I do."

"An accident," I echo. I run a hand through my hair and force a slow, deep breath. "Look at my kitchen. That chicken has to marinate for at least six hours, and now it's all over the floor. It'll have to be off the menu for tonight, and that—"

"I can figure out a new chicken dish for you," Tatum says. She steps forward, her expression earnest. "I can help."

She can help? Because she's so much more qualified than I am?

The urge to be *away* for a minute—away from this situation, from her—washes over me again. I hold my hands up. "I think you've done enough. Now if you'll excuse me, I have a kitchen to put back in order."

"Lennox, I'm really sorry."

I step forward, closing the distance between us until I'm only inches away. I catch the scent of her, something floral and light that reminds me of Stonebrook's apple orchards in the fall. She lifts her eyes to meet mine, and I hold her gaze for a long moment. I told Olivia I would try, that I could be mature about this whole situation, but it already feels like I'm back in time, complete with all the insecurities and uncertainties that plagued me when I had to compare myself to Tatum every single day.

Whatever transfixed me before has lost its hold. I don't need Tatum's help in my kitchen.

I don't *want* Tatum's help.

"Just stay out of my kitchen, Chef," I say, my tone cool. "And I'll stay out of yours."

CHAPTER TWO
Tatum

I heft a box out of the U-Haul and carry it toward the restaurant's back door, nudging Toby ahead of me. "Come on, boy. This way." If only I could strap a box onto *him,* then he could help instead of just getting underfoot. If he were half as good at hauling boxes as he is at destroying kitchens, we'd finish in no time.

But it's fine. I'm a strong, independent woman. Carrying all these boxes by myself is no. big. deal.

I *loaded* the trailer by myself, after all, though then, I was warmed by the California sunshine and fueled by a healthy dose of righteous indignation. Funny how strong *not wanting to look weak* can make you. With Dad looking on, expecting me to change my mind at any moment, strong was my only option.

A bead of sweat trickles down my face, despite the cold outside, and I will myself to ignore it. My nose twitches with the effort, but the box is too heavy to shift. If I stop and lose my momentum, I'll never make it up this narrow stairwell.

How many steps even are there? Eighty? Eight hundred? This has to be longer than a normal flight of stairs. My biceps are seconds away from giving out when suddenly, I'm at the top, standing on a small landing next to Toby. I drop the box to my feet with a grunt then fish a key out of my pocket.

Olivia planned to show me the apartment, but then she was called back to the farmhouse to handle a disgruntled future bride, and she left me to my own devices, promising she'd be back tomorrow to introduce me to my staff and give me an official tour of the farm. Not that I'm in any hurry to see *any* of the Hawthornes again, after making such a memorable first impression.

I insert the key into the lock, a wave of trepidation washing over me. For the first time, I'm doing something all by myself, *without* my father standing beside me.

"I'm here," I say to myself. "I'm here, and it's *fine*." If I keep repeating it, maybe I'll start to believe it.

I take a steadying breath, and Toby stands, like he senses how monumental this moment is.

The door swings forward, creaking on its hinges, and I take a tentative step inside.

The small space could fit inside my last place fifteen times, but overall, it isn't half bad. The kitchen looks like it's been recently remodeled, and the furniture is clean if a little dated. Everything has a sort of rustic, mountain charm that makes me feel surprisingly at home, even though this place couldn't be more different than what I'm used to.

Above the couch, a double window reveals the rolling pastures of Stonebrook Farm, then just beyond, the Blue Ridge mountains melting into the distance. It's an incredible view, but I'm not sure there's a *bad* view anywhere on Stonebrook. The place looks like it belongs in a movie.

I press my palms into the small of my back and arch backward, relishing the stretch of my tired muscles. Toby nudges against my leg then nuzzles my hand with his cold, wet nose until I shift and start scratching his ears.

"This trick, huh?" He leans in, and I tangle my fingers in his silky goldendoodle coat. He needs a trim—I can hardly see his eyes, his hair has grown so long—but I left California so quickly, I didn't have time to get him in to see the groomer before I was tossing things in a U-Haul.

Moving slowly wasn't an option. My father can be very persuasive, so I had to strike fast, before I lost my nerve, or I never would have made it out of the state.

After my run-in with Lennox this morning, I'm wondering if I should have gone a little slower. Would it have been so terrible if Dad had managed to convince me to stay home?

Home was safe. Predictable.

But it was also a life that didn't feel like mine. At least not at two a.m. when I chased a wild hair and actually applied for this job, though I've second guessed myself a thousand times since then. Sheer momentum carried me forward, but I'll admit there's a certain comfort in knowing that if I go back to California, Dad will be waiting for me with open arms.

In fact, I think he probably expects it, something that makes me all the more determined to make this work. I love my dad. I'm grateful for everything he's done for me, but it's thrilling to be doing something—anything—without him holding my hand.

Even if my *new and independent life* isn't exactly off to an auspicious start. Honestly, I don't think my first day at Stonebrook could have started any worse.

I leave Toby lounging on the couch like he's king of the apartment while I head back down the stairs to get another load of stuff from the U-Haul. I stop halfway down, my way blocked by a giant box moving *up* the stairs.

"Hawthorne complimentary moving service coming through," a deep voice says.

I backpedal until I'm in my apartment, my eyes wide as the box follows me, held securely in the arms of—is that Lennox?

No, it's only someone who *looks* like Lennox. Same jawline. Same eyes. He's a little lankier, his hair a lighter brown, and he doesn't have a beard like Lennox does, but still. He has to be a brother. Especially since he just called himself *Hawthorne moving service.*

The man shifts the box onto the table, but before I can say thank you, or even hello, another man appears in the doorway, also carrying a box.

If it's even possible, this man looks even more like Lennox than the first. His features are a little darker, and he's maybe a little more broody? Though I could just be noticing the contrast between him and the other brother, who hasn't stopped smiling since he walked in.

Either way, Hawthorne family genetics are *strong*.

With the invasion of so much testosterone into my tiny space, Toby is immediately by my side, his body tense.

I drop my hand to his ears, giving him a good scratch and shushing him so he knows he doesn't need to worry.

"Sorry to barge in," the first guy says. "Olivia said you were moving in and thought you might need some help." He extends his hand. "I'm Brody Hawthorne. This is my brother, Perry."

I smile. "Right. Lennox's brothers." It's hard not to be overwhelmed by the sheer manliness that has just entered my very tiny kitchen. Both of these men are married, wedding bands clearly visible, but that doesn't keep me from noticing they are both *gorgeous*.

Like, put them on a calendar and hang them in my kitchen gorgeous.

Almost as gorgeous as Lennox *gorgeous*.

You know. In a strictly observational, not at all interested because that would be delusional kind of way.

Once, back in culinary school, I briefly entertained the possibility of Lennox being *more* than just my publicly declared enemy. Or, I don't know. Maybe *enemy* is a strong word. It's more like we were rivals. We both wanted to be the best, and I was the one standing in his way, and he was the one standing in mine.

He was just as handsome back then, not to mention charming, frustratingly brilliant, and clearly interested in dating because he always had women with him or around him or even just following him around.

But it didn't take long to discern that Lennox never looked at *me* like he did the numerous women he dated. I could have been a robot with arms made out of rolling pins and spatulas for hands for all the attention he paid to my physical appearance.

In hindsight, I think the fact that he *didn't* notice me in that way might have fueled my indignation and resentment, making me want to beat him even more.

But then, for a split second, when I burst into the kitchen and tumbled into Lennox this afternoon, our eyes locked and something sparked, heat growing and filling my limbs like some inexplicable force.

The thought seems ridiculous now, Lennox's dismissal echoing through my mind.

Just stay out of my kitchen, Chef. And I'll stay out of yours.

Me and Lennox?

Ha. Good joke, Tatum. Good freaking joke.

Another set of footsteps sounds on the stairs, and this time it *is* Lennox. The sleeves of his chef's coat are pushed up, his forearms flexing with the effort of holding an enormous box in his arms. The box is bigger than both the ones his brothers were carrying, the word BOOKS written across the side in thick, black Sharpie.

Somehow, I know Lennox picked that box on purpose.

To show me that he could—to demonstrate that if this were a competition, *I* couldn't have carried my heaviest box up the stairs by myself.

And that smug look on his face. I know that look. I saw it every time he scored higher on an exam or managed to garner the highest praise in kitchen evaluations. It's a look that says, *You can't touch me, Tatum Elliott.*

My jaw tightens reflexively. So this is how he wants to play it.

When I took this job, I hoped we'd be able to move past whatever tension kept us at each other's throats and get along like professionals, if not friends. I hoped we might be able to laugh about how immature we were, how silly our competitiveness made us.

Back then, if I'd had a choice between being second to Lennox's number one or tenth to Lennox's number eleven? Oh, give me tenth place, baby. Winning wasn't nearly as important as *beating him.*

But I can't keep up that dynamic now. I just walked out on my entire career—all the connections, the opportunities. I didn't exactly burn bridges, but I'd rather avoid crawling home with my tail between my legs, thank you very much. Especially since that's exactly what my father expects me to do.

Like it or not, I *need* this job to work out. At least for now.

If Lennox is still gunning for a fight, I just have to choose to react differently.

Because *I'm* different now. More mature. More self-aware.

I almost have myself convinced when Lennox lowers my box onto the floor like it's filled with feathers instead of books. And there's that look again, his lips tilting up into a sly, taunting grin.

That's when I open my big, stupid mouth.

"So, I have to stay out of your kitchen, but you get to waltz right into my apartment uninvited?"

I have no idea where the retort comes from. Old habits die hard, I guess.

Lennox lifts an eyebrow. "The way your dog waltzed into my kitchen uninvited?"

I scoff. "Can you blame him, really? I think you might be taking the idea of *farm-to-table* a little too seriously, Lennox."

He smirks and folds his arms across his chest. "Maybe it's just that we do things a little differently . . . *out here in the sticks.*" He says this last part pointedly, and I immediately recall the number of times I insulted him based on where he grew up.

Where I come from, I always said, all full of sanctimony and condescension. Like I had so much more experience than he did.

It's not lost on me that even though I *did* have more experience, even though I was the one given more opportunities after graduation, he's the one who has the career I envy.

I saw press releases about Lennox's restaurant online. I scoured the internet for anything I could find about him after accepting this job, and that included reading his menu at least a dozen times.

But I wasn't prepared to see the place in person.

Before Toby turned into Satan's minion and demolished Lennox's kitchen, I stood by the bar, open-mouthed, and gawked. Hawthorne is perfect. Gorgeous rock work lining the entryway, a tasteful, casual elegance in the dining room.

And if OpenTable reviews are any indication, it isn't just the atmosphere that makes it that way.

I shake my head, irritated that I still find his success so irritating. I should be over this by now. When I decided to take the job, I thought I *was* over it.

Still, it's oddly thrilling to be doing this with him. My pulse is racing, adrenaline coursing through me like it always did whenever we sparred back in school.

I take a step toward him. "You're saying a goat in your kitchen is a regular occurrence?"

He steps forward too, bringing us close enough to touch. "I'm saying Penelope wasn't a problem until your dog showed up."

I bark out a laugh. "The goat has a name? This keeps getting better and better. And how could I have possibly prepared for that? *Hold on, Olivia. I better put my usually perfect dog on a leash in case there happens to be a large farm animal hanging out at Lennox's salad station.*"

Lennox's jaw tightens, fire flashing in his eyes as he steps even closer, his folded arms close enough that I feel the warmth of him radiating off his skin. He's so much taller than I am, I have to look up to keep my eyes on him—probably the whole point of him stepping so close.

"You could have left your dog outside," he says, his deep voice sliding from his lips like smooth caramel dripping off a wooden spoon.

I roll my eyes. "But I *live* inside, which means so does he. How else was I supposed to get him into my apartment?"

Brody clears his throat and steps forward, laughter dancing in his eyes. "Should we give you two some privacy for whatever this is?"

Lennox's gaze darts to his brothers, and the tension building between us snaps and dissipates. He takes an enormous step back, his expression suddenly guarded.

"We're happy to keep moving boxes if you need some time to *catch up,*" Perry says, his words thick with double meaning. The smirk on his face tells me he thinks this thing happening between me and Lennox is some sort of playful, flirty banter.

Which it absolutely is not. Is it?

My face heats, and I press my palms to my cheeks to cool them.

What just happened? What is *still* happening?

"We should all get more boxes," I say a little too quickly. "Right now. I'll go first." I dart out the door, not even looking to see if any of the Hawthorne brothers are following me.

I'm only halfway down the stairs when I hear them scuffling behind me, their whispered voices almost as loud as their footsteps.

I'm too far away to understand them, at least for the most part, but I do catch Lennox whispering a hurried, "Stop it. Don't even think about it," to one of his brothers.

I can't know exactly what they're discussing, but even just the possibility of it being me makes my stomach flip-flop.

When we reach the trailer, I step aside while Perry and Brody grab the only piece of furniture I brought—my favorite, overstuffed reading chair. The apartment is already furnished, but Olivia assured me there would be room under the window in the living room. It'll be a little tight now that I've seen the space, but I'm still glad I brought it.

With his brothers out of the way, Lennox steps up beside me, reaching for the closest box. My hands are already on it, so I pull it toward me.

"I've got it," he says as he tries to tug it out of my hands.

This particular box isn't heavy at all because all that's in it is my underwear and a Harry Styles throw pillow my sister gave me as a gag gift.

Thanks, but no thanks, Lennox Hawthorne. This box, I'd like to carry myself.

I pull it against my chest. "Don't you have somewhere else you need to be?"

He tsks. "Touchy, touchy. You know, I agreed to help my brothers unload your stuff because I thought it might give me a nice chance to apologize, but now? I've changed my mind."

I drop the box onto the edge of the trailer and press a hand against my heart with dramatic flair. "Lennox Hawthorne apologizing? May I live to see the day."

Lennox takes advantage of the moment and grabs the box like he's won some kind of victory, but I immediately grab the opposite side, tugging it toward me. "Seriously, Lennox. Go clean your kitchen or something."

"My kitchen's already clean. I have a very efficient staff."

I roll my eyes and yank a little harder, but he doesn't let go. So help me, I will battle like this all day if it means keeping my underwear out of his hands. "Are they well-practiced in cleaning up after farm animals? Is that a routine part of training this far out *in the sticks?*"

His gaze narrows. "You should try the food before you knock the restaurant, Tatum. Otherwise, you just look jealous."

"Ha! Jealous. That's a good one." And a little too close to the truth.

"Just let me carry the box," Lennox says, that same silky voice wreaking havoc on my insides.

"It's fine. I can get this one." I motion toward the back of the trailer. "That one over there is heavier anyway. You can carry that one."

Lennox's expression shifts, like he's finally figured out what I'm up to. He tilts his head to the side, shifting the box just enough for him to read the upside-down label scrawled across the side.

He smirks. "You afraid I'll see your granny panties, Tatum?"

I scoff. "Wouldn't you like to know what kind of panties I wear." I wrench the box away from him, the force of the movement jostling the box enough that the top pops open, and (can you SEE where this is going?) my underwear go flying *everywhere.*

I stare stupidly for five solid seconds before I move, but Lennox isn't moving either.

Which, maybe that's understandable. He's the one who has a lacy black thong on his shoulder.

And—*oh geez*—is that my bra draped over the azalea bush right next to the truck?

This. Is. Not. Happening.

The goat chase through the kitchen wasn't enough? The universe needs to humiliate me by tossing my underwear around too?

Lennox clears his throat, startling me out of my stupor, and I jolt into action, grabbing the thong from his shoulder and the bra from the bush before turning my attention to the ground around us.

Oh my word. They are everywhere. Like tiny, lacy flags of humiliation.

Look. I have to wear the same thing to work every single day. It's a small thing, but having fancy underwear is one way that I can feel pretty when my work wardrobe is so lame. I wear them for me, but I'm still more than a little satisfied that the underwear Lennox is seeing are definitely *not* granny panties.

He's holding the top of the box open for me when I return with the last armful of underwear.

"Like what you see?" I say saucily as I close the box and take it from him. He lets it go easily this time, and I head toward the stairs.

"Careful, Tatum," he says as he comes up behind me, the heavier box in his hands. "You're sounding a little flirty."

"*I'm* sounding flirty? You're the one who—"

Perry appears in the open doorway ahead of us, and my words immediately stall in my throat.

My eyes dart to Lennox. Olivia gave me an overview of the farm's management structure during the interview process and made it clear she'd be the one overseeing my employment. But Perry is CFO to her CEO. They work together. Impressing him is *just* as important as impressing Olivia.

And I've been bickering with his brother like I'm a middle schooler with an ancient bone to pick and an impulse control problem. And now we're talking about my *underwear?*

"Is everything okay?" Perry asks, his gaze shifting from me to Lennox.

"Perfect!" I say a little too quickly. "We're just, um . . . talking about cookbooks. I collect them."

Lennox chuckles as he moves past me and starts up the stairs. "Sexiest cookbooks *I've* ever seen," he mumbles under his breath.

"Seriously, Lennox?" I say to his back.

I turn to see Perry studying me closely. Did he hear Lennox? Do I need to explain?

"Perry, I'm—Lennox was just saying—and I—"

Perry holds up his hands, cutting me off. "Nope. Don't say anything. I'm not your boss today. Just a guy unloading some boxes." He pauses before moving toward the truck. "Besides, I know how Lennox can be. It's kinda fun to see him up against someone who knows how to handle him."

"What's that supposed to mean?" Lennox yells down the stairs. "How can I be?"

Perry shoots me a knowing expression, like Lennox has proven his point by even opening his mouth, then goes to grab another box.

The thought of *handling* any part of Lennox sends another wave of heat to my cheeks, and I hurry up the stairs, willing the color to fade before I have to turn around and face him, or either of his brothers, again.

I don't know what's happening to me. I'm a professional. Here to work.

Less than five hours on site, and Lennox is already messing with my focus enough that other people—including my boss—are noticing. No matter what reassurance Perry just gave me, this isn't the first impression I wanted to make.

It takes all my effort, but I manage to ignore Lennox's taunting expressions while we move everything else upstairs. Twenty minutes after the four of us began, the trailer is empty, and my living room is a sea of boxes. I still have a lot to do, but the hardest part is done, and it would have taken me three times as long had I been doing it alone.

Brody offers to drop the U-Haul off at the rental place up the road on his way home, assuring me he knows the guy who works the counter, and he won't care if I don't bring it back myself. It's more kindness than I expect, though I'm getting the sense this is just how the Hawthornes operate.

I watch as the three brothers work to unhitch the trailer from my SUV and hook it up to Brody's truck. The three of them move with and around each other in a way that makes it seem as though they've done this countless times. Not unhitched a trailer, necessarily. It's just clear they're used to working together. Which makes sense. They grew up on a farm, probably doing all kinds of farm things. Mending fences. Driving tractors. *Tending goats.*

A mental image of Lennox, not in his chef's whites but in a pair of ratty jeans and a faded T-shirt, dirty and sweaty from a day of manual labor, pushes into my mind's eye. I swallow against the sudden dryness in my throat, and a tiny sheen of sweat breaks out across my forehead. I wipe it away with a grunt of frustration.

"Okay," Perry says, clapping his hands together and snapping my attention back to the present.

"You've got Olivia's number if anything comes up. And Lennox is almost always around the restaurant. I'm sure he'd be happy to help you with anything you need," he says, shooting his brother a questioning look. "Won't you, Lennox?"

"So happy," Lennox repeats, his voice thick with sarcasm. "*Enormously* happy."

I frown. Lennox is having way too much fun tormenting me.

Perry looks from Lennox to me, then back again. "Right. Okay," he says, his amused tone implying he has no idea what to make of us.

Well that makes two of us, Perry. I don't have a clue either.

The thing is, even though it was a late-night, possibly wine-induced impulse that made me apply for the Stonebrook catering job, I can't pretend knowing Lennox was here didn't play into my decision. I'd just had a horrible argument with Dad, and the idea of working on the other side of the country sounded blissful. But I was also tired of feeling like everything in my life was so . . . I don't know. Fake? Scripted? Like I was just some set piece Dad could move around at will.

Back in school, Lennox was the one person who didn't seem to care that I had a famous father. He was never afraid to be honest, and right now, I'm craving honesty like it's water, and I'm stranded in the desert without a canteen.

Perry heads up the hill toward the giant, white

farmhouse looming in the distance—I assume this is where the main offices are—leaving me alone with Lennox.

"Thanks again for your help!" I call to Perry's retreating figure, hoping again that I haven't already done irreparable damage to my reputation in the eyes of my employer.

Lennox leaves too, heading toward the opposite side of the building and the front entrance of his restaurant. He turns and takes a few backward steps. "See you around, Elliott," he calls.

Elliott?

I might as well be right back in the kitchen at the Southern Culinary Institute, watching him saunter off with his flavor of the week while I'm working harder and longer to get my flambé perfectly torched.

"Not if I see you first, *Hawthorne*," I yell to his retreating form.

He turns around. "Hawthorne. Sounds familiar. Almost like it's the name of a *very* successful restaurant." He makes a show of looking at the wood and metal sign overhead, the name *Hawthorne* gleaming in the late afternoon sun. "Oh wait. Is that the name of *this* restaurant?" He grins wide. "Dinner's on me if you want to come in tonight. I've heard the filet is delicious."

He disappears into the restaurant, and I barely keep myself from shaking my fists with a frustrated harrumph.

The nerve of that man. The gumption. The stupid sexy arrogance.

"*No,*" I amend as I stomp toward the back door. "He's *not* sexy. Definitely, definitely NOT sexy."

CHAPTER THREE
Tatum

I pace around the oversized pantry at the back of my kitchen and take slow, even breaths, a lame and completely ineffective way to calm my racing heart. Just outside, my staff is gathering, ready to meet me for the first time.

I was standing *in* the kitchen until five minutes ago when a sudden bout of nerves had me darting into what I thought was my office to hide.

To be fair, my office door is only a few feet away from the pantry, so it was an honest mistake. But there are already so many people here, I can't correct it now. My only option is to stay and hope everyone thinks I came in here on purpose.

There *is* something soothing about the familiar, earthy smells filling the enormous room. I've never worked in a restaurant with a pantry storage this size, though this one makes sense since it serves two kitchens. Crates of fresh produce line one entire wall. Potatoes, onions, leeks, mushrooms. Brussels sprouts still on the stalk hang from a shelf nearby, and bunches of garlic adorn hooks near the door. There are nuts and grains of every kind. Oils and vinegars, and every spice you can imagine.

There's something magical about the possibilities that fill this room. Maybe it isn't such a bad place to hide after all.

I pick up a perfectly ripe tomato, sliding my thumb across the tender flesh. I haven't toured the gardens yet, but Olivia gave me the impression during one of our many conversations that almost all of the produce used on the farm is grown on location, either in the expansive kitchen garden just behind the restaurant, the greenhouse on the other side of the farmhouse, or in one of the many commercial fields that feed the wholesale side of Stonebrook's operations.

I suppose that's the whole idea of *farm-to-table* dining, though most restaurants who make the claim aren't actually located *ON* the farm. That's probably part of Hawthorne's charm. That, and the restaurant's incredibly annoying chef.

Annoying.
Irritating.
Presumptuous.
Sexy.
That last thought pops into my head unbidden for the second time since I've arrived, and I shove it aside. *Again.* I'm here as a professional. Remaking my career on *my* terms. Fraternizing with the enemy is *not* on the table.

But that doesn't stop me from wanting to eat his food.

There are at least a dozen things on Lennox's menu that I would love to sample, but after his snarky invitation to have dinner on him, I'm going to hold off as long as humanly possible. I definitely couldn't give him the satisfaction of going in last night. Mature of me, I know, but I am the one hiding in a pantry right now, so maybe maturity isn't really my thing.

In the end, I drove to the grocery store, stocked up on the basics, and went home too tired to cook but happy to have a bowl of cereal before collapsing into bed. Not exactly the dinner of champions, but it tasted better than humble pie, so I'm not complaining.

My phone buzzes with a text, and I pull it out of my pocket, smiling when I see the message from my older sister.

Bree: Hey! Did you make it? Are you safe?

My sister and brother are eight and ten years older than me, so we've never been particularly close. They were mostly grown and out of the house when Dad's fame really took off, so in most ways, it feels like Dad lived two lives. One with Mom and Bree and Daniel, and one with his fame . . . and me.

But lately, I've been texting Bree more. Mostly since deciding to quit Dad's restaurant and move to the other side of the continent. When I called to let her know my plans and ask if I could stop in St. Louis to see her on my drive across the country, she cheered like I'd just told her I won the lottery.

"It's about time you get out from under his thumb," she said. "He's been using you for too long, Tatum. I'm so proud of you."

Her words gave me pause. Was that really how my sister saw my life? Like Dad has been using me? She probably just doesn't understand. Because we share the same profession, my relationship with Dad probably looks different to people on the outside. But we have something special.

Or, we *did* have something special.

Until I panicked and fled and moved myself across the country. But who's keeping score?

In the time it takes to pull up and read Bree's message, two more pop up.

> **Bree:** I want to hear all about the farm. Do you love it? What do you think?
> **Bree:** Also, did you see this Instagram post yesterday?

A screenshot pops up of a post from @*therealTylerMarino*. The photo features a bandana-wearing goat—the very same one Toby chased around Lennox's kitchen yesterday. The caption reads: *Penelope's regular Tuesday: a stroll to the on-site restaurant to say hello, a slightly scary dog chase, and a midday snack with the chef. #specialprivileges*

The fact that Tyler heard about the dog chase makes my stomach tighten. I have to hope it was Olivia who filled her husband in, and not Lennox. Somehow, Lennox telling an embarrassing story about me—or my dog—feels so much worse.

Before I can respond, yet another text pops up. I'm beginning to expect these one-sided conversations, and that thought makes me happy. I like that my sister has enough confidence in our relationship that she'll bombard me with messages even if I don't respond.

> **Bree:** When I read dog chase, I wondered if it was Toby. Please tell me it was. I want your dog to have chased the world's most famous goat!

I glance at the like count on the post. It's already over a million, and it can't be more than twenty-four hours old. Penelope probably *is* the world's most famous goat, which, admittedly, makes Lennox mentioning her by name yesterday a little less weird.

> **Tatum:** It was Toby. He deserved one very serious timeout.
> **Bree:** Um, HELLO. You should put him in timeout and post a picture! And tag

Tyler. I bet he would share! Toby could become internet famous too! He totally has the look for it.

My older sister has a degree in social media marketing, so this is not a surprising suggestion from her. I spent two nights crashing on her sofa on my trip out, and she walked me through an entire plan she created for launching my *own* brand without the overshadowing influence of Christopher Elliott.

I appreciate her efforts, but I'm beginning to think I'll like my life a lot better when people forget Christopher Elliott even has a daughter. I always thought I wanted Dad's life. The TV show. The branding deals. But now? I'm not so sure.

> **Tatum:** I don't want my dog to be internet famous. Also, I think it's weird that you know so much about Lennox's family.
> **Bree:** I only know a lot about *Tyler*. And only because of Penelope. You know how I feel about adorable animals on the internet.

I do know this. I've also learned, from the steady stream of shared TikTok videos she's been sending since we reconnected, that she is particularly moved by dog adoption videos, children with unexpectedly mature singing voices, and cats who eat weird people food. (I have no idea.)

> **Bree:** So how are you feeling about things? Was it weird to see Lennox again?
> **Tatum:** Very weird.
> **Bree:** Is he totally hot? I mean, I remember the picture you showed me. But in person?

I hesitate, because how can I possibly answer that question? Lennox was *hot* back in culinary school. But now, with the broader shoulders and the closely trimmed beard, surrounded by tangible evidence of his brilliance and success? *Hot* doesn't even begin to cover it.

But I'm not saying that to my sister.

> **Tatum:** It's not particularly relevant, is it?
> **Bree:** OF COURSE IT IS. Just answer the question and stop trying to be so diplomatic and mature for a second.
> **Tatum:** Fine. Yes. He's incredibly handsome. He's also incredibly irritating, and clearly, he feels the same way about me.
> **Bree:** Shut up. You're the sweetest. If he doesn't see that, he's crazy.

Tatum: I'm not sure sweet is a word Lennox would ever use to describe me.

Seconds after I hit send, my phone rings with a video call, the screen lighting up with Bree's face.

"What," I groan, as I answer the call.

"I don't even want to hear you talking like that," Bree says, using a big sister bossy voice I didn't know she had. "You're the sweetest, Tatum. The literal sweetest. Also, where are you? Are those brussels sprouts hanging behind you?"

"You're biased," I say. "And yes. I'm in the pantry."

"Why are you in the pantry?"

"Because I thought I was going into my office, but I wound up here instead and now there are too many people to—you know what? Don't worry about it. The point is, you used to call me sassy pants when we were growing up. Which is it? Am I sweet or sassy?"

She scoffs. "You were so sassy when you were little. But now? I'm not buying it."

"That's the trouble. The minute I saw Lennox yesterday, I immediately turned into Sassy Pants. But that's not really how I want him to see me."

"This is an easy problem to fix," Bree says. "You just have to show him how you've grown up."

I glance toward the door. Olivia won't be here

for another ten minutes or so, but I still don't want anyone barging in on my conversation. Especially this one. "How would I even do that?"

Bree almost cackles. "Oh, honey, that's the easy part. You live above his restaurant, right? Just wait until everyone has gone home and he's working late, pounding some bread dough or something, and then go downstairs to get a drink of water in your sexiest pajamas. Shorty shorts. A breezy top. The girls free and loose . . ."

"Bree!" I say, cutting her off. Something thuds behind me, like a shoe bumping into the wall, and I spin around. There's no one there, but I drop my voice anyway. "I thought you were going to give me real, actual advice! It's not going to be like that. No free and loose anything. And pounding bread dough? Where are you getting these things?"

"It's all inside my brain, baby. Scary, right? Have you met any of his brothers? Have you met Flint?"

I roll my eyes. "Flint doesn't live here. But the other brothers helped me unload the moving trailer."

She sighs. "Every time I watch Flint Hawthorne in a movie, I'm going to pee a little thinking about you living on his family farm with all his sexy brothers."

"Seriously. The genetics in this family. I've never seen anything like it." I glance at my watch, sensing the need to wrap things up so I'm fully available when Olivia shows up. "Hey, I should go. Olivia is going to be here any minute to introduce me to my staff."

"Oh, awesome. You're going to do amazing. But first, I actually had a point in calling."

"Oh. Okay. What's up?"

"I just got a box full of Mom's things. I guess her brother sent it from France?"

A pang of sadness flits across my chest, squeezing my heart. I wasn't close to my mom. She moved to Europe when I was twelve, right after she and Dad split, and I only saw her once a year after that, even less once I graduated from high school and started college. When she died last year—breast cancer, aggressive and resistant to treatment—I think that distance made my mourning more complicated. Because mingled in with my sadness was a deep sense of regret.

"What kinds of things?" I ask.

Bree shrugs. "Um, kitchen-y things, I think. A rolling pin, a corkscrew, a whole bunch of other utensil-looking things I can't name. Oh, and there's a set of wooden spoons that are gorgeous. I don't remember what else. Some cookbooks, maybe? Anyway, I was thinking you might want them."

"Oh. Um, yeah, I guess. Sure. But only if you or Daniel don't."

Bree scoffs. "You know how I am in the

kitchen. And I already checked with Daniel, and he agrees with me. You're the one who loves cooking like Mom did. I think she would want this stuff to go to you."

"Not Dad?" I ask, which earns a derisive laugh from Bree.

"Definitely not Dad." She's quiet for a beat before she says, "I'm sorry you didn't get to know her better, Tatum. And that she didn't get to know you."

I shrug. "Yeah. Me too."

"You're a lot like her, you know?"

"Am I?"

"Definitely. You have her spunk. Also her boobs, which I'm still in favor of you using to impress one particularly irritating chef." She grins saucily into the phone, and I roll my eyes.

"Oh my gosh. How old are you, Bree?"

"Seventeen for the rest of my life." She tosses her hands over her head. "It's the only way to be."

"I really have to go now."

"K. Don't forget to breathe. You're going to be great. And text me your address so I can send you this box!"

I end the call and breathe out a long slow breath, trusting that at least this advice from Bree is worth taking.

I smooth my hands down the front of my chef's coat and move toward the door. As I round the corner into the narrow hallway, I stop, startled, because Lennox is standing directly in front of me, his arms folded while he leans against the wall, a devilish smile on his face.

My hand flies to my chest. "Gah. You scared me."

"Sorry. I heard you were on the phone. Didn't want to interrupt."

I freeze. He *heard* that I was on the phone? As in, he heard the general noise of muffled, unintelligible voices? Or he *heard* heard me on the phone? I can only hope it's the former.

"Oh," I say as casually as I can. "That's, um, thanks for that. I was just talking to my sister."

"Ah."

Ah? What does that even mean? *Ah, I already know this because I heard you talking?* Or *ah, that's nice. Thanks for letting me know?* I wish I knew this man well enough to be able to interpret his noises.

We stand there, locked in some kind of staring contest until he finally lifts an eyebrow. The air crackles between us, so similar to all those times we faced off in SCI's student kitchen. Only, there's something new here—a sexy undercurrent of tension that I don't remember feeling then. I suddenly wonder if it was there all along, and I was just too inexperienced to recognize it for what it was.

"Can I go into the pantry now?" Lennox finally asks.

I shift to the side, too distracted by the possibility of him having heard my conversation to protest. He lightly touches my elbow when he passes by, then looks down at me with a familiar smirk. "Hey, Tatum? If you get thirsty later, I'm going to be working pretty late. You know how it is. *Pounding* that bread dough."

Ohhhh, I hate my sister so much.

Lennox disappears into the pantry while I close my eyes, one hand pressed to my forehead.

Because it's definitely going to help if I just stand here stupidly, not moving, not saying anything, not—.

"Tatum. There you are," Olivia says. She pulls her fiery red hair over her shoulder. "Hey, whoa. You okay?"

I open my eyes and force a breath out through my nose, wiping any lingering irritation from my face.

Get control of yourself, woman, I think as I clear my throat.

"Yep! Great. Ready to go."

Lennox reappears, a giant bag of basmati rice in his hand, and Olivia looks from him to me, then back again, her brow furrowed like she's solving a logic problem.

"Lennox," she says slowly.

"What's up, Liv?" he says casually, but I'm not sure Olivia buys it. Her forehead stays furrowed as Lennox asks, "What are you doing here?"

"Just here to introduce Tatum to her staff." She looks at me and smiles. I don't know her well yet, but Olivia Marino has very expressive eyes, and right now they're asking me, *Are you okay? Did he say something to you? Do you need me to punch my brother on your behalf?*

Her concern is just the boost I need to forget about Lennox and dive into work.

But in the back of my mind, I can't help feeling like Lennox Hawthorne just got the best of me.

CHAPTER FOUR
Lennox

"Chef?"

I turn to see Brittany, one of my line cooks, standing a few feet away, her hands on her hips and a furrow on her brow. "What's wrong?"

"I got this," Zach says, motioning toward the counter where I've been expediting orders. When I'm acting as expeditor, I don't cook. Instead, I oversee everyone who is, calling orders as they come into the kitchen and making sure everything is prepared correctly and served efficiently. "Things are slowing down. You can see what she needs."

I step aside, letting Zach take my spot, and walk toward Brittany.

"I can't find the parmesan," she says as soon as I reach her.

"It isn't in the fridge?"

"It *was* in the fridge, but now it's *not* in the fridge, and three plates are waiting for parm."

I follow her to the walk-in, immediately seeing the empty spot on the shelf where the giant wedge of parmesan used to be. It was there as recently as this afternoon—something I know because my pantry chef is out on maternity leave, so I was the one checking on inventory.

The fact that it isn't here can only mean one thing.

I sigh and leave the fridge, making eye contact with Brittany who's waiting for me right outside. "Go do a quick walkthrough and double-check it isn't somewhere else in the kitchen."

She nods and disappears, and I turn away from my kitchen, heading toward the cavernous space where the catering staff works. The room is almost empty, which means everyone is probably up at the farmhouse providing a dinner service to whatever event is scheduled for the evening.

Tatum's voice sounds behind me, and I spin around to see her hurrying into her kitchen. "No, I'll grab them," she says to someone out of sight. "You go on and I'll be right behind you."

She slows when she sees me, her lips lifting in a smile as she turns and walks a few backward steps. "Are you lost, Hawthorne?"

It's not an unreasonable question. It's been two weeks since Tatum moved in, and we've seen each other around plenty. We've even had the chance to argue about: one, the frequency with which her dog pees in my garden; two, the way we organize the shared walk-in fridge; and three, who has first dibs on the produce that comes out of Stonebrook's greenhouse. But generally, we stay out of each other's way when we're at our busiest. There's too much work to be done to do otherwise.

Before I can respond, one of Tatum's cooks steps up beside her, a tray holding four covered dinner plates in her hand. "The specials, Chef."

"Perfect, Jessie. Thank you. And you double-checked for pecans?"

"Double and triple-checked," Jessie says.

Tatum lifts the lid covering one of the plates and peers under it before replacing it and picking up the tray. "I want you with me at the farmhouse, all right? It's your job to make sure the servers get each of these specials to the right people. Nothing like ruining a wedding by sending Aunt Edna into anaphylactic shock because the catering staff ignored her nut allergy."

Jessie laughs. "Understood. I'm on it."

It's not the first time I've noticed the way Tatum interacts with her staff. They all love her—*really* love her—and it's easy to see why. She's firm but fair, and she talks to them like they're real people with real lives outside of work. I've been around the catering kitchen enough to know how stressful it can be to manage so many people's individual needs, from food allergies to finicky couples with weird tastes. But Tatum makes it look easy. I respect that about her.

"Hey Elliott, can I get a minute before you leave?" I ask, proud of myself for sounding so normal. Yesterday, Olivia caught us bickering over a bushel box of celery hearts and scolded me until I promised I would try harder to communicate with Tatum like a professional and not a caged animal.

I couldn't quite explain to my sister that even though Tatum and I might sound like we're arguing, our interactions don't have the same edge that they did in culinary school. I can't speak for Tatum, but it almost seems like we enjoy them. At the very least, we're both energized by them.

Tatum glances at me, eyebrow raised, then turns back to Jessie. "Take this out to the van, and I'll be right behind you."

Jessie hurries out of the kitchen, but Tatum moves at a slower pace, sauntering toward me like she's got all the time in the world. "What can I do for you?" she asks when she finally reaches me.

"Where's my parmesan?"

"You're holding up Aunt Edna's plate to ask me about cheese?"

"I'm sure Aunt Edna will be fine for two more minutes. My parm is missing, and you or your staff are the only ones who could have taken it."

Tatum starts toward the walk-in. "I know which side of the fridge is mine, Lennox. I didn't take your cheese."

"Somebody did," I say, following after her.

"Has Penelope visited lately?" Tatum says, her

eyes flashing with laughter. "Maybe she ate it."

"All twenty pounds of it?"

"Two weeks ago, she was wandering through your kitchen like she owned the place. You can't tell me it isn't possible." She opens the heavy door of the walk-in, and I follow her inside.

"Possible, maybe. But not probable. The cheese was here this morning."

Tatum frowns as she makes a slow circle, her eyes quickly scanning the shelves.

"This is where my parmesan *was*," I say, pointing to the empty spot on the shelf.

"Ah," Tatum says. "I see what happened." She steps forward and hefts a quarter-wheel of parmesan out from behind a giant block of cheddar. "Here."

I glance at the label. "This isn't mine."

She sighs. "I know. It's mine, and apparently, my staff couldn't find it and accidentally grabbed yours instead. It was an honest mistake, and I'm sorry it happened."

I'm already shaking my head. "I can't use this. The parm I use is aged over a hundred months. This won't have the same bite."

"You're right. But what can I do about it now? Call back every plate from the wedding reception so I can scrape off your fancy cheese and replace it with something else?"

She presses the cheese wheel against my chest, which is no easy feat. The thing has to weigh at least twenty pounds. "Do you have plates waiting?" she asks, pushing the parm back into my chest. "Just use this. It's better than nothing."

I don't like that she's right, but she *is* right. I do have plates waiting, and slightly less bitey parmesan is better than no parmesan at all. *Barely* better, but still better.

"Fine," I concede. "But we aren't done talking about this."

She presses a hand to her chest with mock enthusiasm. "I am giddy with excitement at the thought," she deadpans.

As I turn back to my kitchen, the snarky sarcasm in her tone stays with me, except this time, it feels more challenging than annoying. And I've always been a man who loves a challenge.

No one complains about the subpar parmesan, and I make it through the rest of the night without any major mishaps, though my staff seems more tired and disgruntled than normal. I need to figure out why, but it can wait until tomorrow when I'm not bone-deep exhausted and my brain doesn't feel like whipped meringue.

I turn off the lights in the main kitchen and head to my office where I shed my chef's coat, dropping it into the laundry bin that will get picked up in the morning. The t-shirt I'm wearing underneath is damp with sweat, and I pull it away from my skin. I need a shower. And about twenty hours of sleep. Which is impossible, seeing as how I have to be back at the restaurant in less than twelve.

"You're still here," Tatum says from behind me.

I turn to see her standing in my office doorway, clutching what looks like the rest of my parmesan in her hands. She looks as exhausted as I feel.

"I could say the same about you." I drop into my desk chair, which bumps the mouse connected to my laptop and wakes up the screen. "You getting the hang of things?" The question feels normal—*neutral*—and I almost wonder what's wrong with me.

Tatum eyes me, like she doesn't quite trust that we're having a regular conversation either, then she shrugs. "For the most part. Moving food all over the farm is a little different, but I'm learning." She leans against the door jamb. "Some things are the same. Like how exhausted I feel at the end of the night."

I nod toward the cheese in her hands. "Did everyone rave about the incredible parm?"

She rolls her eyes as she moves into my office, setting the wrapped cheese on my desk. "It annoys me to admit it, but *yes*. Three different people mentioned how delicious it was." She sticks her empty hands into her pockets. "I'm sorry about the mix-up. I talked to my staff and reminded them that borrowing from the Hawthorne kitchen isn't acceptable crisis management."

Okay, now things are feeling *really* weird. We're having a calm, reasonable conversation. I don't even know what to make of it. But also, I maybe, sort of, like it?

"Whoa, what's that?" Tatum says, her eyes on my laptop. "Is that Stonebrook?"

I look at my laptop screen, open to the live feed coming from the various game cameras positioned around the farm. I don't normally have the feed open, but Dad messaged me earlier, saying something about deer in the apple orchard visible from his back porch. He and Mom live on a secluded corner of the farm, and after his stroke a few years back, he isn't so great at getting around. But he's quick to reach out to one of us if he feels like something needs to be done. It's too early for there to be fruit on the trees, but deer in the orchard means a breach in the fence, and I was hoping activity on the cameras might help me figure out where that breach might be.

Ultimately, it'll be the farm manager's job to fix the problem, but there's no getting away from the *family* nature of a family-run farm. Even Brody pitches in, and he's a chemistry teacher at Silver Creek High. His job doesn't have anything to do with the farm, but he's still here almost as frequently as the rest of us.

"It *is* Stonebrook," I say, answering Tatum's question. "We've got game cameras set up everywhere. Helps to keep an eye on the wildlife."

She stiffens, her hands curling into fists. "Wildlife?" she says, her voice a little softer than before.

Huh. This could be fun.

"Sure. Bobcats. Bears. Wild boar. They can get pretty aggressive."

Her eyes widen. "And they're just . . . *on* the farm? Should I not let Toby out?"

I bite my bottom lip, trying not to smile. "Probably not. It's pretty wild out there. I heard there was a crocodile in the pond the other day."

"A croc—*wait*. You're messing with me."

I finally grin. "Tiny bit."

Tatum huffs. "I hate you so much right now."

"The cameras are mostly to keep an eye on the deer," I say. "They'll eat whatever they can get to. It helps if we track their movements, stay ahead of them."

She nods. "That makes sense. So all those other animals. Bears. Bobcats. Those don't live around here?"

There's real fear in her voice, and I suddenly feel guilty for teasing her, especially since now, I have to tell her the truth, and I don't want to give her actual reasons to worry.

"They do," I say carefully, "but you don't need to worry about them. Bobcats are more scared of you than you are of them. And the bears, too. We only have black bears around here. We see them pretty frequently, but they'll stay away if you have Toby with you."

"But like, not *now*, right?" she says. "They're all still hibernating."

I almost smile at the hope in her voice. "It's pretty much spring, Tatum. It's still cold, but nature's waking up. It knows what's coming."

"Oh good. Great. Love that."

"I promise you'll be fine. We've never had a bear attack at Stonebrook." I nod toward the parmesan sitting on the desk, sensing a change of subject might do her some good. "Did you try it?"

She shakes her head. "I didn't."

I stand and pick up the parmesan, then carry it into my kitchen where I unwrap the cheese, grab a knife, and slice off a chunk.

Tatum follows behind and takes the cheese when I hold it out to her, her fingers brushing against mine as she does.

I watch as she lifts the cheese to her mouth, already knowing how she's going to react. Still, I'm unprepared for the way my pulse speeds when she closes her eyes and a low moan escapes her lips. "Oh my word. That's . . ." Her words trail off as she finishes the bite. She picks up the cheese and studies the label. "Where did you get this again?"

"I know a guy in Italy. He does small batches. Ages it twice as long as most." Any authentic Parmigiano Reggiano is only going to be produced in one very small region in Italy, so having an Italian supplier isn't all that surprising. But my source isn't just any supplier. "His name is Gianni Rossi. His family has owned a farm in Emilia Romagna for centuries. He mostly sells to restaurants in Italy, but there are a few of us in other places. I'm the only one in the US."

"How did you even find him?" Tatum asks. "For real. That's the best parm I've ever had. I'm suddenly so sorry to have wasted it on a bunch of thankless wedding guests."

"Dumb luck, mostly. I was vacationing in Italy, and I just happened to be in the right place at the right time."

She eyes me suspiciously. "Right place, right time? There's got to be more to the story than that."

I carve off another few slivers of cheese, taking one for myself and offering the other to Tatum. Her fingers brush against mine, slower this time, almost like she's lingering on purpose.

It takes me a minute to respond because then she's lifting the cheese to her mouth and I'm watching as her tongue darts out to catch a crumb that's stuck to her bottom lip.

Focus, Lennox. FOCUS.

"I, uh . . ." I clear my throat. "What can I say? I was in this tiny Italian bistro, Gianni stopped by, and we struck up a conversation—"

"He just randomly started a conversation with you? Then discovered you were a chef and offered to fly his artisanal, small-batch, world-class parmesan halfway across the world because he liked your smile?"

I grimace and run a hand through my hair. She isn't going to let me off the hook, and I *really* wish she would. "It's possible I was dating his daughter at the time." I breathe out a sigh, slowly lifting my eyes to meet hers. For reasons I cannot define, I don't want to talk about my dating history with Tatum.

"Ahh, there's the catch," she says. "I knew there had to be one. And knowing what I know of your dating history, this totally tracks."

The comment about my dating history cuts, but I ignore the sting as I slice off another piece of cheese for Tatum. I can't argue about the impression she has of my dating history because it's the right one. I dated *a lot* in the four years I attended culinary school, never settling down with any one woman. At least not after my first year when Hailey Stanton carved my heart out of my chest and ran it through a meat grinder.

Gruesome imagery, I know. But in this instance, it totally fits. And I'm still not over it. Whenever I think about getting serious with someone, my body breaks out in a cold sweat, a visceral reaction I never see coming and can't prevent.

I don't *want* to be a player. And in the sense that most people mean the term, I'm not. I might go on a lot of dates, but I never lead women on.

But defending my reputation would mean talking about why I keep everything so casual in the first place, and that's not a conversation I want to have. At the end of the day, it's easier to take the label and let people think what they want to think.

"Must be nice walking around the world so handsome and charming, people just waiting to lavish you with shiny, fancy things," Tatum says.

I push the negative thoughts away and focus on Tatum. "Are you telling me you think I'm handsome?"

She reaches for the cheese and I pull it back right before she can grab it. She frowns and tries again, this time wrapping her fingers around my wrist and sending a burst of sensation up my arm. She holds my hand steady as she takes the parmesan out of my fingers. "I'm telling you I think you're ridiculous," she says. "The cheese is delicious. But *you* are ridiculous."

"Better watch it, Tatum. If you're nice to me, I could probably hook you up with your own artisanal parmesan." I really *could*. It wouldn't be hard to order enough from Gianni to cover the catering kitchen's needs as well as Hawthorne's.

"I don't need your handouts to be fabulous, Lennox," Tatum says saucily.

The air around us shifts just slightly, and I hold her gaze for a long moment. She really *is* fabulous.

The thought feels foreign in my brain, especially when I slide it in next to all the *hating* we did to each other back in school, even next to the bickering we've been doing since she arrived at Stonebrook.

"Hey, can I ask you a question?" I ask on impulse.

She must sense I'm being serious for once because her playful expression fades. "Sure."

"Don't get me wrong. I know everyone here is happy to have you. But why did you take this job?"

The light in her eyes fades the slightest bit, but then she shrugs dismissively, like the question is no big deal. "Why not?"

I narrow my eyes. "Tatum. Come on. Your father is—"

"Not in charge of my career," she says, cutting me off. "I needed a job. This seemed like a good one. I don't ever want to be a chef who thinks *any* job is beneath me. Catering is a new challenge that I was excited to try. It really isn't more complicated than that."

Pretty sure it's *a lot* more complicated than that, but I'm not about to push Tatum for an explanation she isn't ready to give.

"Fair enough," I say, and her shoulders relax the slightest bit.

She might not have answered my question directly, but she told me plenty anyway.

I've met her father, after all. It isn't hard to guess what the gaps in her story might look like.

Tatum says goodnight and heads toward the back door while I wrap up the last of the cheese and return it to the fridge, then grab my keys and lock up my office.

When I make it outside, Tatum is on the landing beside the loading dock, her eyes following Toby as he makes his way across the grassy lawn to the left of the restaurant.

"Oh hey, he isn't in my garden. What a nice surprise," I say.

"I tried to send him there, but he just wouldn't listen," Tatum says without missing a beat.

I chuckle as I walk to my car. Toby runs over to greet me, and I give his ears a good scratch. Despite my grumbling, he's actually a pretty great dog.

"So I *don't* need to worry about bears, right?" Tatum calls.

"You don't need to worry about bears."

She nods, but there's an uncertainty in her eyes that says she doesn't completely believe me. "You promise?"

"I promise," I say. And then, because I think she needs the distraction, I add, "Better rest up, Elliott. I'll be here early in the morning, and I'm willing to fight for the best bell peppers."

"You won't have the chance if I get here first,"

she says. "Since I live right upstairs, I'm thinking my odds are pretty good."

I open my car door and rest my hand on the top of the window. "But *I'm* the one who gets personal text messages from Shelton."

I've been spoiled without a catering chef on staff, getting first pick of whatever Stonebrook's produce manager brings over and leaving the rest for catering to work with. But Tatum is serious about her vegetables. Last week, she shoved four entire endives into her shirt just to keep me from snatching them out of her hands.

"How do you know he doesn't text *me?*" Tatum asks.

I let out a dramatic scoff. "Are you *flirting* with Shelton to get first dibs on produce?" The thought of *anyone* flirting with gray-haired, mild-mannered Shelton is hilarious. The poor man would probably quit his job if he even thought it was a possibility.

"Absolutely not. But if I was, would it be any different than you flirting to get parmesan cheese?"

"I didn't *flirt.*"

"You say to-may-to, I say to-mah-to."

"Now you're the one being ridiculous."

She calls Toby and he trots toward her. "Goodnight, Lennox," she sing-songs.

I climb into my car, shaking my head as I pull

out of the parking lot onto the long, winding drive that cuts through the farm.

I don't realize until I pass the wide stone sign at the Stonebrook entrance that I've been smiling the entire time.

CHAPTER FIVE
Tatum

"Your butter's too soft, Tatum."

I flush at the sound of Lennox's voice somewhere over my left shoulder, the hairs on the back of my neck standing up.

What is he doing here? I swear, since our conversation last week about his stupidly delicious parmesan, it almost feels like he's been finding reasons to be in my kitchen.

Not just running into me around the farm, but *here,* in my space. Making me feel all flustered and out of sorts.

I wish I could say I didn't like it.

I set a bowl onto my food scale and zero it out before dumping in several scoops of almond flour. "My butter is *not* too soft," I say without turning around. "Are you lost *again,* Lennox? Do you need me to draw you a map so it's easier for you to stay in your own kitchen?"

"Just here to preserve the reputation of the farm. If you make pastry with butter that soft, it's going to be flat." He reaches over my shoulder and nudges the still-wrapped butter with his knuckle. "Flat pastry? Unhappy wedding guests. Unhappy wedding guests? Bad reviews. Bad reviews?"

I spin around, cutting him off. "I get the point. But it's a *moot* point because my butter is *not* too soft. It's room temperature. It's fine."

He quirks an eyebrow. "Room temperature works if it's seventy-two degrees. But what if it's seventy-three?"

His eyes spark with humor, and I press my lips together as I wipe a bead of sweat from my forehead. It might actually be a little warmer than seventy-three degrees, which is unusual considering I'm the only person here. The only thing we served today was breakfast for a family reunion up at the farmhouse.

We have a wedding tomorrow night, but all the prep work is done, so I'm here alone, finishing up a small batch of gluten-free pastries for the bride's gluten-intolerant siblings. My pastry chef worked late last night finishing up the regular pastries, so I told her I would handle these.

With no ovens on, no cooking happening anywhere in the vicinity—it shouldn't be so warm in here.

I take a step closer, my arms folded across my chest. I'm only inches from Lennox now, who is mirroring my stance. If I weren't so much shorter than he is, our arms might be touching. Instead, his arms are more in line with my collar bone. "You seem awfully concerned about the temperature, Lennox. Makes me wonder if someone turned up the heat on purpose."

"Are you accusing me of sabotage?"

I'm suddenly aware of his delicious body heat, of the smell of his clean chef's coat mingled with something woodsy and uniquely Lennox. It's completely disconcerting. I didn't come to Stonebrook with any thoughts or hopes about a relationship with Lennox Hawthorne. Did I hope we'd be able to co-exist peacefully as co-workers? Sure. Does that mean I want to flirt—argue?—my way into something more? Absolutely not.

Which makes this interaction feel a little like smelling an apple pie in the oven when you're allergic to apples. It might smell delicious, but if you actually eat it, you're going to break out in hives.

I'm not *positive* Lennox will give me hives. But I just made a drastic life change. Changed jobs. Moved across the country. Logically, this should not be something I'm ready for.

Still, the way he smells—it's all I can do not to breathe in enormous lungfuls of Lennox-scented air whenever he's close by.

"You brought up sabotage first," I say, my voice alarmingly breathy.

Why am I breathy?

If Bree were here, and I told her I wasn't flirting, she would laugh right in my not-flirting face.

"I didn't sabotage anything," Lennox says,

his voice low. "But I did see one of your chefs messing with the thermostat yesterday. You might want to check on that."

I prop my hands on my hips. "Oh. Well thanks, then. I'll do that."

Lennox reaches forward and tugs on a curl that's come loose, stretching it down before it springs back into place. "If I were you, I wouldn't make your pastry until you do," he says. "Because that butter is too soft."

"You're too soft," I grumble, smacking him in the stomach and leaving a trail of almond flour on his chef's coat.

Except . . . *oh. Oh my.* His stomach is *not soft.*

It takes exactly three seconds for me to realize my hand is *still* on his abdomen. Sliding down the ridges of muscle like they're there for my amusement.

"Find something you like?" Lennox says with a smirk, and I pull my hand back like I've touched a flame.

"Ha!" I say, a little too quickly. "You wish." I clear my throat, resisting the urge to lift my hands to my fiery cheeks. It would probably only draw more attention to them. "I was . . . only trying to dust off the flour," I say.

The laughter in his eyes says he senses the lie in my words as well as I do, but I'm not about to back down. He raises an eyebrow. "That's all, huh?"

Fine. Yes. Call me a liar. It's better than admitting I was just feeling up Lennox's abs.

When his expression doesn't shift, his grin cocky and sure, I use both hands to playfully shove him away. "Uggh. Just go. Take your muscles and let me get back to work."

He chuckles lightly as he saunters off, stopping in the doorway long enough to say, "I'm going to remember this, Elliott."

I wait until he's well and truly gone to pick up my butter, testing its softness with the pad of my thumb. I swear under my breath, hating that he's right. Butter that's too soft makes flat, gummy pastry that isn't light and flaky at all. I really *can't* make pastry with this.

I carry the butter back to the fridge, stopping on my way to check on the thermostat. It's set to seventy-six, which is entirely too warm. I make a mental note to talk to my staff about it, then abandon the pastry and head upstairs to take Toby for a walk. I'll come back later when the kitchen—and the butter—are both a little cooler.

Before I make it more than a few feet, shouting from Lennox's kitchen draws me in the opposite direction. I tiptoe down the hallway and peek around the corner to see two of his cooks locked in some heated exchange, a giant bin of sliced onions on the counter between them. Lennox is standing off to the side, his forehead pressed into the heel of his hand.

"I hear what you're saying," Lennox says, dropping his hand. His tone is measured, like he's fighting to maintain control. "We can talk about it. But right now is not the time to hash out—"

I duck back into the hallway, feeling suddenly guilty for eavesdropping and not wanting Lennox to see me.

I can't know exactly what's going on in Lennox's kitchen, but this isn't the first time I've seen some of his staff locked in disagreements like this one. I've also noticed a few things about his set up that are making things more complicated than they need to be. The flow of a professional kitchen can make or break the way a team works together, and his could use some tweaking.

I peek back around the corner, my eyes scanning the space. If the island in the center of his kitchen is modular, he could turn it ninety degrees and create larger pathways for the chefs moving from prep to the grill. That would also open up a little more space for the sauté cooks, who, based on Lennox's menu, are probably the busiest in the kitchen. It would mean chefs would have to take a slightly longer walk to get from the pantry to the prep counter, but the improvements would be worth the sacrifice.

Still, it's not my place to tell Lennox he isn't running his kitchen the right way. Every chef does things a little differently, and my opinions are just that—opinions. Unless he were to specifically ask for my help, I'd never feel comfortable volunteering any suggestions. At least not with our relationship like it is now.

I move back down the hall to my apartment steps and make my way upstairs. I truly feel for Lennox. He has a hard job—especially since he's building an entire operation from the ground up.

When I started as head chef of my father's restaurant, Le Vin, the staff was already highly trained with refined systems and procedures in place. They hated working with me—I was basically there for show—but I worked my tail off anyway, and I learned. I grew. I got better at the job.

I may not have deserved the leadership position my father prematurely foisted upon me, but I tried to make the most of it anyway, and eventually, my staff begrudgingly accepted me. Most of them were better chefs than I was—than I *am*. But they learned to trust my strategic brain, and I discovered I am very good at helping chefs maximize their efficiency.

It's probably why the transition to catering hasn't been too bad for me. Event catering, especially for larger events, has a lot of moving parts. The logistics matter almost as much as the food, so it's been nice that my brain seems to be wired for the kind of problem-solving the job requires.

What I'm not loving about catering? My obligation to come up with new seasonal entrees every couple of months. It's not that I can't do it. I can. I have the training, the knowledge. But I've always felt more overwhelmed by menu creation than inspired by it.

I know. Daughter of the famous Christopher Elliott, graduate of the acclaimed Southern Culinary Institute, former head chef of Le Vin, a world-renowned restaurant, and I'm intimidated by creating some new catering menus. I realize how ridiculous it sounds. That doesn't make it any less true.

When I reach the top of the steps, there's a photo taped to the center of my apartment door.

What the?

Someone actually came all the way up to my apartment door to give me a picture? Am I going to find a message made out of magazine clippings next?

But then I really look at the picture.

It only takes a second to recognize it.

Our last year of culinary school, Lennox and I represented the Southern Culinary Institute at a Christmas fundraising event for the Atlanta Arts Foundation. They had a British Baking Show-style bakeoff with eight participants ranging from pastry chefs at Atlanta's finest restaurants to TikTok-famous home chefs and, of course, to students from SCI. The event had three rounds, with two chefs eliminated in each of the first two rounds until only four of us were left for the final segment of the competition.

Lennox and I both made it to the final round, but then he nailed his gingerbread man cupcakes and my peppermint cake totally flopped. *Literally.* Like, the entire thing collapsed in on itself seconds before it was my turn to present to the judges.

The photo Lennox taped to my door—because who else could have possibly done it?—is the one the Atlanta newspaper printed in their Sunday edition featuring the young phenom chef who won the bakeoff and would surely "take the culinary world by storm." Lennox is smiling wide, holding up a cake-shaped trophy while standing next to a table featuring his prize-winning dessert.

The picture is creased along one side, a third of the photo tucked under, so I unfold it to its original size . . . and burst out laughing.

Because *I* am on the other side of the photo looking absolutely furious. My arms are folded across my chest, my hip is cocked, and I'm frowning, my eyes narrowed to tiny slits.

I am the picture of poor sportsmanship—a textbook definition of what NOT to do when someone else wins and you lose.

The Motion Picture Academy should take notes. They could do an entire workshop on how actors should and shouldn't react when their rivals win Oscars using just my face.

I have no idea why the paper didn't print the entire photo—the version that went to print definitely cropped me out—but I'm so glad they didn't. The media would have had a heyday over Christopher Elliott's daughter exhibiting such classless behavior.

I laugh again as I let myself into my apartment and greet Toby, who meets me at the door.

If this were a competition—it's not, but let's just say, hypothetically, if it were—Lennox is winning a billion to zero. Granny panties. Pounding bread dough. Crocodiles in the pond. And now this photo, which is admittedly hilarious, but STILL. He has made so many jokes at my expense, and I've been too busy learning how to do my job to push back at all. (You know. When I'm *not* feeling up his abs.) Of course, I've also been trying to be professional—to make a good impression. I've never had to rely on my own merits like I do now. I haven't wanted to do anything that might screw that up.

But now that I have my feet under me, it's time I start to push back a little.

And I think I know just the way to do it.

CHAPTER SIX
Lennox

I pull another order off the ticket machine and read it over. The board is already full, and this order isn't going to make my sauté cooks happy. They've already got six items on the board, and I'm about to give them three more. "Ordering," I call. "Two scallops, one halibut, and a filet, medium rare."

I listen as my cooks echo back the order, then turn my attention to another ticket. "Plating one tenderloin, one chicken pot pie, and a pork belly," I call.

Off to my left, Griffin swears as a pot clatters to the stove.

"Griffin, how are we on that sauce?"

"Working on it," he calls.

Two plates slide into the window ready to go, so now we're only lacking the tenderloin. Zach is at the grill, but the apple brandy reduction is what makes the dish, so without Griffin's sauce, we're at a standstill on the whole table.

"Behind you!" another cook calls out, followed by a string of expletives.

I frown. The energy in the kitchen is good, but our rhythm is off. Cooks are tripping over each other, getting in each other's way. Twice, plates have made it out of the kitchen before I put eyes on them which isn't supposed to happen. When things are working like they should, I'm the last one to see every plate and guarantee that every single person in my dining room is getting the best possible meal.

But when I'm having to fix an oversalted she-crab soup—a staple and a favorite on our menu—or fill in for Zach because he's filling in for my salad chef who called out for the fourth time in two weeks, it's hard to keep things running the way they should.

Zach slides the tenderloin onto a plate, then adds the charred broccolini and the mushroom risotto.

Griffin swoops in, ready to ladle the sauce over the tenderloin, but the sauce looks thin. I lift a hand, stopping him just in time. "Wait." I dip a pinky into the sauce and taste it. It *is* too thin. And not sweet enough. "What is this?"

Willow appears beside Griffin. "I told you it didn't reduce enough." She reaches for the sauce pan. "Here. I'll fix it."

"We don't have time to fix it," Griffin barks. "Reducing takes time."

"No, but I can thicken it with a beurre manie. It won't be perfect, but it's better than what we've got."

Griffin hesitates, his grip firm on his saucepan and his jaw tense.

"Let her do it," I say. I look toward a line of cooks working at a long silver counter across the room. "You go help Brittany with prep. Willow, you're saucier for the rest of the night."

"You want me on prep?" Griffin asks, his tone incredulous.

"You're off your game tonight, man, and we can't afford another mistake. Go. We'll talk about this later."

"Yes, Chef," Griffin grumbles as he moves aside, leaving Willow alone at the sauces station.

I grab another ticket and call the order, hesitating when I see Tatum standing near the back door. I'm not sure what she's doing in my kitchen at this time of night, but her eyes are roving over everything, almost like she's cataloging the way I'm doing things. A surge of discomfort—or maybe defensiveness?—rises in me, which feels strange, considering how much our old rivalry has recently shifted into something a little more enjoyable. I haven't felt a real sense of competition with Tatum in weeks. Still. Hawthorne is my heart and soul right now. Criticism from *anyone* would probably make me defensive.

"One salmon, one filet, rare," I repeat, when my cooks don't call back the order. Still nothing. "Zach, one salmon, one filet, rare."

"One salmon, one filet, rare," Zach calls back, "but I'm swamped over here, Chef."

I hear Zach's frustration, but there's not much I can do to help him. The orders won't slow for at least another half hour. "Willow, we're out of time," I say. "I need sauce now."

"Here. It's here." She steps across the counter and holds out her saucepan. I taste it and lift my eyes to meet hers. "Well done."

She smiles. "Thank you, Chef."

She ladles the sauce over the tenderloin, I wipe away a few extra drips from the rim of the plate, then pass it off to the server waiting behind me.

I allow myself one more glance in Tatum's direction before grabbing the next ticket, but she's already gone.

Long after the last dinner guest has left, I sit in the center of my clean kitchen, notebook open in front of me, and review the night's feedback—a long list of notes I took during my final check-in with my cooks and waitstaff.

The night was all right overall. Customers were happy, which is most important. My cooks aren't compromising on the quality of the food they prepare even when they're stressed and stretched thin. But I see how tired they are, how much they're getting on each other's nerves, and that's not how I want them feeling at the end of the night. I need to tweak our process, but I'm not sure how to do it.

Then there's the problem with Griffin. It could

be he just needs more training. It could also be that he isn't up to the job.

A knot of anxiety tightens in my gut. I haven't had to fire anyone yet, and I don't relish the thought.

I sigh and read the last few items at the bottom of the list. The waitstaff mentioned two different complaints about the salmon being too salty. And there were at least that many about the she-crab soup.

Zach appears beside me. "I'm heading out," he says, his bag slung over his shoulder. "See you tomorrow, man."

I nod slowly, not looking up from the list in front of me.

"Hey, you all right?" he asks.

"Just trying to decide if we have a *salt* problem or a *staff* problem."

"Ahh," he says. "Good question."

A door creaks across the room, and I look up to see Tatum walking toward us, a small dish in her hands. I didn't see her again after I spotted her in my kitchen during the dinner rush, and her kitchen has been quiet for a long time, so it's a surprise that she's here now.

Not an unwelcome one, though, and I suddenly find myself hoping whatever is in that dish is something she's bringing for me.

Tatum's chef's coat is gone, revealing a black tank that's hugging her in all the right ways, and her curly hair is loose around her shoulders. I . . . *do not* remember her having those curves back in culinary school.

Zach makes a low sound of appreciation which immediately irritates me, and I grunt my disapproval.

"Hands off, Zach," I say under my breath.

He lifts an eyebrow. "So it's like that, then?"

I don't know how to answer him—I'm not even sure where the warning came from. "Nope," I say, though Zach doesn't look convinced. "But it's not like that for *you,* either."

Tatum pauses directly across us.

"I'm not giving back the broccolini, Elliott," I say. "You better not be asking."

We didn't quite come to actual blows last time we divvied up the weekly produce, but had I not sacrificed ten pounds of brussels sprouts in exchange for the broccolini, we might have.

"You can keep your broccolini," she says. "I came to return this." She pulls out the picture I stuck to her apartment door the other day and tosses it onto the counter. "I found it stuck to the bottom of my shoe and thought you might want it back."

"Come on," I say. "You can't tell me you didn't laugh."

Her lips twitch, her eyes dancing, but she doesn't crack. "I don't know what you're talking about." She clears her throat and lets her gaze slide away from me. "Anyway, I'm actually here for Zach." She smiles at my sous chef, her expression warm and friendly. "I'm so glad you're still here."

Wait, what? Zach? She's so glad *Zach* is still here?

Suddenly, I'm back in middle school, watching April Henderson give my best friend Beau a valentine instead of me.

"Oh yeah?" Zach shoots me a look, then steps forward and crosses his arms, his biceps flexing. Tatum reaches out and touches his arm, and I barely restrain myself from standing, pulling Zach away from her, and tossing him out the back door.

"I was hoping you could help me," Tatum says. "I've been experimenting. Trying to come up with a new salad dressing to use for the bridal luncheon next month. I need to make a good impression, and I *really* want everyone here at Stonebrook to like me."

Tatum's eyes dart to me for a split second before they zero back in on Zach. She wants everyone to like her? Why do I wish she were only talking about *me?*

"Will you try this for me and let me know what you think?" She extends the dish she's been holding in her hands.

"Of course." Zach puts down his bag, takes the salad dressing, and lifts it to his nose.

I watch on, my irritation growing by the second. When, in just a few weeks, have the two of them had the opportunity to get so friendly? It's not like our schedule allows for tons of free time where we get to just stand around and make friends. Especially not Tatum's schedule because she's often serving three meals a day—breakfast, lunch, *and* dinner.

Nothing about their chumminess makes sense unless they've been hanging out *outside* the kitchen. My hand curls into a fist and I press it into my thigh, the slight discomfort keeping me grounded. I am *not* jealous of Zach. I have *no reason* to be jealous of Zach.

After a more thorough sniffing than Brody's basset hound trailing a rabbit, Zach dips a finger into the dressing and lifts it to his lips.

His expression sours as he tastes it, his eyes scrunching up. "Oh man," he finally says. "That's—" He clears his throat and swallows. "Is it—could it be—?"

Tatum presses her lips together, watching Zach with wide, innocent eyes.

"I think you might be using a little too much lemon," Zach finally says, rubbing at his jaw.

"Really?" Tatum says. Her gaze finally shifts to me. "That's funny. I used a recipe I got from Lennox."

From me? When would she have gotten a recipe from me?

Zach looks at me, eyebrows raised. "Really?"

Okay. I'm so over this. I reach for the salad dressing. "Let me see."

"It got him all kinds of attention back in culinary school," Tatum says as Zach hands me the dish. "I'm sure Lennox remembers."

I taste the dressing, her words catching up with me a beat too late. I wince as the overly sour flavor makes my jaw clench and my face contort.

The salad dressing tastes terrible. But it isn't just terrible. It's also *familiar.*

I should have known.

Nothing about Tatum asking Zach for an opinion on her salad dressing felt right. And the way she was looking at him, all wide-eyed and innocent, it's almost like she was *too earnest.*

I lift my gaze to Tatum who is smiling wide, her bottom lip caught between her teeth and her hands propped on her hips.

No, I take it back. She isn't smiling. She's *smirking,* her eyes glittering with mirth.

I have one hundred percent been *played.*

"Ha, ha, ha. Very funny," I say dryly.

"Wait, what? What's funny?" Zach asks.

Tatum leans forward onto the counter and props her chin in her hand. "What do you think? Does the dressing have too much lemon? I was going for subtle."

The lemon in the vinaigrette is about as subtle

as a semi-truck barreling down the highway. Exactly as it was the one and only time I completely bombed an assignment in culinary school. I don't know what possessed me to add three lemons' worth of juice to the simple dressing. I was trying to be bold, probably, prove that I could buck the rules and still come out shining. But adding enough sweet to combat that much tartness would have turned the dressing into lemonade. By the time I realized as much, the damage was already done.

My instructor used me as an example of what not to do for weeks.

I slide the dish back onto the counter. "How did you even remember the recipe?"

"Honestly, with that much lemon juice in it, does the rest of the recipe really matter?"

I roll my eyes. "I'll never forget the way you looked that day," I say, a slight challenge in my voice. "Almost as smug and condescending as you look right now."

"I still need someone to explain what's going on," Zach says.

"I was not *smug*," Tatum says tartly, and I'm weirdly happy she doesn't break our gaze to answer Zach's question.

I scoff. "You took an actual victory lap around the kitchen after our instructor declared it a catastrophe."

She leans forward. "Maybe I was just happy to

see the great Lennox Hawthorne knocked down a peg or two."

"Hello?" Zach says. "Do either of you want to clue me in?"

"The great Lennox Hawthorne?" I say. "That's rich coming from Christopher Elliott's golden child. How is daddy dearest?"

She rolls her eyes. "Golden child? Says the guy literally working on his family's farm?"

I stand up and lean over the counter, bringing my face level with Tatum's, and place my palms flat against the cool stainless steel. "Hawthorne might be sitting on family land, but it's still my restaurant. I'm the one doing the work and making it successful."

The bravado sounds false to my ears, especially after the night I just had, but I won't equivocate in front of Tatum.

She breathes out a chuckle. "It must be so exhausting," she says. "Doing all that work while lugging around *such* an enormous ego. The muscle definition in your shoulders is probably something else."

It's finally my turn to smirk. "I'll show you my shoulder definition if you show me your granny panties."

"Okay, I give up," Zach says as he backs away. "I'm going home unless either of you still needs me here?"

"We don't need you," Tatum and I say in unison.

Zach mutters something unintelligible on his way out the door, but all I care about is that he's gone.

Tatum crosses her arms and gives me a saucy look. "Still dreaming about my underwear, are you? Maybe you should get out more, Lennox. Get your mind off of something that is *never* going to happen."

The *never* hits me differently than it would have two weeks ago. I don't know exactly what it means. I just know Tatum Elliott is getting under my skin.

I lean even closer, close enough to see the flecks of gold in Tatum's gray-blue eyes. "It's *never* going to happen?" I repeat. I tilt my head like I'm studying her. "Do you promise?"

Her expression hardens—all but her eyes. Those stay bright and flirty, like she's enjoying this exchange as much as I am. "A promise, a solemn vow, a guarantee," she says. "Whatever you want to call it."

My eyes drop to her lips, but I force them back up. Because she said *never*. Because there is *nothing* happening between us. Because I am definitely *not* thinking about kissing Tatum Elliott.

Kissing her would be madness.

Ridiculous.

Reckless.

I shift and lean back, clearing my throat and

making a mental note to never stare into Tatum's eyes.

"Well that's a relief," I finally say.

"Definitely a relief," she echoes. She mirrors my posture, standing opposite me across the counter. "So glad we're on the same page."

I swallow. It *does* feel like we're on the same page, but I'm not sure it's the one we're admitting to out loud.

"So, you and Zach?" I ask on impulse, wanting to know why they seemed so familiar with each other, but still regretting the words as soon as they're out of my mouth. Mostly because I sound jealous, and I'd rather not give Tatum that kind of satisfaction.

"We're just friends," she says. "Not that it's any business of yours."

I shrug like I'm only mildly interested. Like this doesn't feel like the most important conversation I've ever had with Tatum. "It's my business if you're distracting my sous chef."

"By being his *friend?* Is this the rule you have with your employees? No friendshipping allowed?"

I purse my lips. She's got me there. I don't really care if people on my staff date, so long as it doesn't interfere with their work, so I have zero grounds for questioning her.

"I don't care who you're friends with," I say. "I was just curious. You can do whatever you want." I look at the discarded bowl on the counter between us. "Just as long as you don't actually serve *that* anywhere."

Her gaze follows mine, but it skates right over the bowl and lands on the list of notes I was reviewing before she and Zach interrupted me. She leans sideways like she's trying to read the list, and I snatch it away from view. I close the notebook and drop it onto the stool beside me.

Tatum's tone shifts and her eyes soften. "I used to do the same thing," she says, like she's already forgotten our previous conversation. "Go over complaints at the end of the night."

"More like compliments," I say a little too quickly.

She nods, but then she tilts her head, considering me for a long moment. "Lennox, if you ever want to talk about anything work-related, I'm happy to listen."

I lift an eyebrow. We talk about work-related things all the time, which means she's hinting at something specific.

Apparently, an eyebrow lift is all the encouragement Tatum needs.

"I'm not saying you need my help," she says, wringing her hands in a way that makes me think she's nervous. "But I did spend five years running a kitchen twice the size of yours, and I know a few things about efficiency. And it's possible I *may* have noticed a thing or two that might make things easier on you."

I think of her standing at the back of my kitchen, her narrowed eyes taking everything in.

"Is that what you were doing earlier?" I ask. "Spying on me?"

"No! Not at all," she says. "I was just passing through." She gives her head a little shake. "And it was just a few casual observations. It isn't really a big deal—more of an *only if you're interested* kind of thing," she says. "I'm sure what you're doing is working just fine."

My pride flares, making me itchy and annoyed. So every time she passes through my kitchen, she's looking for weaknesses? Ways she could swoop in and make everything better?

At the same time, I was just thinking about what I could do to improve things in my kitchen. It's hard not to be curious about what her "casual observations" might be.

Still, this is Tatum Elliott we're talking about. Tatum *freaking* Elliott. I may be willing to tease her and joke about who gets the bigger brussels sprouts, but that's surface-level stuff.

My kitchen? My livelihood? That's real. I'm not sure I'm ready to go there with Tatum, even if we are getting along.

"Thanks, but no thanks," I hear myself say. "I've got things under control."

I *do not* have things under control. But I'll

figure it out. I've got the experience. The knowledge. I have a few problems to solve, but I'll solve them. I'll fix things.

Tatum studies me for a long moment, like she can somehow see the battle playing out in my mind. "It's okay to ask for help, Lennox," she finally says, her tone soft.

As gentle as they are, her words still make me queasy.

I'm not supposed to need help. I told my family I could do this—I could make this restaurant work.

And they invested in Hawthorne because they believed me. They *trust* me.

And I'm not going to let them down.

I push away from the counter. "I appreciate it, Tatum. I do. But I'm good. Things are running fine."

She nods, taking a step away from the counter. "I'm sure they are," she says simply, but the dancing light in her eyes is gone, and it's that worried expression that stays with me for the rest of the night.

CHAPTER SEVEN
Tatum

Honestly, I should probably buy a winter coat. It's technically almost spring, but it doesn't feel like the weather has gotten the memo. Either way, March in Western North Carolina is a very different experience than March in Southern California.

I pull on my warmest leggings and a base layer, then add another long-sleeved shirt and a hoodie. It makes me a little bulkier than I like, but at least I'll be warm.

Finally bundled up, I grab Toby's leash and we head down the stairs for a late afternoon walk. I might not even use the leash—as long as we don't see any goats, Toby should be fine—but I like to have it on me anyway just in case. Especially since Lennox freaked me out with all the bear talk.

I pause at the base of the stairs and look toward my kitchen. The light is off, and I relax knowing now, I'm truly off the clock. We had both a breakfast and a lunch service today, but we only served twenty-five people, so I worked with less than half my regular staff and we had a pretty chill day overall. I left my dishwashers finishing up the last of the dishes, and Jessie scrubbing down the stove when I went upstairs, so I'm glad it didn't take them long to finish.

I felt guilty cutting out early, but Toby has been holed up inside a lot the last few days. We both need a nice, long walk around the farm.

Outside, we walk past Lennox's garden, and Toby pauses to pee in his new favorite spot.

"Toby!" I whisper yell, though honestly, I'm still feeling a little salty about the way Lennox dismissed me the other day, when I offered to help with his kitchen. Maybe I don't really care if Toby pees in his garden.

Maybe I don't care about Lennox at all.

Stupid, prideful man. It's not like I meant to insult him. Honestly, I didn't plan to offer at all. But then I saw all his notes, and I just—I remembered what that was like.

He has a really hard job. I just wanted him to feel like he had someone on his team.

But no. Lennox doesn't need anyone. Especially not me.

"Come on, Tobe," I say, ushering him out of the garden and back onto the path. We walk a little further, looping around the giant pasture below the restaurant, passing the pavilion where, when the weather warms, we'll hold outdoor weddings and other events.

Olivia told me about a trail that cuts through the woods on the opposite side of the main drive, so we cross over and find it, then take it past a little spring and up a hill steep enough to make my quads burn before the trail spits us out next to the goat barn. From there, we head over to the farmhouse, then catch the trail meant for guests who want to take a more scenic route to get down to the restaurant.

When I'm hauling a dinner service up to the prep kitchen at the back of the farmhouse, I use the main drive. But the meandering path through the woods is storybook perfect, right down to the gazebo lit with twinkle lights year round. I can only imagine the hundreds of wedding photos that have been taken in this spot.

Maybe it's the way the whole farm is nestled into the mountains, but it feels like there are all these little pockets of solitude, places where you might be minutes from a restaurant full of people or a barn full of goats or an orchard full of workers, but you still feel like you're completely alone.

This is exactly what I needed when I took this job. It's not that running the catering kitchen isn't stressful. But the pressures feel completely different. Nothing is quite as personal as it was when I had Dad observing every single decision I made, micromanaging my career in every way I would let him.

I drop onto the gazebo steps while Toby wanders off to sniff around the trees. On my phone, I scroll through half a dozen texts from my father—all sent in the past twelve hours.

So far, I've ignored every single one. But if I keep that up too much longer, he might do something drastic. Like actually *call* me. Or worse, fly out here to talk to me in person.

That's probably not a fair assessment. I'm sure he's just worried about me. But if I talk to him, he's going to try to convince me to come home, and that's not a battle I feel like fighting. Before responding to Dad, I distract myself by texting my sister. A dose of Bree's humor and optimism should go a long way to give me the courage I need to stand up to Dad's coaxing.

> **Tatum:** Tell me I can respond to Dad's text.

Instead of texting back, Bree calls me.

"Of course you can," she says when I answer the call. "You're a strong, independent woman who doesn't need him *or* his money."

"I am," I repeat. "I am those things."

"Yes you are," she says through a grunt that makes my eyebrows rise up my forehead.

"Bree, what are you doing?"

"Yoga," she says, her voice still strained. "My doctor says working on my core will help me stop peeing on myself every time I laugh."

"Oh, geez. That's—wait, is that a thing? That really happens?"

"Welcome to motherhood, baby," Bree says. "The twins wrecked my body. Sweet of them, right?"

"It's the gift that keeps on giving," I say. "I won't keep you. Just needed to hear you tell me I'm tough."

"You are so tough," she says. "Don't let him manipulate you, Tatum. You're living your life. Just say no to his guilt trips!"

A surge of gratitude for my sister and all her quirky weirdness fills my heart. "Thanks, Bree."

I hang up the call and pull up the thread of texts with my dad.

> **Dad:** Did you see the revised offer I had the studio email over? Note the salary. I pushed them to double it, and they agreed. Let me know when you're ready to sign.
> **Dad:** Double, Tatum.
> **Dad:** Did you see that part?
> **Dad:** You know, offers like this don't come along every day.
> **Dad:** It's a primetime slot, too. They're really excited about it. We just need you on board.

In his last message, his positivity finally starts to crack.

Dad: The studio won't keep waiting for you, Tatum. I need your thoughts on this ASAP.

I sigh and tap my phone against my hand.

I recognize that having a major television network offer me a primetime cooking show is a big deal—the kind of thing chefs all over the country dream of. This particular show would be something my dad and I did together—some sort of father/daughter bake-off thing featuring us both.

But when the offer first came in? All I felt was *suffocated.* It was just another thing in the long line of things Dad has pressured me to do over the years. Open my own restaurant. Sign onto his merchandising deals. Be head chef at Le Vin. And now, become a television star right next to him.

It was three days after he told me about the offer that I applied to be Stonebrook's catering chef.

Still, I haven't told the network *no.* Not explicitly. I've just told them I'm not ready to say yes.

Dad's patience is wearing thin, but I'm not going to cave.

I have never, in all of my life, made a decision about my career without Dad's opinions weighing heavily in the conversation. Maybe I will do the tv show, but if I do, it's going to be because I want it, not because Dad wants it for me. And I'll take whatever time and distance I need to figure it out.

Fortifying my nerves, I key out a response to Dad's messages.

> **Tatum:** Dad, if they don't want to wait for me, then don't wait for me. I'm not ready for this. I'm not even sure I want it.

His response comes through with lightning speed, like he's been sitting and waiting for my reply since he sent the first text late last night.

> **Dad:** You're being silly, Tatum. Eventually, you'll get over this little farm life you're playing at, and you WILL change your mind. But by then, it may be too late.

His words sting more than anything else he's sent. It isn't like him to be so harsh with me.

Toby barks somewhere in the distance, and I look up, scanning the wood line for his familiar black-and-white form. I don't immediately see him, but he never stays out of sight longer than a moment or two, so I don't stress as I type out a response to my dad's last message.

Tatum: I guess that's on me, then. I like where I am, Dad. I like what I'm doing.
I'm sorry that's not the answer you want.

Now leave me alone about it.
Toby barks again, only, this time, it sounds a little more urgent. I still can't see him, and a pulse of alarm snakes through me. I slide my phone into the pocket on the side of my leggings and stand up. I lift my fingers to my lips to whistle, but then I freeze, my eyes locked on a black bear standing at the edge of the woods.
An actual. Real. Living. Bear.
I swear and take a step backward, climbing onto the first step of the gazebo.
Lennox said the bears wouldn't come around if I had Toby with me.
He *said* the bear would be as afraid of me as I was of it.
Or did he say that about the bobcat?
Either way, he made it sound like what's happening right now would absolutely *not* happen.
That's when I see the cubs playing at the base of a tree a few yards away.
Oh geez.
Cubs mean the bigger bear is the mama, and I'm pretty sure the expression about *mama bears* is rooted in real, actual science. Meaning, that mama isn't going to let anything—or anyone—harm her babies.

Maybe, if I stand here silently long enough, she'll wander back into the woods and take her babies with her.

Maybe—

Toby comes charging out of the trees, barking like the crazy fool he is, and completely evaporates my hope. My stomach drops to my feet.

"Toby, no," I say, and his barking cuts off, his eyes lifting to me for the briefest second. But then the mama bear ambles forward a few steps and lifts onto her back legs.

Toby backs up, a low growl sounding from his belly.

Think, Tatum. Just think!

There has to be a way to scare the bear away. With grizzly bears, you're supposed to play dead—something I know thanks to the closed captions on the nature documentary my seatmate was watching the last time I was on an airplane—but this isn't a grizzly bear.

What are you supposed to do with black bears? Still play dead? Yell and scream and scare them away? Whatever the answer, what I *really* don't want to do is see my dog get into a fight with *any* kind of bear. Brown, black, polar, grizzly, smoky. NONE of the bears are preferable. I want ZERO bears.

Behind me, the sound of a gun cracks through the air. I flinch and turn to see Lennox walking toward the gazebo, what looks like a long hunting rifle in hand.

I shake my head and close my eyes, like I'm in some kind of dream and sharp movement might jostle me out of it. But when I open my eyes, Lennox is still there.

Nothing about the sight of him makes sense. It's close to dinner time, which means Lennox should be in his kitchen. Instead, he's outside, still in his chef's whites, scaring off a bear with a rifle.

My eyes dart back to the bear who has dropped back down on all fours. Her cubs are closer to her now, but there's a low sound rumbling in her belly, not all that different from Toby's growl, that makes me think she isn't quite ready to give up the fight.

Toby inches forward and lets out a snarling bark. I've never heard him make that kind of sound.

"Tatum," Lennox says slowly. "Walk behind me and cross over to the big oak tree. Do you see it?"

I manage a jerky nod. "I see it."

"From there, call Toby and see if you can get him to come to you."

"I'm not . . ." I swallow. I understand what he's telling me to do, but I'm having a hard time moving my feet.

"Tatum." Lennox's voice is calm and steady.

"Listen to my voice, all right? *You* are the reason Toby isn't backing down. He thinks you're in danger. If he can get to you without going through the bear, he probably will."

This, finally, logs in my brain, and I'm able to propel my feet down the step and behind Lennox to the massive oak tree across the lawn.

"Toby!" I whisper-yell. "Here, boy!"

Toby looks my way, then looks back at the bear.

"Come on, boy," I call, my voice quivering.

Toby barks one more time, a short, growling yelp, then darts over to me.

I drop to my knees and wrap my arms around him, curling my hand around his collar as Lennox fires another shot into the air. Toby flinches at the sound—he would probably bolt if I wasn't holding onto him—but I tighten my grip and he settles, leaning his weight against me.

The bear jerks, shaking her head before heading into the woods, her cubs following close behind.

Lennox is in front of me in a second, the gun dropping to the ground beside him as he pulls me to my feet. His hands wrap around my shoulders and slide down my arms, then lift to my face like he's cataloging every inch of me, making sure I'm whole and well.

"You're okay," he says softly as his thumbs slide across my cheeks, wiping away the tears I didn't even realize were falling. "You're okay," he repeats.

I fall against him, taking a deep breath as his arms wrap around my back. His embrace is warm and strong and stabilizing in all the best ways.

"Just breathe," Lennox says, his voice close to my ear.

Toby nuzzles my palm with his nose and lets out a soft whimper, and I keep my hand on his head, as much to steady myself as to steady him.

Somewhere in the back of my mind, I sense that later, I will remember things about this moment—about Lennox—that I'm unable to process right now.

How good he smells.

The feel of his strong arms around me.

The concern reflecting in his green eyes. But right now, I'm only repeating one thought.

I'm safe. Toby is safe. We're safe.

Also. Lennox knows how to fire a gun.

Listen, it's not like I sit around and dream about being a damsel in distress. But I *was* in distress, and seeing Lennox come to my rescue? It's an experience I didn't know I needed until right now.

And I'm not sure I'll ever be the same again.

I slowly lift my head and meet Lennox's eye.

"How—" My words catch, and I clear my throat and swallow, then try again. "How did you know I was out here?"

Lennox's hands are still pressed against my back, slowly rubbing up and down as if to soothe me. I hope they stay there if only to hold me up.

"I didn't," he says. "Not until I got out here. Perry saw the bear on the game cam. He called me."

I nod at his explanation, but I still have questions. "You said no bears, Lennox. You promised."

"I know. I'm sorry. Usually, there aren't any."

"But *you promised*," I say, suddenly feeling borderline hysterical as the adrenaline coursing through me starts to wane.

"*I know* I promised," he fires back, "but I saved you, didn't I? I'm here. I won't let anything hurt you."

I breathe out a gasp at his protective words, a surge of heat coursing through me at the admission I didn't expect.

The surprised look on his face says he didn't expect it either.

The words hang between us for a long moment before Lennox's grip on me loosens the slightest bit. "Are you sure you're okay?" he asks, his voice soft.

When I nod, he drops his arms and takes a step back, pushing his hands into his pockets.

So this is where we just *forget* that he turned all *knight in shining armor* on me, declaring his protection with a certainty in his voice that nearly melted the bones right out of my body.

Fine. There are other things we can sort out.

Like when Lennox turned into some sort of wilderness superhero.

"You fired a gun," I say stupidly, as if it hadn't been obvious.

"I did," Lennox says, like my statement amuses him.

"How do you know how to fire a gun? You're a chef."

He chuckles. "A chef who grew up on a farm."

"Well, right. But still. I was here, and the bear, and then you were just . . . *here*. With a gun."

He nods along, a smile playing at the edges of his mouth. "I keep it in my office."

In his office? "For what?!"

He shrugs. "Target shooting with my brothers, mostly. *Annnd* to scare off the occasional bear."

I press my palms against his chest and give him a tiny shove. We already had this argument but now I feel like we need to have it again. "Why didn't you tell me that the other night?"

He frowns. "I'm sorry I didn't do a better job preparing you. But honestly, had the bear not had cubs with her, Toby's bark probably would have frightened her away."

This argument makes sense—logically I know I can't really blame him—and I slowly release the breath I'm holding. "Would you have shot her?"

Lennox shakes his head. "It's against the law without a permit. I was just trying to scare her."

I hold his gaze, suddenly wishing he still had his arms around me. "You saved me."

He grins. "More like I saved your dog."

I drop my eyes to Toby, who is sitting at my feet, tongue lolling out of his head like he doesn't have a care in the world. A sick feeling creeps over me at the thought of something happening to him. "You saved my dog," I repeat.

Lennox crouches down and picks up the gun. "I need to get back. I don't think the bear is coming back, but just to be safe, you should probably put Toby on a leash and stay a little closer to the restaurant."

I nod. "Yes. Good idea." I retrieve the leash from where I left it on the gazebo steps and hook it to Toby's collar. Lennox waits for me, and we walk toward the restaurant together.

I'm surprised when he reaches over and takes my hand, giving it a reassuring squeeze.

I'm even more surprised when he doesn't let go. Except, the gesture doesn't feel like he's making a move. It just feels like *comfort,* and it sends warmth up my arm and right to my heart.

We pause at the base of the stairs that lead up to the restaurant's back door.

Lennox drops my hand and shifts his weight from one foot to the other.

Suddenly it feels like we're on a date and this is the awkward moment where we try to figure out how to say good night. A handshake? A hug? A kiss on the cheek? A full-on back-against-the-door make out?

"Not going to finish your walk?" Lennox asks and the make-out imagery floating in my brain disappears.

"I think Toby's had enough excitement for one day."

Me. It's me who has had enough excitement.

"Fair enough," Lennox says. Then he just stands there. Staring at me. Like there's something he can't quite figure out.

"Hey, look at us," I say breezily. "This is the first conversation we've had where we haven't argued about something."

He wrinkles his brow, his lips pulling to one side. "Haven't we though? I think we argued about bears a little."

"That one is totally on you," I say. "But . . ." I hesitate and bite my lip. "But the walk back was nice."

Heat warms my cheeks at the blatant admission—why, again, was I so blatant?—but Lennox smiles easily like he doesn't notice.

"Don't get used to it," he says. "I expect everything to go back to normal tomorrow."

"Hey, Lennox?" I say, stopping him before he can leave me alone. "I'm sorry about the other night. It wasn't my place to say anything about how you run your kitchen."

He pushes his hands into his pockets. "The great Tatum Elliott apologizing? May I live to see the day." His words echo the ones I said to him the day I moved in, right down to the inflection and tone of my voice.

I gasp, though I can't keep from smiling. "I did not deserve that! I just gave you a really sincere apology!"

"You did, you're right," he says. "And I appreciate it. But you don't need to apologize. You were only trying to help."

I *still* want to help. But I won't say another word about it until he asks me.

"So we're good?"

He nods. "See you around, Elliott."

"Not if I see you first, Hawthorne," I say to his retreating form, though my words are so soft, I'm not sure he even hears me.

I turn and head up the stairs, a new unsettling thought taking root in my mind.

Lennox said he expects everything to go back to normal tomorrow, but what he's asking is completely impossible.

Because I'm pretty sure I'm actually starting to *like* Lennox Hawthorne.

CHAPTER EIGHT
Lennox

"You know it's weird that you're standing here staring, right?" Zach leans against the wall beside me, his arms folded, and follows my gaze into Tatum's kitchen.

I'm not *in* her kitchen, necessarily. I'm more standing just outside it, in an area that I could, technically, also be standing in if I were on my way to the pantry.

"I'm not staring."

"You're definitely staring."

"I'm observing. That's different. Also, I'm working on inventory. Getting an order ready." I look over my shoulder into the pantry where I am not, actually, inventorying anything.

"Uh-huh, that's why you haven't written a single thing down."

I look down at the still-blank paper on my clipboard.

Whatever. Zach can call me out if he wants.

I motion toward Tatum with my chin. "Her staff really like her, don't they?"

"Ahh, so we're here about Tatum. That makes this way more fun."

"Shut up and just answer the question."

"I'd say hero-worship is more like it," Zach says. "They're always gushing about her."

"Why is that, do you think?" I've been noticing the same thing lately. As well as how cohesive her team seems to be—more than they were before she arrived. And she's only been here six weeks.

Zach shrugs. "She's good with people. Makes them feel seen. And I heard Jessie talking about some changes Tatum made to their order of operations that I guess made a big difference? I was only half-listening. But I'm sure Jessie would tell you about it if you asked her."

Or I could just ask Tatum about it.

I run a hand through my hair. It still rankles my pride, but the reality is, I *do* need help. Last night wasn't terrible, but it wasn't great either. Griffin is still giving me trouble, and for mostly stupid reasons, we had three plates returned to the kitchen with problems.

One is too many. Three is absolutely unacceptable.

I told my family I could do this on my own, but I'm not too proud to ask for help when I need it.

I'm *almost* too proud to ask Tatum Elliott for help, but for Hawthorne, I can get over myself.

Tatum is *here,* and she offered. Worst case scenario, I hate everything she suggests, I don't make any changes, and I'm no worse off than I was before.

Tatum walks toward me, heading for the pantry, probably. She lifts an eyebrow when she passes by. "You've been staring into my kitchen for a long time, Lennox. Do you have a purpose, or do you just think I look cute today?"

Zach chuckles, and I reach out a hand, stopping him from trailing me when I follow Tatum into the pantry. I stand behind her while she sorts through a bin of apples, setting aside the ones she wants. "Can I help you with something?" she asks without looking up. "I'm a little busy right now. I've got apple pie to make, and my butter will be the right temperature *any second*." She shoots a teasing look over her shoulder that makes something in my chest flutter to life.

"How are you feeling after last night?" I ask.

"You mean how am I feeling after I almost got eaten by a bear? I didn't sleep very well, for all the worst-case scenarios running through my mind, but I'm sure my brain will settle down eventually."

After I closed the restaurant and went home, it took all my willpower not to text Olivia and ask for Tatum's number. I wanted to make sure she was okay—that the bear encounter hadn't freaked her out too much.

Honestly, it freaked me out, and I grew up here.

But begging Tatum's number off my little sister would have given Olivia the wrong impression, and she would have passed that wrong impression on to Mom, and then the whole family would start talking about something that isn't even a thing.

Maybe isn't a thing? Do I want it to be a thing?

"I'm glad you're okay," I say. Because it's true, and because it feels safe. As a fellow Stonebrook Farm employee, I *am* glad she's okay.

She looks up. "I'm glad you were there to make sure I was okay."

The feel of Tatum in my arms pops into my brain, making my neck flush with heat.

I need a subject change, but my brain is not making it easy.

I have to say something though. I *followed* her into the pantry. I could probably start taking an actual inventory, but something tells me Tatum would see right through me.

"Your staff really like you," I blurt out. *Okay,* I guess we're doing this now then.

She drops a few more apples into the bin on the shelf beside her. "I hope so."

I scratch my jaw. "And your kitchen—you run it well."

She props her hands on her hips. "Thanks."

"And I guess—I guess what I'm saying is that if you have any suggestions for how to make the Hawthorne kitchen run a little smoother, I could use the help."

She cocks her head. "What happened to *thanks but no thanks?*"

I sigh. "*Thanks but no thanks* came from an

overly cocky guy who didn't want to admit to his college rival that he could use some help. But then he had another bad night in the kitchen, and he decided his business was more important than his pride."

She raises an eyebrow. "Keep talking."

"I can't let Hawthorne fail. But I think I must have some blind spots, and I can't fix a problem that I can't see."

She presses her lips together and takes a few steps forward, bringing herself close enough that I could reach out and touch her. She smiles playfully. "That was really hard for you to get out, wasn't it?"

I breathe out a little laugh, grateful that somehow, she knew lightening the mood would help. "You have no idea."

"So, you want my thoughts just right off the top of my head?"

I nod. "Bring it."

"Okay, first you need more room for your sauté cooks. They're getting in each other's way, and since your menu is so sauté heavy, you need to make their workspace as efficient and comfortable as possible. You can't move the grill, but you could move your saucier. Give sauté a little more elbow room."

I nod along as she talks. It's a relatively easy change, but I can see how it might make a difference.

"Okay, that's actually a good suggestion."

"Do you really have to sound so surprised?" she says, her tone teasing.

"Sorry. You're right. What else?"

"Your prep counter is modular, right? You can break it up? Move it around?"

I nod. "Yeah. For the most part, anyway."

"I'd turn it ninety degrees if I were you. It'll create a wider path from prep to your busiest stations and keep people from bumping into each other so much." She reaches down and picks up the apples. "And fire Griffin. He's rude, and he doesn't listen to you. And he talks a lot of trash. I overheard him in the parking lot the other night, and it wasn't pretty. If he were a genius in the kitchen, it might be worth keeping him on and seeing if you could temper his attitude, but he's not. I'd let him go."

"Sheesh. Who knew Tatum Elliott was such a cutthroat?"

She pauses at the door and looks back. "Um, do you remember *anything* about culinary school?"

Okay, fair point. But this seems different somehow. Culinary school didn't always feel real. We were isolated, working in practice kitchens, and spending *a lot* of energy trying to one-up each other just for bragging rights. But this is real life, and she just synthesized three ways I can improve my kitchen in less than five minutes. I guess I shouldn't be surprised, but this is the first time I've had all of Tatum's sharp wit working for me instead of against me.

"Thank you," I manage to say. "I appreciate the suggestions. I can't promise I won't ask for more."

She shifts the bin of apples to one hip, holding it against her body, then lifts her free hand to pat my chest as she passes by. I swear it feels like her hand lingers, her fingertips pressing into my chest for an extra-long moment. "Anytime, Len."

Len. It's mostly my family who uses the nickname, but there's something right about hearing it coming off her lips.

Zach is still waiting outside the pantry when we emerge.

He raises his eyebrows at me, but then Tatum captures his attention. "Zach, how's your mom? Is she feeling better?" she asks as she passes by.

"Much better. Thanks for asking," he calls to her retreating form.

She lifts a hand in a backward wave. "I've got a little more of that soup if you decide she needs it!"

Zach and I turn and make our way back to the Hawthorne kitchen. "Your mom is sick?"

He nods. "She flew down to visit and must have picked up something on the airplane. Tatum made her some chicken noodle soup."

I . . . don't even know what to say about this. I thought I knew Tatum, but here lately, every conversation I have either with her or about her just shows me more ways that I was wrong.

"In other news," Zach says as we approach my office, "can we talk about how Tatum actually *is* your type, you really *do* have a thing for her, and when you told me I better keep my hands off, it was *absolutely* because you're into her?"

I step into my office, turning my body to block the way so Zach can't follow me. I do get *some* privileges as the boss.

"We aren't going to talk about any of that." I hold up a finger. "But the hands-off rule still applies."

I shut the door in his laughing face, then move to my desk, anxious to have a few minutes of solitude before our pre-dinner service team meeting.

I'm glad I talked to Tatum, and I think her suggestions will help, but I need to have a conversation with Perry and Olivia about the restaurant anyway. They deserve to be in the loop, especially if I wind up firing Griffin.

I drop into my desk chair, hesitating when I see a small gift box on top of my closed laptop. I untie the ribbon and tug off the lid to reveal a hand-carved black bear about the size of my palm. The variegated colors of the wood swirl together like marble, and it's been polished to a glossy sheen. The craftsmanship and artistry of the carving are next level. At the bottom of the box, there's a handwritten note from Tatum.

For the hero I didn't know I needed. Thanks for saving me. I'll never forget it!

I set the bear on my desk and stare at it for a long moment.

I like Tatum.

I like that she's so thoughtful. That she gets to know people. That she's so smart and perceptive. I like that she pays attention and *sees* things others miss. Details. Nuances. People.

I like her, and that scares me. I don't usually give myself enough time to like someone before I cut things off.

But Tatum is here. Around me every day.

I couldn't cut that off even if I wanted to.

And I *really* don't want to.

So now what am I supposed to do?

CHAPTER NINE
Tatum

I bounce up and down on my toes, the cold concrete of the loading dock behind the restaurant seeping through my fuzzy socks and chilling me all the way to my bones.

I keep my eyes on Toby, watching as he wanders around the small lawn beside the restaurant. This early in the morning, he shouldn't venture far, and we aren't close enough to the woods for there to be bears—at least I don't *think* we are.

When Lennox said the bears wouldn't come back, did he mean they wouldn't come back *ever*?

I'm going to tell myself *yes*. Otherwise, I might never come outside again.

A sharp wind blows, and I rub my hands up and down my bare arms. I should have grabbed a hoodie on my way down the stairs. But Toby was anxious to go out, and I keep forgetting how cold it is outside until I get there. I'm too used to Southern California where the weather is pretty much hoodies optional three hundred and sixty-five days a year.

At least there's no one else around. Which is good because I'm wearing tiny pajama shorts you can hardly even see underneath my oversized T-shirt. My fuzzy socks complete the look, branding me, if nothing else, as an idiot who has no idea how to dress appropriately for the weather.

Even worse, my outfit is uncomfortably close to what Bree suggested I wear in front of Lennox to try and grab his attention—a realization that makes me all the more anxious to get inside before he randomly shows up and sees me. The last thing I want is for him to think I'm wearing this outfit on purpose. I may be growing more comfortable with whatever *feelings* are happening, but I'm not going to woo him *like that*.

Gravel crunches behind me, and I turn to see Lennox's dark sedan pulling into the parking lot.

Oh, fabulous. This is exactly what I need. It's like I wished him into existence with the force of me *not* wanting him here. The universe clearly has a sense of humor. Or it hates me.

With the way the evidence is piling up, it's probably that one.

I glance down at my ridiculous outfit and scowl.

What is Lennox even doing here so early? He *never* comes to the kitchen this early.

"Toby!" I call, quickly moving toward the stairs. "Come on! Let's go inside. You want breakfast? Let's go get breakfast!"

Toby woofs and moves toward the edge of the

parking lot, crouching low in the grass like he's a mountain lion stalking his prey. With a playful wag of his tail, he leaps forward, landing on a fallen leaf.

"Toby!" I call again, but it's pointless now. Lennox is already out of his car and walking toward me.

I fold my arms across my braless chest—it's cold outside and the girls are in full salute—and act like it's absolutely no big deal for me to be standing outside in the freezing cold in nothing but my pajamas.

Lennox eyes me as he approaches, his expression neutral. He totally caught me off guard when he asked me for help yesterday. When he followed me into the pantry, I'd expected some sarcastic remark, but then he'd asked for my opinions and offered a real and genuine thank you.

I almost fell over on the spot from the shock of it.

Now that we aren't trading barbs all the time, I have no idea what to expect from him. Will he still needle me and tease me? If I start flirting more openly, will he reciprocate? Do I want him to reciprocate? Do I really, truly want to pursue something with Lennox Hawthorne?

It isn't why I came out to Stonebrook at all. But as I take in how good he looks—even at this ungodly hour—and think of how safe I felt in his arms, it's hard to remember any of the reasons why I wouldn't.

He pauses across from me and takes a long sip out of the travel mug he's holding. I catch a faint whiff, and my stomach grumbles. Whatever coffee he's drinking, it smells delicious.

"Tatum," he says by way of greeting. His eyes drift over my outfit, and his lips quiver like he's fighting a smile, but he doesn't say anything.

I lift my chin and give him my haughtiest glare. "Lennox."

He looks down his front, surveying his own outfit, which is fabulous, even in its simplicity. Jeans. A dark wool pea coat. The man can wear anything, apparently. Chef's whites. Jeans. All of it looks equally delicious.

"It's a little cold outside," Lennox says.

I shrug casually. "Oh, I don't know. I'm pretty comfortable." Another breeze cuts through the air, lifting my hair, and I suck in a breath.

"Tatum, come on. You're freezing." Lennox holds out his coffee cup. "Here. Hold this."

I take the mug, loving the warmth that seeps through to my fingers.

Before I can fully process what's happening, Lennox pulls off his scarf, and steps closer, close enough for me to feel the heat of his body and catch his clean, masculine scent.

He drapes the scarf around my neck and ties it loosely at my throat. "I don't know how they do March in California," he says softly, "but out here, it usually means cold."

Oh my. WHAT is even happening right now?

Who needs a scarf to feel warm? All I need are Lennox's words delivered with that smooth baritone, and I could stand out here in the cold all day.

"I must have missed the memo," I say. "You should have Olivia add a section to the employee handbook."

Feeling bold, I lift his mug to my lips and take a slow sip. The coffee is delicious, warm, and perfectly creamy.

Lennox watches, eyebrows raised, but makes no move to stop me. In fact, the way he's tracking my movements makes me think he doesn't mind at all.

I don't know what to make of it. *Of him.* A month ago, I thought Lennox Hawthorne would barely tolerate my existence when I showed up on his family's farm. But now he's looking at me with bedroom eyes while I drink his coffee, making my body feel warm all over.

What does he really think about me being at Stonebrook?

What does he really think of *me?* Not just as a chef, but as a person?

In my periphery, I see Toby pounce on another leaf, chasing it when it catches on the breeze and swirls into the air.

Lennox follows my gaze. "He seems to really like it here."

I let out a little laugh. "You mean minus the bears?"

He grins. "Speaking of bears. Thank you for the gift."

I bite my lip, suddenly feeling shy. "I hope you like it."

He holds my gaze for a long moment. "It's perfect."

Nope. He's perfect. Ridiculously, perfectly perfect.

Another sharp wind blows, and Lennox looks to the sky. "They say a snowstorm is coming next week."

I wrap my arms around my middle and sink down a little further into Lennox's scarf, which—*oh, mercy,* it smells so much like him. A little herby, with hints of citrus and sandalwood. I could breathe this in all day and never get tired of it.

"Is snow in March normal?" I ask, wanting to prolong the conversation despite the golf ball-sized goosebumps popping up on my legs. I shift my feet and take another sip of Lennox's coffee. "There are blooms on the apple trees—I saw them when I was walking Toby the other day. I guess I thought it meant spring was pretty much here."

"It's a little late for snow, but it's happened

before." He moves to the door, his hand resting on the handle. "Come on. Even with my stolen coffee to warm you up, your teeth are going to start chattering if we don't get you inside."

I don't miss the way he says *we,* or the way it makes my insides flop around when he does. I really like the sound of *we.*

"The coffee is delicious, thank you."

"Yeah," Lennox says on a laugh. "I know."

I whistle for Toby, who, as if sensing his audience, takes the long way back to the steps so he can pee in Lennox's garden one more time.

Lennox eyes me, a dubious expression on his face.

"Oh come on, it's not like he's peeing on actual vegetables," I say. "It's just dirt. How much harm can he really do?"

"It isn't about the vegetables," Lennox argues. "Eventually, he'll impact the pH of the soil, which will matter when we plant next month."

"We, huh? You do the planting yourself?" The remark comes out snarkier than it should because it absolutely wouldn't surprise me if Lennox does the planting. Especially not after seeing him wield a rifle like some mountain wilderness version of Jack Ryan. The man grew up here. Of course he knows how to garden.

Before Lennox can answer me, another car pulls into the parking lot, and Toby darts off the landing like he's the official Stonebrook employee welcoming committee.

"Oh geez," I say, casting another glance down at my wardrobe. "I really don't want anyone else to see me like this. Why is everyone getting here so early today?"

"It's deep cleaning day," Lennox says. "The rest of my staff will be here soon. Here." He opens the door for me. "You go on in. I'll get Toby and bring him up to you."

I don't even hesitate as I dart inside and into the stairwell as Lennox closes the door behind me. I'm halfway up the steps when I hear Lennox's laughter ringing just on the other side of the exterior door. I pause. As long as whoever comes inside doesn't lean over and look up the stairwell, they won't see me when they enter the building. And I really want to know who made Lennox laugh.

Another few seconds pass before the door creaks open and voices float up the stairs.

I don't recognize the woman's voice, but it's definitely a woman, and not one who is on my staff, so she must work for Lennox.

The woman laughs—a light, breathy, flirty sound—and my jaw clenches.

I turn and flee up the remaining stairs, throwing myself into my apartment and shutting the door behind me, my back pressed against the worn wood.

I'm jealous.

The feeling is as clear and potent as it is annoying.

I don't want to be jealous. I'm just getting used to the idea of possibly, maybe sort of liking the man. It's one thing to observe his sexiness, to bask in the warmth of his scarf or enjoy his scent or banter with him over bushels of vegetables.

Those things are all surface level.

To feel real, actual jealousy?

That feels deeper. More significant.

But the way that woman was talking to him—*laughing* with him—all I want to do is storm back down the stairs and punch her right in her pretty-sounding throat.

A knock sounds on the door behind me, and panic spikes in my chest.

I can't face Lennox.

Not now.

Not now that I've realized how I'm actually feeling.

I worried I *might* like him after the bear attack—bear encounter?—but now I'm certain of it. Why else would I feel so irrational?

I drop Lennox's coffee mug onto the counter and back away from the door, putting as much space as possible between me and it.

"Come in!" I call, hating how shaky my voice sounds.

The door swings open, and Toby trots in,

tongue lolling to the side, and jumps up on the couch. Lennox hovers in the doorway, his eyes going wide as soon as he takes in my expression.

"Whoa. You okay?"

I prop my hands on my hips, forgetting that they were the only thing shielding the very free and loose situation happening under my t-shirt.

Lennox's eyes drop for the briefest moment, and I immediately regret my decision, but to his credit, he zeroes back in on my face lightning fast.

The fact that he was laughing with some other woman seconds before he's *noticing* me only fuels the (admittedly irrational) fire coursing through my veins.

"Fine. I'm totally fine," I say, trying—and failing—to sound casual. "Are you done with all the flirting that was happening?" I ask with a dramatic wave of my hand.

He frowns and glances down the stairs, then steps into my apartment and shuts the door behind him.

"I wasn't flirting with anyone."

"You were. I heard you. I heard *her*."

"Tatum," Lennox says calmly. "I don't know what you think you heard, but I run my kitchen with professionalism, and I never cross lines with my staff. I had a two-minute conversation with Brittany—who is married with two kids, by the way—and then I came up here."

"Then what did I hear? Why did she sound so . . . so breathy and *trembly?*"

He shrugs, like he can't even believe we're having this conversation.

Honestly, I'm not even sure why we still are. It's only my pride driving me forward now—pride I'd like to take downstairs and run through the trash compactor.

"She was probably nervous," Lennox finally says. "She's new. We don't know each other all that well yet."

"Nervous because you're so intimidating?" *Oh my gosh, WHO AM I? WHAT AM I SAYING?*

"Yes," he says firmly. "My family owns the whole farm. Sometimes people are intimidated by that." It's the first time he's ever raised his voice, though he's not even close to yelling. Still, the passion he's feeling is evident. And also *sexy*.

Lennox props his hands on his hips, his face turned away like he's pondering the world's problems and carrying the weight of them on his shoulders. His unbuttoned coat falls open to reveal a navy blue henley that looks soft enough to touch. I suddenly remember I'm still wearing his scarf, and I lift my hands to hold onto it. It's a flimsy anchor, but I'll take anything I can get. Because this conversation doesn't feel like banter anymore.

It feels like . . . like *feelings*.

"I realize you're probably coming to this

conversation with ideas about the kind of man I was when we were in school. And I get that. But that's not who I am anymore. It hasn't been for a long time. I'd appreciate it if you'd keep your wild accusations to yourself so you don't give anyone else the wrong impression."

His words are deadly serious, which makes my heart feel tight with regret.

He thinks I lashed out because I was judging him. *Accusing* him.

"You're right," I say, quickly backpedaling.

I can fix this, right? I just have to tell him I was wrong.

"I've seen you with your staff, and you're right. You're never anything but professional." I lift my shoulders in a resigned shrug. "I'm sorry I freaked out."

There. Done. See? That was easy.

Lennox studies me closely, tilting his head to the side. "What's really going on?" He takes a slow step forward. "What are you not telling me?"

I take a step backward, erasing the ground he gained, and breathe out a little laugh. "Nothing is going on. I was wrong, I admitted it, end of conversation."

"Nope. That's not all of it," he says, taking another step closer. He folds his arms across his chest. "Want to know what I think?"

I back up another few steps until I bump into the living room wall. I press my palms flat against the smooth surface and squeeze my eyes closed, peeking one open to look at Lennox who is moving toward me like some sort of wild animal stalking its prey. "Something tells me I really don't."

He grins as he presses one hand against the wall behind me and leans close. "I think you freaked out because you got jealous."

I scoff. Just because he's right doesn't mean I have to admit it. But two can play at this game. "As jealous as you were when I was talking to Zach the other night?"

He smirks, his expression completely shameless as he says, "Maybe not that jealous."

Ohhh man. So he *was* jealous of Zach.

What does that mean?

What do I want it to mean?

"So . . . I've been thinking," Lennox says, his smooth voice completely melting my insides.

I cross my arms over my chest even as I start to plot my exit strategy. "Oh yeah? What about?" I could hover in the warmth of this man's intoxicating gaze all day, but in my currently braless state, I'm feeling the need to escape sooner rather than later. It's hard to have any kind of serious conversation when my arms are acting as permanent nipple shields.

Lennox holds my gaze. "I was just thinking . . . maybe we could try getting to know each other *without* arguing."

My eyebrows go up. "What, like . . . be friends?"

He shrugs. "Something like that." He steps back and pushes his hands into his pockets. "What do you think? I could make dinner for us."

There is a measure of boyishness to Lennox right now that is doing strange things to my heart—a vulnerability I've never seen but really like.

Do I want to have dinner with Lennox? A tingle of excitement sparks in my chest, radiating out to my fingertips. I'm thinking that means *yes, yes I do.*

"Dinner here?" I ask.

He immediately shakes his head no. "Come to my place. We both spend too much time here as it is."

Oh my. Dinner at his place sounds like a date. Does he think this is a date? I said *friends,* and he said *something like that,* which could mean *YES, friends,* but could it also mean *more than friends?* I almost ask him, but I bite back the words before I can. One, because I'm spiraling, and two, if he *isn't* thinking date, asking will only imply that I am, and I'm not ready to make that kind of a declaration when I don't know where he stands.

I manage a nod. "Dinner at your place sounds great."

Once we pull up the farm's event calendar, we have to count out nine full days before we both have a night off at the same time.

There are other ways we could swing it.

We could have a late dinner in the restaurant kitchen after closing. Or we could change our plan to have breakfast or lunch when we both have an hour to spare. But now that Lennox has put the idea of dinner at his house in my head, I don't really want to settle for anything else.

It's also possible I'm happy to buy myself a little time. I could use a minute to breathe, to think, to figure out what kind of headspace I'm in. I just upended my entire life and moved across the country in an effort to find myself and figure out what I want. Will those efforts get cloudy if what I decide I want is a man? What if that man is Lennox Hawthorne?

I need to get my head on straight before I expose myself to a private meal prepared by the hands of America's sexiest chef.

Once we have a plan in place, Lennox leaves me with the last of his coffee *and* his scarf, insisting I can return them both the next time I see him.

Note: having Lennox's scarf in my possession is absolutely *not* going to help with my getting-my-head-on-straight efforts.

Also note: I'm going to wear it for the rest of the day anyway.

CHAPTER TEN
Tatum

I step outside and wave as Olivia pulls up in a Stonebrook Farm Gator.

The restaurant is closed on Mondays, and I don't have any events until the evening, so the place is pretty much abandoned, but I notice Lennox's sedan parked in the corner. I didn't see him when I passed through his kitchen to get outside, and I tell myself not to even wonder where he is. His office, maybe? Or maybe he was in the deep freeze when I walked past?

Or—*no. Not thinking about it. Don't care. Don't care. Don't care.*

I mean, of course I care. But I'm trying not to obsess. So we're having dinner next week. It's *just* dinner. There is no reason to act differently.

"Hey! You look adorable," Olivia says.

I look down at the cashmere cardigan I splurged on just before leaving L.A. I mostly put it on because it's the warmest thing I brought with me, and I'm pretty sure spring is on permanent vacation in North Carolina. But as a bonus, when paired with my favorite jeans and a fitted tank, it's an outfit that makes me feel cute in an easy, casual way. Which somehow felt important for lunch with Lennox's mom.

Yes—yes, I am having lunch with Lennox's mom. But as far as I know, this lunch has everything to do with me being the new catering chef and nothing to do with me being the woman whom Lennox just invited to dinner. (A work dinner? A strictly platonic friend dinner? I WISH I KNEW.) Regardless, whether justified or not, I'm feeling extra anxious about making a good impression. I want Lennox's mom to *like me,* so it eases a bit of my nerves to hear Olivia's compliment.

If nothing else, at least I've managed to get my outfit right.

"Are we not leaving the farm?" I ask as I climb into the Gator, tugging my sweater close against the chill in the air.

Olivia shakes her head, making no move to start the engine. Instead, she pulls out her phone. "Mom doesn't like to leave Dad for too long, and her studio is right by their house, so we're meeting there. You already know Brody's wife, right? Kate? She'll be there. And Lila, too. She's Perry's wife. I hope that's okay."

Oof. So I'm having lunch with *all* the women in Lennox's family? That . . . doesn't feel like pressure at all.

I swallow the lump in my throat. "Sure, of course," I say. "I do know Kate, and she's great. But I've never met Lila."

"Lila is the sweetest. You'll love her, too. Oh, hey," Olivia says, "before I forget, that box back there is yours. I guess the UPS guy couldn't find your place, so he just left it at the farmhouse."

I turn back to see the box, recognizing my sister's name and address on the return label. "Oh, awesome. Thanks for bringing it down." It must be the box of my mom's things Bree said she'd be mailing over.

A beat of uncertainty pushes through me. Maybe going through Mom's things will be good for me. It's been so long since she was a regular part of my life, sometimes I go days, even weeks, without thinking about her. But since she passed away, she's been on my mind more frequently, and I think it might do me some good to have a reason to spend some time processing what I'm feeling.

I lift a hand to my sternum and rub the spot just over my heart, as if I can rub away the ache, then file my thoughts away for later when I can sort through the box *and* my feelings in private. Definitely not *today,* when I'm already feeling the pressure of meeting Lennox's mom and spending time with his sisters.

"Seriously, where is Lennox?" Olivia asks, her gaze trained on her phone.

"Is he coming too?" I glance at Olivia, sounding way more chill than I feel.

"Definitely not." Olivia types something on her screen while I breathe out a relieved sigh. "I just need him to bring out the food."

"Wait. Lennox is feeding us? Isn't today his day off?"

Olivia meets my gaze, clearly sensing my incredulity.

"I know it sounds like a big ask, but if there's one thing that will *always* hold true for Lennox, it's his desire to take care of his mom. All she has to do is ask, and he'll make her whatever she wants."

Oh my word. Lennox loves to feed his mom?
This is so great. Exactly what my heart needs.

"Trust me, if *I* asked," Olivia continues, "he'd laugh in my face. Or agree and then make me a liverwurst sandwich."

"Who's making liverwurst sandwiches?" Lennox says from behind us.

Olivia turns and looks over her shoulder, but I intentionally keep my eyes forward. I wasn't expecting to see him, and now I feel like I need a minute to put on my armor.

"*You* would make liverwurst if I were the one who asked you for lunch," Olivia says. "I was just telling Tatum that only Mom gets the good stuff."

In my periphery, I see Lennox drop a picnic basket in the back of the Gator. "Don't go knocking liverwurst," he says. "In the hands of the right chef, it's not that bad."

I scoff without even realizing it, my hand flying to my mouth as if to stop any more errant noises from escaping.

"Hey, Tatum," Lennox says, a playful note to his voice. "You don't agree with me?"

I finally lift my eyes and turn to face him. And *oh, good grief.* He's wearing a pair of joggers and a fitted running shirt, the long sleeves hugging every curve of his trim, muscular arms.

I couldn't school my attraction to this man even if I wanted to. When he looks like *that?* Resistance is futile.

I lift a shoulder in what I hope looks like an easy shrug even though on the inside, my internal organs are melting into goo. "I mean, it's not foie gras," I say. "You don't exactly see *liverwurst* on fine dining menus across the country."

"Probably because it's called liverwurst," Olivia adds. "Who would ever order it?"

"I don't know that I'd order it somewhere else," Lennox says. "But could I make it taste good in my kitchen?" He offers that cocky grin I've seen a few times since arriving at Stonebrook, his hands lifted as if weighing the imaginary odds.

I don't doubt that he could, but I'm still glad when Olivia snarkily says, "You should bake it into some *humble pie.* See how that tastes." She cranks the engine on the Gator and shifts it into reverse. "Are you seriously going to run in this weather?" she asks, looking back at her brother one last time.

"It's perfect running weather," he says. "Race you to the studio?"

"Oh, you're on," Olivia says, and then we're squealing out of the parking lot, gravel flying behind us.

Surely Lennox can't *actually* beat us when we're driving and he's running. But as we round the bend toward the east apple orchard, I see him hop over a fence and cut across the goat pasture, which, if my sense of direction is worth anything, will take him right to the orchard while we're driving around the barn and the rest of the outbuildings to get there.

I hang onto the hand grips, shutting my eyes as Olivia rounds another curve, this one sharp enough that I'm surprised two of our wheels don't come off the ground. I'd ask if this kind of thing is normal, but by the way she's driving, it has to be.

Finally, we crest the top of the hill, and I see a white building trimmed with dark shutters in the distance. Just beyond it, Lennox is sprinting through the orchard, closing in on what must be Hannah Hawthorne's studio.

"Gah!" Olivia yells, as she increases our speed, but it isn't enough.

Lennox is standing in front of the studio, hands resting on his knees, when we finally skid to a stop.

Olivia's eyes are wide as she turns off the Gator. "He's never done it before," she says. "He's never actually beat me." She looks at me, a smile playing on her lips. "I wonder why he tried so hard *this* time."

She climbs out of the Gator and grabs the picnic basket, leaving me to wonder what she meant by *that* comment.

Does she think he was trying to impress me?

Was he? If so, then mission accomplished. Not that I needed yet *another* reason to be impressed with the man.

"Well done, Len," Olivia says as she passes by. "In honor of your win, I'll make sure we only tell Tatum *some* of the embarrassing things we know about you instead of *all*."

Lennox frowns, and I press my lips together to keep from smiling.

I'd like to know *all* the embarrassing stories about Lennox, please and thank you.

But also, Olivia is talking like Lennox and I are a thing. Like I've just come over to meet the parents and they're about to slide out his baby pictures.

Does she know we're planning to have dinner? Did Lennox tell her?

Is that why she invited me to eat lunch with half his family in the first place? Because she knows we might be a thing?

Or maybe she knows nothing and she's just hoping?

Or . . . *maybe* it's time for me to get my wayward brain under control and stop with all the questioning. I can almost feel myself spiraling, which absolutely isn't like me.

Also, it's incredibly presumptuous for me to be asking these questions in the first place.

Dinner with Lennox is *just* dinner. Not even a date.

And this is probably *just* a meal to welcome me to the farm as catering chef.

I lift my hand and offer Lennox a little wave, then follow Olivia to the door of the studio. She disappears inside, but I pause when Lennox calls my name.

"Hey, Tatum?"

I turn to face him.

"Make them go easy on me?" He props his hands on his hips, accentuating the breadth of his shoulders and his tapered waist. "And don't believe everything they tell you, all right?"

I bite my lip, suddenly liking this power I have over him. "Oh, I'm going to believe every word."

I love Hannah Hawthorne's studio almost as quickly as I love Hannah Hawthorne.

Despite the chilly temperatures outside, inside the studio is light and bright and full of warmth. Art supplies and a variety of easels and differently sized canvases fill one half of the space, and beyond that, it looks like there's a kitchen, but the back corner feels more living room than studio.

An overstuffed sofa is pressed against the back wall, a striped afghan in every color of the rainbow draped over the back. Several mismatched chairs sit opposite the couch, all in funky colors and textures, and piles of throw pillows are stacked in every corner.

The room has the same easy, welcoming vibe as Hannah herself. Everything about her seems to say she's happy in her own skin—in her own life. Her soft gray hair hangs in easy waves to her shoulders, framing her face and accentuating her warm, friendly eyes. An ache forms deep in my chest. I want this for myself. I want to belong somewhere like Hannah belongs in this room, surrounded by her art, her family, and so many other reminders of her place in the world.

After a round of introductions and a hello hug that makes my heart squeeze, Hannah motions me toward the couch. "You come sit with me, Tatum. I want to know everything about how you're settling in."

"Start with the bear attack," Olivia says as she unloads the picnic basket. "I want to hear your perspective."

"Perry told me something about that," Lila says, leaning forward, her dark hair cascading over her shoulder. "Were you terrified? I would have been so terrified."

It's a dangerous subject, because I can't talk about the bear without talking about Lennox, and

I'm not sure I can talk about Lennox without my crush bleeding through.

"Forget the bear," Kate says. She pulls her legs up and folds them crisscrossed in her chair. "I want the dirt on what Lennox was like in culinary school."

Olivia looks at me, a question in her eyes. She has to know something of the tension that existed between me and Lennox because she was there the day we met and Toby chased Penelope through his kitchen. But we haven't really talked about it since, so I have no idea how much she truly knows—how much any of them know.

"Ignore that question, Tatum," Hannah says. "I didn't invite you up here to grill you about my son. I just want to get to know you." She eyes the other women around the room. "That's what we all want, isn't it?"

I smile gratefully, appreciating the course correction, and easy conversation carries us through lunch. The women talk easily—about their lives, their jobs, their kids. Olivia's son, Asher, just started walking, and we all ooh and aah over the video she has on her phone, then Lila shows us a video of her son, Jack, at his first piano recital. All of it feels effortless and natural. These women really like each other. Like, I'm pretty sure they would be friends even if they weren't related.

And the food—it's absolutely delicious. Thick

slices of ham and gruyere cheese on soft sandwich bread, with fresh greens and some kind of homemade honey mustard that is bright and flavorful. There's also a winter vegetable salad with sweet potatoes, brussels sprouts, and pecans, with this balsamic glaze dressing that makes me want to cry.

I hate to admit it, but Lennox probably *could* make liverwurst taste delicious.

After we polish off half a plate of almond pillow cookies—these make me cry *for real*—I don't miss the way all three of the younger women shift in their seats, leaning forward the slightest bit when Hannah's questions turn more personal.

"So, tell me, Tatum. Did you leave anyone special back in California?" she asks. "A boyfriend, maybe?"

"Oh." I hold up my hands. "Definitely not. My schedule was too crazy. I dated occasionally, but nothing ever really stuck."

Hannah reaches out and pats my knee. "Well maybe the move will be good for you in that respect, too. Sometimes, we need to shake things up a bit. Get a change of scenery, if you know what I mean."

"Well I definitely managed that. This place couldn't be more different than L.A., and I mean that in the best way possible."

I think of my last interaction with Dad, and I have to fight the urge to cringe.

"Do you think you'll ever go back?" Olivia asks. "Is that totally rude of me to ask?"

"You should probably clarify if you're asking as her employer or as her friend," Lila says gently. "Otherwise, you're kind of putting her on the spot."

Olivia's eyes widen. "Oh. Oh my gosh. You're right. I'm totally asking as a friend," she says to me. "I mean, as your employer, I want you to stay forever. But even when I hired you, I doubted that would happen. You're Christopher Elliott's daughter. I thought we'd be lucky to hang onto you for a year, two tops."

When Olivia first interviewed me, she hinted at the possibility of highlighting me as a part of the farm's marketing. After all, having the daughter of the famous Christopher Elliott cater your wedding would be an easy sell. I awkwardly explained that I was actually trying to distance myself from my famous father, and Olivia immediately shifted gears and told me that was totally fine. It's not like the farm's hurting and needs the extra marketing.

But she's still looking at me like I'm special—assuming some level of greatness that I don't deserve, that I don't feel like I ever truly earned. It's not Olivia's fault, but there's no way I can explain all of that without making her doubt her decision to hire me.

And she shouldn't doubt. I might not be the star

Olivia thinks I am, but I can still do this job at least as well as your average catering chef. What I lack in passion and innovation, I make up for with scrappiness and efficiency. I might not love everything about the job, but I'm not going to let her down.

"I appreciate your transparency," I finally say, "but I'm not sure I can give you an answer either way. I don't really know what happens next or even how long I'll stay at Stonebrook."

I think of the television show still hanging over my head. Dad's been more persistent with his texts lately, but the longer I'm here, the less I want to even think about going back to California.

I curve my hands over my knees and press my palms against them, suddenly feeling bold. "But I'm pretty sure I don't ever want to go back to California."

A tiny thrill pulses through me as I say the words out loud. Could I really just *not* go back? Stay here longer than a year or two, or move on and make a name for myself somewhere else? *I could.* I can. The realization fills me like a deep breath of air.

Bree would be proud of me for owning my future like this—even if I have no idea what it's supposed to look like. Who am I really if not Christopher Elliott's daughter?

I might not be sure about who I *am* just yet, but

I *am* sure about who I'm not. And that's as good a place to start as any.

Olivia and her mom exchange a look. "Well you know you're welcome here as long as you want," Hannah says. "We're thrilled to have you." She reaches for another cookie. "And I wouldn't worry too much about what happens next. I've often found the thing we're looking for is right under our nose, even if it takes us a while to figure it out."

CHAPTER ELEVEN
Lennox

I make it through six reps before my arms start to tremble. Seven, and I'm struggling to get the weight all the way up.

Brody's hands tighten around the center of the bench press bar. "Okay, you need to be done. Your muscles are toast."

"Not yet," I manage to say. "Three more."

"Three more? Dude. What are you trying to prove? You're pushing it twice as hard as you usually do."

"I'm fine. I've got this."

Brody lets go of the bar, but he keeps his hands close. I groan as I crank out one, then two more reps, but on the third, my muscles completely give out, and Brody has to grip the bar before it falls onto my chest. He lifts it enough to keep me from hurting myself, but *not* enough for me to get it back onto the rack.

"Brody, what are you—"

"Will you tell us what's going on with Tatum?" he asks, cutting me off, and suddenly, I realize what this is.

My idiot brother is holding me hostage under two hundred and fifty pounds of iron while Perry watches from the sidelines.

Most of the time, I'm grateful to have brothers who know so much about my life.

But today? I'd rather they take a long hike and leave me alone.

I suddenly wish I'd used the impending snowstorm as an excuse not to work out with my brothers. We get together to lift in Brody's garage every Saturday morning since that's the only time that works with our schedules.

But I should have skipped this morning. My brothers think they know why I'm feeling off, but they're wrong. And the real reason is not a conversation I feel like having.

Trouble is, I also don't want to stay here all day, and there's no way I'm getting this weight up without Brody's help.

"Come on," I say on a groan.

"Will you talk?"

"There's nothing to talk about. Perry, are you seriously going to let him do this to me?"

"Sorry, man," Perry says. "You've been sullen and silent for the past hour, working out like you're training to go pro. You'll feel better if you talk."

"Ugh, fine," I finally say, and Brody immediately pulls up the bar, helping me reposition it on the rack.

I sit up and tug my shirt over my head, then use it to wipe the sweat from my forehead. It's unseasonably frigid outside, but space heaters are running to make things a little more tolerable in the garage. If the weather forecast is correct, it'll start snowing within the hour.

"Okay," Brody says, handing me my water bottle. "Start talking." He grabs a folding chair from where it's leaning up against the wall and flips it around so he can sit backward, straddling the chair with his arms resting on the back.

I take a long drink of water and try to organize my thoughts. My brothers think I've got Tatum on the brain, and I do. It's been almost a week since we made plans to have dinner, and I've spent more than a little time thinking about how that's going to go.

But she isn't the reason I'm feeling off this morning. That honor goes to my restaurant, which suddenly feels like it's on a slippery slope sliding into chaos, and I have no idea how to fix it. I've made the changes Tatum suggested, and they're helping, but when I fired Griffin, the conversation devolved into him basically railing on me for an hour, questioning my leadership and management abilities, insulting Zach and other cooks in my kitchen. He even said something hateful about Tatum.

Annnddd that's when I almost punched him.

Had Zach not walked by at just the right moment, stepping between us and stopping me, I would have created one enormous pile of paperwork for Stonebrook's HR guy.

I owe Zach for that, and I ended up having a long conversation with Olivia just in case Griffin decides to file a complaint anyway. I told her everything—minus the insult Griffin tossed at Tatum. No one's ears need to hear those words ever again.

Olivia was understanding, but she made me promise I would talk to Perry and fill him in. Pretty sure that's why I'm in such a foul mood. I'm here. I need to do it.

I just don't want to.

If I were only talking to him as my brother, it wouldn't be a big deal. But he isn't just my brother in this situation. He's the financial brains of the farm, and he was the slowest to get on board with the idea of an on-site farm-to-table restaurant. Olivia finally convinced him the idea was worth the risk, giving me the opportunity to live my dream and build my own place, which just means there's no way to have this conversation without making Perry think he made a bad call.

I don't think Perry made a bad call, but jerk that he is, Griffin still managed to get in my head. And now I'm questioning everything. I don't know what the answer is, but I'm finishing every night feeling like I've run back-to-back marathons only to get up the next morning and start all over again.

"Lila had lunch with Tatum the other day,"

Perry says, clearly still thinking Tatum is the source of my low mood. "Well, not just her," he continues. "Mom, Lila, Olivia, and Kate had lunch with Tatum. They had sandwiches at Mom's studio."

"I *made* the sandwiches," I say, "so I know." And I've been wondering what Tatum thought of the women in my family ever since. I'm also curious to know what she thought of the food. As far as I know, she still hasn't eaten at the restaurant, and I find myself wishing she would just so I can ask her what she thinks.

"Are you feeling weird about her eating lunch with the family?" Brody asks.

I run a hand across my beard. Olivia did make it seem like they had every intention of talking about me, but she could have just been messing around. And it isn't so crazy to think that Mom just wanted to invite Tatum over for lunch to make her feel welcome. Still, knowing Mom, she could definitely have some ulterior motive. "Should I feel weird about it? Did Kate say anything to you?"

"Only that Liv and Mom seemed to be dropping a lot of hints about you. Is that actually something that could happen? Are you guys even getting along?"

I don't *hate* the idea of Liv and Mom dropping hints but admitting that would derail the conversation I *need* to have with Perry. It's smarter to do it here, while Brody is around to play peacemaker. He's the middle kid in the family. Peacemaker is a role he knows well.

I breathe out a sigh. "I'm getting along with Tatum," I say. "But that isn't what's on my mind."

Brody lifts an eyebrow. "What is it then?"

My gaze slides to Perry. "Things are not great at the restaurant right now," I finally say.

My older brother's eyes narrow. "What are you talking about? The financials look great."

"I know. Money, reviews. Everything looks good on paper, but my kitchen is floundering. I just lost a chef, and I'm running myself ragged trying to keep up with everything, and it's only a matter of time before the chaos behind the scenes starts to trickle outward. How I'm running things right now isn't sustainable, but I don't know how to fix it."

"Can you just hire someone new? To replace the chef you lost?" Brody asks.

"I can, but I'm not sure that's the right call. I'm not maximizing the people I already have on staff."

Perry's quiet for a beat before he leans forward, propping his elbows on his knees. "This is a solvable problem," he says, in the voice he must have used when he was a high-profile corporate consultant. His tone leaves no room for argument or equivocation. "We know there isn't a problem with the food. Your location is solid, and your employees are making competitive wages for this part of the country."

"So what is the problem then?" Brody says.

"It's workflow," I say. "Training. My kitchen isn't running efficiently. I know enough to see the problems, but I'm having a hard time figuring out how to solve them. Tatum made a couple of suggestions, and they've helped, but it's not enough."

"You need a consultant," Perry says. "The restaurant business has those, I'm sure. People who are trained to come in and maximize your efficiency."

"But wait, didn't you just say Tatum made some suggestions?" Brody says. "Can she be your consultant? She's already here. And we're already paying her."

"She's good at what she does," I say. "And she said she's happy to help. I can ask her if she has any other suggestions."

Brody and Perry exchange a look.

"You'd be good doing that?" Perry asks.

I frown. "Why wouldn't I?"

"Uh, because just over a month ago, you guys were fighting over who got to carry the heaviest moving box. You hated Tatum Elliott when you were in culinary school. What happened?"

"I didn't *hate* her."

"Right, you just wanted to beat her at

everything, blah, blah, blah. Either way, it's still surprising you'd be comfortable asking *her* for help," Brody says.

I shrug as casually as I can manage. "It's not really like that anymore though. We're getting along. It's actually been a lot easier than I thought it was going to be."

Brody's expression shifts, like he's got a million follow-up questions to ask, all of them of the relationship-defining sort, but Perry beats him to it, and his question is all business. "Can we trust her?"

"Why couldn't we trust her?" Brody asks.

"I'm not saying we can't," Perry says. "I'm just saying that on paper, someone like Tatum Elliott shouldn't be running a catering kitchen in Silver Creek, North Carolina. With her connection to her father and the experience she's had working with him, she could work anywhere. Why here? Are you sure she doesn't have an ulterior motive?"

"What, like, she's spying or something?" Brody asks. "I don't really get that vibe. And why didn't that come up when Olivia hired her?"

"Olivia trusts her," Perry says. "And we probably can. But having her run the catering kitchen as an employee is different than pulling her into Lennox's circle of trust and giving her access to all of his trade secrets."

My *lack* of trade secrets is more like it.

Also, circle of trust? I'm not sure we need to make this so serious.

I hold up a hand, stopping before Perry can start drafting a nondisclosure agreement. "It's not like I'm in danger of going bankrupt. I don't need to tell her any secrets. I just need help sorting out some management stuff."

Perry nods slowly, as if considering. "Okay. Well, if you think she has the experience, and you're comfortable asking her, I say go for it."

"She has the experience," I say. I swallow the last shreds of my tattered pride. "I'll talk to her."

"Has she told *you* why she came to Stonebrook?" Brody asks. "Now that you bring it up, it is kind of weird how she wound up way out here. Did she know this was your family's place when she applied for the job?"

"She hasn't told me. But—" I hesitate, rubbing a hand across the back of my neck. "Maybe it'll come up when I make dinner for her next week."

I guess all I needed was a *tiny* crack in the dam for all my secrets to come tumbling out.

I roll my eyes as my idiot brothers erupt in a chorus of cheers and guffaws, pounding me with good-natured backslaps.

"Stop," I say, though I can't hide my grin. "It's just dinner."

"When you're cooking, it's never just dinner. You could probably propose after the appetizer, and she'd say yes," Perry says.

The sincerity in Perry's words gives me pause. Lila has *really* done a lot to counter his grumpiness. But even though I appreciate his vote of confidence, it doesn't give me the same boost it usually would.

If only amazing food were the only thing you needed to run a restaurant.

"So do you really like this woman?" Brody asks. "Is she planning on staying in Silver Creek long term?"

The question of how long Tatum will stick around has occurred to me, but I've tried not to focus on it too much. I don't want to get ahead of myself or make Tatum feel any pressure when we don't even know what this is between us. My brothers—they're the kind of guys who are thinking long term seconds after they learn a woman's name. But that isn't me.

"I like her," I finally say. "But I'm not trying to rush into anything. Our relationship has changed a lot in the past few weeks. I just want to see what happens. Get off my back and let me have dinner with the woman."

"You know what they say about the line between love and hate," Brody says.

"True," Perry adds. "Imagine channeling all the passion you guys put into arguing into something else."

Annnnd that's my cue to leave.

"Okay, time to go," I say as I stand. If I don't

bail now, the jokes and jabs will only get worse from here.

"Oh, Lennox, you're the macaroni to my cheese." I hear my brother Flint's voice behind me, which doesn't make any sense because Flint is in L.A. The voice is pitched high in an exaggerated falsetto, but it's *definitely* him. I spin around to see Brody holding up his phone, Flint's face filling the screen in a video call.

I shake my head even as I start to laugh. Flint just illustrated exactly why I want to bail, but it's Flint, so I can't really bring myself to care. "How long have you been listening?"

"Long enough," Flint says, his grin wide, though he's looking a little bit rumpled. I lean forward and look closer. "Dude, were you asleep?"

He yawns. "Maybe. But you know how much I hate it when you guys are together without me."

"You could always move home," Perry says.

"Actually, I've been thinking about doing just that. But right now I want to hear Brody's best food-themed pick-up line for Lennox to use on Tatum."

Brody immediately brightens, and Perry groans. "Not this again."

"Ohh, I've got it!" Brody says with the boyish enthusiasm only he can pull off. "Are you full of jalapenos?" He pauses and bites his lip like he can't contain his own laughter. "Because you're making my heart burn."

I make eye contact with Perry. "Has he been talking to Lila?"

"They never stop," Perry says. "He texts her with new puns at least twice a week."

"But these aren't just puns," Brody says. "They're pickup . . . *limes*."

Flint's groan dissolves into laughter, but Perry only scowls. Must only be Lila's puns he's willing to smile for.

"But for real, man," Flint says. "Keep us posted on how dinner goes. I won't even care if you leave me behind as the only lonely sibling."

"You should make that the name of your next movie," Perry says.

I laugh at Perry's joke but make a mental note to text Flint later. That's the second thing he's said in this conversation that has given me pause. He's thinking of moving home *and* he's lonely? That's worth a follow-up conversation.

"I'll keep everyone posted," I say, "but none of you say anything to Mom, all right?" I hold up a warning finger. "Or Dad. They'll start in on their whole-life happiness stuff, and I don't need them getting any ideas in their head."

Whole-life happiness is a Hawthorne family term, coined by my parents and used to measure how they think their children are *really* doing. It never has anything to do with how much money we're making or whether we're successful in the world's eyes. It's all about the stuff that *truly* matters.

In other words, until I settle down, find a wife, and have a couple of kids, or, at the very least, get a dog, my parents will never believe I'm *whole-life happy.*

Kate appears in the garage doorway. "I hate to break it to you, but your mom is already talking about your whole-life happiness. *Regularly.* And fair warning—she *really* likes Tatum."

I sigh. Why did I move home again?

Kate turns her attention to Perry. "Hey, the snow is really coming down now. Lila just texted and said it's time for me to kick you out."

"On my way," Perry says. He claps me on the back as he slides past. "You're not going to open tonight, are you?"

I shake my head. "I don't want employees to risk coming in."

"Enjoy the night off then. It sounds like you could use one." Perry yells a final goodbye to our youngest brother as he disappears out the door.

"All right, I'm out too," Flint says. "I'll be waiting for those updates, Len!"

Kate disappears back into the house after Flint hangs up, leaving me alone with Brody. He stays silent while I put my shirt back on, then pull my sweatshirt over my head.

"Hey, should we be worried about Flint?" I say

as my head pops through the neck of the hoodie, mussing my hair. I smooth it down again. "You think he's serious about moving home?"

Brody shrugs. "Nah. He's too restless to live in Silver Creek."

I grab my keys. "Maybe, but you used to say the same thing about me."

"That's true." He follows me out the front door and onto his porch. The air around us is heavy with the silence that only a snowfall can bring, the ground quickly disappearing under a blanket of white. Brody shoves his hands into the pocket of his hoodie and hunches his shoulders against the cold. "So, this thing with Tatum," he says, studying me closely. "Do you feel like things are different with her?"

"Different how?"

He shrugs. "I don't know. I just—" He pauses and clears his throat. "I'm just saying. Tatum doesn't seem like some random woman you picked up at a bar." He scratches his neck like he's nervous. Or maybe just trying really hard to be tactful. "She seems . . . different."

"So I better not be messing around?" I ask, saying what he clearly *wants* to say but won't because he's too nice of a guy.

He nods like he's relieved I owned up to the possibility. "If things went south and it impacted her job, you'd be answering to Olivia, so I'd be careful if I were you."

I don't feel like I'm messing around with Tatum, but Brody's words send a jolt of uneasiness through my chest anyway. Brody's concern is valid because my track record is . . . not great.

I've never been very good at explaining my feelings about relationships to my brothers—especially not Brody, who has been in love with the same woman since he was old enough to realize what love was. Brody was built to be in love—to be committed—so he's never understood my serial dating habits—though those dried up about the time I opened Hawthorne.

But even when I *was* serial dating, I was always up front with women about what I *wasn't* looking for. Nothing serious. No commitments. No expectations.

But now that I'm home, living in Silver Creek, it's harder to live that life. And not just because the dating scene is so dismal. I'm constantly surrounded by my siblings and all their devoted *marriedness,* which is making my reasons for keeping my relationships so shallow look a little flimsy.

I don't really want to stay casually single forever, do I?

"It's only dinner," I say to Brody. I look him right in the eye, somehow wanting to reassure my brother that he shouldn't worry about me, even if I'm worried about myself. "But I get it."

The front door opens, and Kate pops her head out, her gaze zeroing in on her husband before they dart to me. "Oh. You're still here," she says, like she's disappointed.

"On my way out though," I say slowly, like I'm stating the obvious.

Because I *am* stating the obvious. I look at Brody. "You got somewhere you need to be?"

"More like something we need to *do*," Kate says.

"Whoa. Right now?" Brody says. "Like, *now* now?"

"*Now* now," Kate repeats. She disappears inside, and Brody moves to the door to follow his wife. He lifts his shoulders in a sheepish shrug, a small smile lighting his face. "We're trying for a baby," he says simply.

"Whoa. Really?"

He nods. "I know it's kind of fast, but it doesn't really *feel* fast."

"You've known each other your whole lives," I say. I run a hand across my face. "I'm happy for you, man."

"Thanks. But don't say anything, all right? We don't want people to get excited when we have no idea how long it's going to take."

I nod. "Of course."

Brody opens the door. "Be careful heading home, all right? If you wind up needing to drive anywhere later, come borrow the truck."

"Will do. Thanks man."

He disappears inside, the click of the front door sounding loud in the heavy silence of the falling snow.

Brody is trying for a baby.

Perry is running home because his wife is worried about him driving on the roads.

And I'm . . . standing alone on an empty porch.

Geez. Who's the only lonely sibling now?

It's been a decade since I was in a serious, committed relationship, and that one ended badly enough that I can still conjure up the sting of Hailey's betrayal.

If something really is happening with Tatum, can I be different with her?

And if I can't, is it fair for her to get caught in the crossfire?

I don't know the answer. I only know Brody's right. Tatum *does* feel different. And I think that means I have to try.

CHAPTER TWELVE
Tatum

There is SNOW falling outside my window.

Real, actual snow! I mean, it's not like I've never seen it before. I've been to ski resorts. I've traveled to places where snow falls regularly. But I've never lived anywhere where it can just happen, so this feels momentous.

And also *freezing*.

The heat is turned up inside my tiny apartment, but multiple people at work yesterday said that when it snows around here, the power frequently goes out from downed trees and power lines. Brody's wife, Kate, already assured me that they have wood-burning heat at their house, and if we lose power, she'll send Brody to pick me and Toby up, but I'm still going to bed with extra blankets in case it goes out in the middle of the night.

Out my living room window, Stonebrook Farm looks picturesque and perfect. I pull out my phone and take a couple of photos, debating whether I want to put them up on Instagram.

My account has remained mostly dormant since I made the move across the country, which is fine with me. Most of the people who follow me only do so because of my connection to Dad, so it's never really felt like my account anyway.

A handful of friends follow, but short of a few DMs and text messages sent right after I left, I haven't really stayed in touch with anyone back in L.A. The longer I'm gone from the entire scene, the more I think there really wasn't *any* part of my life that felt like mine. Even my friendships.

I slide my phone into the back pocket of my jeans without posting anything.

My photos of Stonebrook can be just for me.

I may not be one hundred percent sold on catering, but I *am* starting to love Stonebrook. It feels right somehow, while I'm still parsing together a new life for myself, to hold it close.

I cross my tiny living room, where Toby is lounging on the sofa, and pull leftovers from last night's dinner out of the fridge.

I finally took the plunge and ordered dinner from Lennox's restaurant. Because I couldn't decide between two entrees, I ordered them both which, obviously, was a brilliant decision and one I'm particularly grateful for now.

I ate most of the filet mignon last night, but I was too full to eat more than a few bites of the pork tenderloin, so that's what I warm up now. Even ordered to go—which can be trying for some dishes—both entrees were beyond delicious. The fried green tomato appetizer I ordered was just as amazing. Bright, balanced flavors, perfect textures and consistencies, sauces that complimented and heightened the dishes without overpowering them. A good sauce can easily be used to mask all kinds of sins, but none of that is happening at Lennox's restaurant. At least not that I've found so far.

Somehow, he knows how to use every ingredient to its fullest potential—something I remember noticing even back in culinary school. The way he sees food—it's a gift I'll never stop envying.

I move to the kitchen table and drop into a chair, then take a bite of the tenderloin. I moan as the flavors explode on my tongue. Apples, brandy, brown butter. It shouldn't still taste this good warmed up on the second day, but *man,* it's the best thing I've eaten in weeks.

It only tastes better when I imagine Lennox's hands preparing it, his bright green eyes looking over my order—even if he didn't know it was for me. Would he have done anything differently if he had known? Would he have wanted to make it extra delicious just for me?

The thought warms my cheeks, and I push it away. These are the thoughts that will drive me crazy if I let them. For all I know, Lennox would have laughed and squirted extra lemon juice all over my meal as payback.

Toby moseys over and drops his head on my

thigh, his unobtrusive way of asking for a bite. I cut off a tiny piece of pork and hold it out to him.

The fact that Lennox's food is so good when his kitchen seems to be falling apart is only further testament to how brilliant he is—or maybe just how hard he's working. I don't think I've seen him take a day off since I got here.

He's probably loving the snowstorm. The restaurant is closed tonight and probably tomorrow too, along with the catering kitchen since all the events scheduled to happen this week have been postponed due to weather.

I'm happy to enjoy the break, but I think Lennox really needs it.

My phone buzzes from my pocket and I pull it out to see a notification from the weather app warning of below-freezing temperatures and recommending that all pet owners make sure their animals are safe and protected indoors.

I glance over to see Toby back on the sofa, already snoring.

A beat of trepidation passes through me. I'm not nervous, exactly. But I do feel like hunkering down to wait out a snowstorm would be more fun if I had someone besides my dog for company.

I turn on the most recent Harry album—it always puts me in a good mood—and clean up my dinner dishes, then move to the tiny closet in my entryway to get the extra blankets I shoved onto the top shelf when I moved in. I reach up, my fingers grazing over the edge of the blanket, and I let out a groan. I'm not *that* short—a hair over five foot four—but it's still short enough that most things on high shelves are just out of reach. I jump up and manage to wrap my fingers around the corner of one blanket, giving it a hard tug as I land back on my feet.

The blanket comes tumbling, followed by something else much less forgiving. A shoebox I've never seen before hits my head with a thunk, then tumbles to the ground, its contents spilling all over the floor of the entryway. It must have been left by whoever lived here last.

I crouch down to gather everything up, pausing when I pick up a picture of Lennox. I shift and sink onto my butt so I'm sitting on the floor, my legs extending toward the front door.

I study the picture closely. It's definitely Lennox, but a much younger version of him. More like the Lennox I knew in culinary school. He's got an arm around a woman I recognize but can't quite place. She was in school with us for a little while, but I don't remember her graduating with us. Kailey, maybe? Or something close to that. Regardless, the way she's looking at him makes me think he definitely meant something to her.

I gather up a few more pictures. They are *all* of Lennox and the same woman. There are also ticket stubs, playbills, a random slip of paper that looks like some kind of dry-cleaning receipt.

So it's *that* kind of box.

The date on the receipt gives me a timeframe—our first year in culinary school.

I barely knew Lennox then. We didn't really start clashing until our third year when our identical degree programs dropped us in most of the same classes. Southern Culinary Institute has multiple tracks and degree programs, but Lennox and I were in the same one, getting bachelor's degrees in culinary arts and food science.

I look through the contents of the box, curiosity building, only pausing when I get to a couple of handwritten notes in a swirly, feminine hand. I drop the letters into the box like they're on fire, suddenly uncomfortable with this weirdly personal window into Lennox's life.

I shouldn't be doing this, pawing through his old memories like they don't matter.

But then . . . maybe they don't. They wound up *here,* after all.

I purse my lips to the side and stare at the box.

I would not want Lennox reading my old love letters.

I *can't* read them.

I shouldn't.

But I really, *really* want to.

"I am not going to read these letters," I say out loud, as if voicing my commitment to the universe will make me more accountable somehow.

But then I turn, checking to make sure I've

picked up everything that fell out of the box, and I see a card lying open on the entryway rug.

I wouldn't even have to unfold it to read it.

Curiosity too strong to ignore, I pick it up and glance at the name at the bottom.

Hailey.

Her last name immediately comes to me. *Hailey Stanton.* She lived a few doors down from me, but we didn't talk much. My eyes rove over the card, catching on a few key words and phrases.

This is a breakup letter.

There must be ten different *I'm sorrys* filling the page. Along with *I didn't mean to hurt you, I hope you can forgive me,* and, my personal favorite, *It's not you, it's me.* Not very original, but at least she didn't send a text. A surge of protectiveness rises in my chest. Who did this woman think she was breaking up with Lennox like this? It was a long time ago, I know, but I still find myself wishing I could ease the hurt somehow, soothe whatever wound might be leftover.

Hailey didn't come back after our first year. I remember that clearly now, though that's not all that uncommon. A lot of people change majors or change degree programs or drop out of school all together. But now I'm wondering if her breakup with Lennox had something to do with her disappearing act.

I close the card and drop it into the box before

pushing the lid on top, wishing I had some masking tape to keep it from ever falling open again.

How did it even get here? Did Lennox live in this apartment before I did?

It wouldn't be all that weird if he did—it's his parents' farm, after all. Maybe he lived here while he was working to open the restaurant.

A pulse of heat moves through me at the thought of Lennox occupying this space. Sleeping in my bed. Using the shower. Lounging in the living room after a long day of work. It's a dangerous thought because it makes it all too easy to imagine the two of us lounging around the apartment *together*, and those are exactly the kinds of thoughts I'm trying to avoid.

Outside my apartment door, footsteps sound on the stairs, and my heart rate spikes. I stand up, picking the box up with me, and take a step away from the door.

Toby sits up, his ears perked.

Who could possibly be coming to see me now? In the middle of a snowstorm? Or, more like the *beginning* of a snowstorm, but still. An hour ago, the parking lot was empty except for my SUV, so to suddenly realize I'm not alone is a very uncomfortable feeling.

A knock sounds on the door. "Tatum?" Lennox calls. "Don't freak out. It's just me."

Oh. *Oh*. Maybe I can stop freaking out over

the possibility of a masked murderer being at my door, but how am I supposed to stop freaking out over *Lennox* being there?

I hurry forward, composing myself as best I can in the three steps it takes me to reach the door. "Hey," he says easily. He's all bundled up in a winter coat and scarf, a wooden milk crate in his hands. "Sorry if I scared you."

"Nothing like heavy footsteps slowly moving up the stairs to get your heart racing." I step back to let him in. "What are you doing here? Should you be driving in this weather?"

He steps inside, and I shut the door behind him. "I borrowed Brody's truck," he says. "And the roads aren't too bad yet." His eyes drop to the box in my hands—*his box*.

Oh no.

What do I do now?

Do I give it to him? Put it back in the closet and pretend like it's mine?

It's an old Nike box—orange with a white swoop—so it's not like it's unique. Unless he recognizes the particular way this box is worn, he could just think it's *my* old shoebox.

I spin around and put it on the kitchen table like it's no big deal. Like I have no reason to hide it from him. Like I didn't just spend half an hour digging through the remnants of his love life.

"Are you a Harry Styles fan?" Lennox asks. *Harry's House* is still playing in the background, but the song that's playing right now is one of the lesser known tracks. I'm impressed Lennox recognized the artist.

"Is anyone *not* a Harry Styles fan?"

He chuckles. "You know, he and Flint are friends."

"Ohhh, don't tell me things that will make me obsess about the degrees of separation between me and Harry. It's cruel."

He smiles. "Noted. So, uh—" Lennox clears his throat like he's suddenly nervous. "I brought you some things to help you get through the storm."

He sets the milk crate down on the table not far from the shoebox.

Oh, this is awkward. Please, please, please, just don't ask me about the box.

"A flashlight, a few candles. Some snacks," Lennox says. "And an extra blanket just in case you need it."

Oh, my heart. He brought me snacks? I lean forward and look into the box, my eye catching on a thermos in the corner. Wait, no. *Two* thermoses.

"There's soup in that one," Lennox says. "And the coffee you seemed to like so much in the other." He shoves his hands into the pockets of his coat, and I get the sense that he's nervous.

He shouldn't be. If he was hoping to charm me, he has succeeded. I'm charmed. Fully. Completely. All-in *charmed.*

I still have the travel mug I stole from him last week when he found me outside in my pajamas. And his scarf, too. I've been meaning to give them back, but I keep forgetting. Maybe because subconsciously, I like having things around that belong to him.

My eyes dart to the shoebox. Better a scarf and a coffee mug than *that*.

Lennox must follow my gaze because he reaches for the box, sliding it into the center of the table. "Is this what I think it is?" he asks slowly.

I frown, and then words tumble out of me like water bursting through a dam. "I'm so sorry, Lennox. I didn't know what it was. I pulled something out of the closet, and it fell off the top shelf and all the stuff inside went everywhere. But I didn't read anything. Or, I didn't read *everything*. And I put it all back."

He lifts the top of the box and pulls out one of the pictures.

His face is impassive, his expression completely unreadable.

"Did you live here? In the apartment?" I ask if only to break the tension building in the awkward silence. Obviously, it isn't the most relevant question, but I'll do anything—*anything*—to avoid talking about the contents of the box. Or the fact that I was just pawing through his stuff.

Lennox nods without looking up. "For a few months. Before the restaurant opened."

If I could rewind time five minutes and put the box back in the closet before opening my front door, I would.

Lennox brought me soup. And coffee. And a blanket to get through a cold night. And now he's looking at pictures of his ex-girlfriend and *not* making eye contact with me.

Fantastic.

If I had a fireplace, I'd torch the entire box of Hailey memories on the spot.

You know.

If Lennox wanted me to.

"If it matters, her break-up letter was total trash," I say.

He finally looks up, the subtle lift of his smile easing the pressure around my heart. "I thought you said you didn't read anything."

"But then I clarified that I didn't read *everything.* I read some. Enough to know that one more *it's not you, it's me,* and I might have poked my eyes out with an oyster fork."

Lennox chuckles and drops the photo back in the box. "I can't believe I saved all of this stuff. I'd forgotten it was even here."

I study him closely. His words are light, like it doesn't bother him at all to look through a box of his old memories, but there's a tightness around his eyes that makes me think it's impacting him more than he's letting on.

Maybe that just means it's time for him to move

on. "Hey." I nudge his arm. "In the mood for a bonfire?"

"That's actually a really good idea," he says through a grin, and I wonder if I imagined his earlier discomfort. But then he glances at the door. "I've got to get going though. I still need to check on Mrs. Sprinkles, and I don't want to be out on the roads too much longer."

Is he telling me the truth? Or is he just looking for a way to escape so he can nurse his Hailey wounds in private? But also—*Mrs. Sprinkles?*

"Hold up. Who do you need to check on?"

"She was my seventh-grade math teacher. She lives alone just up the road. I want to make sure her generator's working in case the power goes out."

"And that's her real name? Mrs. Sprinkles?"

He chuckles as he moves to the door. "If you say it a few more times, you'll get used to it."

Okay. This does not sound like he's feeding me an excuse. So maybe he's fine. Maybe we're fine?

"It's really nice of you to check on her, Lennox."

He shrugs like it's no big deal. "I don't mind."

I might get used to Mrs. Sprinkles's name, but I will never get used to him.

To think I wasted all those years in culinary school thinking this man was some stuck up, full-of-himself, womanizing jerk. Talented, yes. But still a jerk.

But no. Now that I'm truly getting to know

him, he's nothing like I thought he was. He's a man who feeds his mom and grows vegetables and checks on little old ladies who live alone. A man who just brought me snacks and coffee and didn't get bent out of shape over me clearly violating his privacy.

Lennox holds my gaze for a long moment, his green eyes sparkling, before he reaches out and squeezes my shoulder. "Stay warm, all right?"

I nod, but as he pulls away, I stop him, reaching up to grip his wrist. "Lennox, wait."

He stills, his other hand falling from the doorknob. I suddenly get the sense that if I were to ask Lennox to stay, to share the soup he brought and hang out with me through the storm, he'd probably say yes.

If not for Mrs. Sprinkles and her generator, I might ask him to.

"I still don't have your number," I say instead. "If something were to happen, can I call you?"

Outside, a gust of wind rattles the shutters and we both turn toward the window.

"It's on a sticky note stuck to the outside of the box of crackers," he says. "Text me so I have your number too."

"Okay. Be safe, all right?"

He nods, then disappears down the steps.

I run across the room to the window, peeking through the blinds to see him climb into Brody's truck and slowly pull out of the lot. I watch him until he makes it down the main drive and turns out of sight.

Well.

How am I supposed to relax after *that* interaction?

I immediately grab my phone and text him a quick hello, then program his name into my contacts, a little thrill shooting through me at this new connection.

After retrieving the blanket—which smells so much like Lennox it makes my knees feel wobbly—and the coffee he brought over, I settle on the sofa and turn on Netflix.

There has to be something mind-numbing and ridiculous to get my mind off of the man. I pick a romcom I've seen a hundred times that will not require me to work too hard because honestly, my mind is pretty preoccupied at the moment.

No matter how hard I try, I can't stop thinking about how much I'm starting to like it here.

The scenery. The entire Hawthorne family.

Lennox.

There are still worries hovering at the back of my mind. The uncertainty about my future and whether I see myself working in catering—in culinary anything—long term. My relationship with my father. Whether I could truly leave California for good.

But just for a moment, I let my worries go and allow my thoughts to unspool unchecked.

Maybe . . . I don't care if I'm a good enough chef to have my own TV show or run a five-star restaurant.

Maybe it's fine that my strength is in management instead of innovation.

Maybe I can just *stay here,* live in this tiny mountain town and be content.

Maybe Hannah Hawthorne is right and what I'm looking for really *is* right under my nose.

CHAPTER THIRTEEN
Lennox

My phone rings just after two a.m., but I'm too sleep-confused to figure out how to answer it. The call ends, but I can't stop staring at the screen. Why did Tatum call me in the middle of the night? Before I make any progress in sorting things out, she calls me again.

This time, I manage to answer. "Tatum?"

"Hey. Did I wake you?" There's a slight tremor in her voice that immediately starts my heart pounding.

"That's a stupid question. I did, didn't I?" she says.

"What's wrong? Is everything okay?" I finally manage.

"That depends on your definition of okay. A tree just fell on the catering kitchen."

"What?"

"A tree. The big one at the corner of the employee parking lot."

I immediately know which tree she means. There's a mostly dead red oak that Dad has been telling us to take down for years. "Tatum, are you safe? Is Toby safe?"

"We're safe," she says quickly. "It missed my

apartment, though I think the roof above the stairs might be damaged. And my office is completely crushed."

"That doesn't matter. As long as you're okay." I glance around my very still and silent house, missing the hum of working electricity. "Is the power out over there?"

"Yeah. My nose is already cold."

"I'm on my way, all right? Just stay warm. I'll be right there."

I spend the next five minutes calling Perry and Olivia and filling them in. I can't get Brody to answer his phone, but he only lives a few doors down, so I'll just drive over and wake him up. If we're cutting up a tree, he'll want to help.

I grab my chainsaw out of the garage, then hurry out to Brody's truck which I conveniently didn't return last night. Outside, the wind from earlier has died down, leaving the air still and peaceful—a sharp contrast to the stress and urgency I'm feeling. It's also colder than I expect, and there's a thick sheet of ice underneath the snow that makes walking treacherous. The snow isn't deep enough to shovel before I back the truck out, but the roads are going to be *slick*.

I pull out and head toward Brody's, my mind on Tatum the whole time. *Is she warm? Is she safe? Is Toby okay?* Of course, I'm worried about the catering kitchen too. And the restaurant. But those worries pale in comparison.

It only takes a minute to get to Brody's even driving in the snow. I stop on the road, not wanting to bother with pulling the truck in and out of his driveway, then hurry toward his front door.

This far south, this kind of weather won't last long. It'll be fifty degrees by the weekend, and all of this will melt, but the next forty-eight hours will be terrible. I pull my coat more tightly around me as I ring the doorbell, then follow up with a sharp knock.

I wait for what seems like an eternity, banging one more time before Brody yanks the door open. He's holding a camping lantern, his eyes wide, and his pajama bottoms are on inside out.

"Hey," I say a little too cheerily. "Did I wake you?"

He runs a hand through his hair. "What are you doing here?"

"Sorry to yank you from your cozy slumber, but a tree fell on the catering kitchen. I'm headed to the farm to clean up. Want to put some real pants on while I grab your chainsaw?"

"Is everyone okay? Is Tatum safe?"

"She says she is. But I'll feel better when I've seen her for myself."

He nods. "Give me two minutes."

While I wait for Brody, I go to his storage shed out back and pull out a couple of tarps and Brody's chainsaw, adding them to mine in the back of the truck. By the time I finish, Brody is already coming out of the house. He heads to the driver's side, which is fine by me. He has more experience driving his truck in this kind of weather than I do anyway.

I climb into the passenger seat, and Brody's eyes cut to me as he shifts the truck out of park and engages the four-wheel drive.

Brody tries to make small talk as we drive, but I can't focus on anything but getting to Tatum.

I suddenly wonder if this is what it's like. To have someone in your life who you care about more than anything else.

I'm not even in a relationship with Tatum, and yet, since the minute she called and I learned what happened, I've been consumed with thoughts of her well-being.

That has to mean something, right?

The farm is completely dark when we arrive, all but the restaurant parking lot which is lit up by the headlights on Perry's truck and Tyler's SUV.

Perry motions for Brody to back his truck up enough that the beam of his headlights projects onto the roofline of the catering kitchen just like the others.

I get out of the truck and survey the damage.

All I can see is tree.

It's everywhere. Giant, snowy limbs block the back entrance and poke through the back windows.

Perry and Tyler are deep in discussion about how to best go about removing the tree and Brody quickly jumps in. They'd do well to just let Brody take the lead—he's the problem solver in the family—and do whatever he says. Either way, they don't need me, so I make my way around the building to a side entrance and let myself inside.

Light reflecting on the snow outside made it easy to see, but in here, it's pitch black. I reach for my phone to turn on the flashlight, but then something—someone?—bumps into me, knocking the phone from my hand and falling against my chest.

"Ooof. Ow."

I reach out and steady Tatum—there's no one else who could be wandering around the kitchen in the middle of the night, at least no one else who smells this good—and wrap my hands around her shoulders. "Hey, you okay?"

Her hand presses against my chest, then moves to my face. "Lennox?" Tatum whispers. "Is that you?"

"Who else would I be?" Her hand is still cupping my cheek, and I barely resist the urge to lean into her touch and press a kiss against the palm of her hand.

"I thought you might be a burglar."

"A burglar? Right now? While half my family is in the parking lot outside?"

She huffs. "When you put it that way . . ."

"Tell me—are you more or less comfortable with the idea of groping a burglar than you are groping me?" With my hands on Tatum, hearing the sound of her voice, the tension I've been carrying around in my shoulders drains away. She's okay. She's safe.

She drops her hand. "I wasn't groping you. I was trying to make sure it was you in the first place."

"Pretty sure you were groping me."

"Shut up. I was not—whatever. Do you have a flashlight on you?"

"I did, but then someone bumped into me and knocked my phone out of my hand."

"Oh. I did do that, didn't I?"

"Do you have your phone?"

"I put it down when I grabbed the rolling pin."

"You're holding a rolling pin?"

"I needed a weapon!" she says, as if this explains everything.

"Right. For the burglar."

"Exactly."

I'm still gripping her shoulders, and I let one hand slide down her arm until it reaches the rolling pin she's still holding tightly in her fist. I wrap my fingers around it. "Maybe I'll just take this?"

"Right. Yes," Tatum says slowly. "And I'll just get my phone . . ." She steps away from me, and I immediately miss the warmth from her closeness. She stumbles around for a second, at least by the sound of the clanging and bumping I hear, then her flashlight turns on. Silently, she moves toward me, shining the light across the floor until she finds my phone.

She bends down and picks it up, dusting it on the front of her hoodie before she hands it back to me. "Looks like it survived the fall," she says. "Sorry about that."

Side by side, with our phone lights lifted and aimed in front of us, we move silently into the main part of the kitchen, then cross to the back half where the tree's skeletal arms have poked a giant hole in the ceiling. Tatum's office is completely crushed and filled with the bulk of the tree's trunk, but the damage doesn't look like it's extending too far into the actual kitchen space.

"I guess it could be worse," I say as I shine my light over the damage. "At least it missed your apartment. And you'll still be able to cook."

"It could definitely be worse," she says. "How long do you think it'll take to repair?"

"I have no idea. We'll get the tree out tonight, at least, so we can get some tarps covering the hole in the ceiling, then we'll have to wait for the weather to clear up and for the power to turn back on. Then find a crew who can replace the wall in your office and fix the roof. Best guess, a week? Maybe two?"

She bites her lip. "Two weeks. That feels like a very long time."

"At least the kitchen is functional. I'm happy to share my office with you if you need a place to escape every once in a while."

Tatum's eyes lift to mine, her expression playful. "I'm sorry, what was that? Did I just hear Lennox Hawthorne offering to help me?"

I roll my eyes. "You better get used to it. I have a feeling it'll be happening a lot more frequently."

She grins. "Does that mean I'll get all the best asparagus?"

"I won that asparagus fair and square, Elliott. It's not my fault you're terrible at Rock, Paper, Scissors. I did offer to cook for you though. I think that was pretty nice."

"I still think you cheated at Rock, Paper, Scissors." She tucks her hands under her arms and shivers the tiniest bit. "And actually, you already cooked for me."

"Sandwiches at Mom's don't count."

"Those were delicious sandwiches, but I didn't say they did. I ordered a couple of entrees from Hawthorne the other night. The filet mignon and the pork tenderloin."

"Smart choices," I say, sounding more chill than I feel. Tatum ate my food? Did she like it? Was she impressed?

Had I known I was preparing something for

her, I would have taken extra care. "Those are two of my favorite dishes."

"I guessed they probably were," she says.

Nerves tighten my throat as I ask, "What did you think?"

She holds my gaze for a long moment. "Everything was perfect, Lennox. *Of course* it was perfect."

There is nothing but sincerity in her words, and the praise fills me with a sense of pleasure and satisfaction I've never experienced before. It's always rewarding to know people enjoy what I create. But this feels different somehow—more meaningful.

I lift my hand and finger the edge of Tatum's scarf—*my scarf*. It's wound loosely around her throat, but she still looks cold, her nose tinged pink and her cheeks flushed. "Tatum, where is your coat?"

She shrugs. "I don't have one."

"You don't have a coat? Any coat?"

"It doesn't get cold like this in California. And you said yourself this weather is unusual for Spring. I figured I'd get something in time for *next* winter."

I slide my hand down her arm and grab her hand, lacing her fingers through mine. "Come on," I say as I tug her toward my office.

I leave her standing by my office door while I go inside and pull my black puffy jacket off the hook on the back of the door. I prop my phone up on the bookshelf and angle it toward the floor so we still have some light, without it shining right in our eyes. I hold out the jacket. "Here. Put this on."

She makes no move to take it. "You promise you don't need it?"

I look down at my heavy wool coat. "This one has me covered."

"Right," she says, looking a little flustered. "Of course it does."

I open the jacket and motion for her to turn so she can put it on. "I hike in this one," I say as she slips her hands inside. "It should keep you plenty warm."

She turns back to face me, and I pick up the hem of the jacket to zip it up. It's ridiculously big on her. Her hands don't show through the sleeves, and it hangs well past her waist. But she looks cute in it anyway, and not just because I like the look of her in my clothes.

"Thanks," she says softly. "It *is* warm." She lifts a hand and reaches over to touch me, her hand sliding down the front of my chest, and my breath catches in my throat. I've never been so irritated to be wearing so many layers.

"I like this coat on you," she says slowly, her fingers lingering over the buttons.

My heart races at the contact. This is . . . different. *Good* different. More intentional than any of the other times we've touched. Excluding the whole bear episode, but I'm not sure that counts because she was freaking out and I was comforting her.

Now I'm the one freaking out.

"Lennox!" Perry calls, and Tatum and I jump apart. "We need your help."

"Be right there," I respond. "I'm just checking on the generators."

Tatum breathes out a tiny gasp. "Did you just lie to your brother?" she whispers through a grin.

I hold up my thumb and pointer finger, holding them an inch apart. "Tiny lie," I say. "I'm *about* to check on the generators." I grab my phone off the shelf and hold out my hand. "Come with me?"

She bites her lip, only hesitating a moment before slipping her fingers into mine.

Holding hands makes it slightly more difficult to navigate our way through the kitchen in the dark, but I don't care, and the tightness of Tatum's grip tells me she doesn't either.

Together, we check on the generator which is, gratefully, humming away, keeping the fridge cold and the freezer even colder.

"What does the generator power?" Tatum asks.

"Just the walk-in fridge and the freezer. It was too costly to get something for the entire building. And I didn't see the point in keeping an empty building warm. It's not like we're going to open when we have no power."

"You mean the empty building that I live in?"

I grimace. "Fair point." I touch the tip of her nose with my free hand. "I guess you'll have to turn into a popsicle like the rest of us."

She will absolutely *not* be turning into a popsicle, but I need to check with Brody before I offer his house as a refuge. I'd invite her to my place, but she'd be no better off there than she is here.

Tatum follows me to the door, dropping my hand before we step into view of my brothers who are already working to cut away the tree.

We pause at the edge of the parking lot. "You'll be okay here?"

She burrows down into my coat and nods. I reluctantly move toward my brothers to help, but my eyes keep going back to her. Every time I look, her eyes are focused on me.

Perry is already using my chainsaw, and Brody has his, so Tyler and I become the muscle, moving the logs away as they shave away at the massive trunk, chunk by chunk.

We haul the pieces to the edge of the parking lot, leaving them in a haphazard stack. By the time we finish, my biceps are screaming, I can barely feel my fingers, and my nose is numb from the cold.

We use several enormous tarps to cover the opening into the kitchen, anchored and angled in a way to keep snow from accumulating on top.

It's not a great long-term solution, but it should hold until the snow stops, and we can get some professionals out to do the needed repairs.

At some point in the process, Tatum disappears inside—something I sense more than I see—and I become almost obsessive about looking over my shoulder to see if she's reappeared. But she doesn't show. Not even when Tyler and Perry are pulling out of the parking lot and Brody is cranking the engine on his truck, ready to leave as well.

Maybe she went inside and got back in bed? Which I can understand, but I don't want her to have to stay here. She won't be warm here. And neither will her dog.

Dawn isn't far off. The sun is still low behind the mountains, but the sky is lightening, casting a bluish glow over the falling snow. But it could be hours before the power is back on. And even in daylight, the temperatures aren't supposed to get above freezing.

"You okay?" Brody calls from his open window, his arm resting on the truck door.

I scrub a hand across my jaw and move toward Brody's truck. "I just need to check on Tatum. She went back inside, but I don't want her to stay here. Do you—" I hesitate. "Do you mind if I invite her to your place?"

Brody gestures behind me. "One step ahead of you, man."

I turn and look over my shoulder to see Tatum crossing the parking lot, still wearing my jacket, a bag hitched over her shoulder and Toby on a leash beside her.

I push away the sudden disappointment filling my chest. I'm glad she's coming, but I'm sad I wasn't the one who got to invite her.

"Kate invited her," Brody says. "I assume this means you're coming over too?"

I don't have time to answer before Tatum opens the back door of Brody's truck and climbs into the extended cab. "Come on, boy," she says, scooting over and motioning for Toby to jump in beside her.

I climb into the passenger seat and look over my shoulder, my eyes meeting Tatum's for the briefest second.

"Thanks for this," she says to Brody, her gaze sliding away from me. "My apartment already feels freezing."

"No problem," Brody says. He slowly eases the truck out of the parking lot. "The wood stove in the living room does a great job of keeping the house warm. At least the first floor. And Kate loves it when the house is full of people."

"Will the power stay out long?" Tatum asks.

"Not more than a day or two," I answer. "Depends on how long it snows."

"Tyler told me he's taking Olivia and the baby over to Mom and Dad's," Brody says. "And Perry has a fireplace at his place, so I'm sure he and Lila will stay home." He shoots me a questioning look. "So that means it'll just be the four of us?"

Tatum shifts in the back seat, and I look over my shoulder to see her gaze on me—something like anticipation—maybe even excitement?—dancing in her eyes.

I raise my eyebrows in question, and she shrugs the slightest bit. "I think it sounds fun."

Brody eases his truck to a stop outside my house. "It's your call, man."

I unbuckle my seatbelt. "I'll walk down in a bit," I say. "I've just got to get a few things together first."

Get a few things together . . . and shower. And trim my beard and put on clean clothes and do my best to *not* look like I just rolled out of bed and spent two hours fighting with a giant oak tree. The water will be ice cold, but if I'm spending the day with Tatum, holed up by the fire in my brother's living room, that's a price I'm willing to pay.

CHAPTER FOURTEEN
Tatum

The sun is barely up when we pull into the driveway at Kate and Brody's house, but Kate is awake anyway, standing on the front porch to greet us as we climb the steps.

She pulls me into a big hug. "I'm so glad you're safe and everything is okay."

The comment takes me by surprise, only because I hadn't considered the possibility of anyone being worried for *my* safety. It was snowing inside the kitchen, which felt like more than enough reason to be concerned. But they were worried about me, too?

"Come on," Brody says, nudging Kate toward the door. "Let's get inside where it's warm. I'll build the fire up."

Less than ten minutes later, I'm wrapped up in a blanket sitting next to the fire, Toby curled up at my feet. Pale morning light filters into the room, but it's still dim, giving the entire space a sleepy, cozy feel. Considering how long I've been awake, I should probably nap—I'll never make it through the day if I don't. But that would require me to stop obsessing about when, exactly, Lennox intends to show up.

He said he'd walk down in a bit. Does that mean in an hour? Two hours?

The power is off at his house too, so if he waits that long, won't he be cold?

I groan and grab a book off the side table. Lennox is a grown man who can regulate his own body heat. I don't need to worry about him.

Still, as I open the book and flip to the first chapter, I can't stop thinking about the way it felt to walk through the dark catering kitchen holding Lennox's hand. I don't *need* to worry about him.

But maybe I *want* to.

"That's a good one," Kate says as she settles into the chair opposite me. She motions toward the book. "I just finished it."

I turn the book around and look at the cover, which I barely noticed when I picked it up. It's romcom-y and cute and looks exactly like the kind of book I would enjoy. "I was trying to decide if I should read or sleep," I say, stifling a yawn.

"Brody just went up to sleep for a few more hours. You're welcome to stretch out on the couch if you want. If you can get Charlie to move."

The basset hound taking up the left half of the couch thumps his tail against the cushion when he hears his name, but otherwise, he doesn't stir.

I pull my feet up under me and extend them toward the dog, nudging him to the side. "I'm used to sharing a couch with Toby," I say. "I can make this work." Honestly, I'm surprised Toby isn't up here with me too, but I'm glad he's opting to stay closer to the fire. That would be a lot of dog on one couch.

"Try and sleep," Kate says as she stands up. "After the night you've had, I'm sure you could use it."

I nestle down into the couch and read a few pages, but I must doze off at some point, because when I startle awake, the book has fallen to the floor, bright light is streaming through the window, and both dogs have abandoned the room.

I hear them though, collars jingling, paws tapping against the floor like they're excited about something. The front door creaks open, and suddenly, I understand. Either Brody or Kate must be taking the dogs outside.

I stretch my arms over my head to stretch, then glance at my watch. It's already eleven a.m.? *Dang.* I didn't just nap, I *slept.*

"Hey, you're awake," Kate says, appearing in the doorway between the kitchen and the living room.

I rub a hand down my face, still trying to wake up. "I am. Is Toby okay? Did Brody take him outside?"

"Lennox, actually."

I sit up a little taller and lift a hand to my probably sleep-crazy hair. "He's here?"

"He walked down a few hours ago, but he and Brody drove up to the restaurant to get us some lunch and they just got back. Lennox made hot chocolate earlier though. Do you want some?"

In any other circumstance, I might have asked for coffee instead, but if Lennox made the hot chocolate, I'm all in. "That sounds amazing."

She disappears, returning moments later with a sky-blue mug with the words *I once made a chemistry joke, but there was no reaction* printed on the side.

She holds it out to me. "The mug was a gift from one of Brody's students."

"Punny," I say as I take the mug, and Kate smiles. "How do we even have something hot?" I say as I take my first sip. *Oh. Oh my word.* I let out a low groan. "Is this even for real?"

"Delicious, right? Brody got out his propane camp stove and set it up on the back porch."

The hot chocolate is perfectly creamy with a hint of something on the backend that I can't quite identify. Whatever it is, it's absolutely delicious. "Honestly, is there anything Lennox hasn't perfected?" I take another sip. "What does he put in this?"

"Mascarpone cheese," Kate says. "And nutmeg."

As soon as she says it, I recognize the acidy sweetness of the mascarpone. But I never would have thought to add it to hot chocolate. It's brilliant and delicious and somehow very Lennox.

I take another long sip just as the front door opens and Lennox himself steps inside, the dogs dancing around his feet. He's wearing the same wool pea coat he had on this morning, the black fabric speckled with snow. His scarf is a deep blue, and unlike the wool one of his I'm *still* currently wearing, this one looks handmade, like something his mother or a grandmother could have knitted for him. I watch as he unwraps it from his neck, then slips out of his coat, revealing a thermal henley the same color as his scarf. It fits him well—like it was made for him, and I . . . am paying way too much attention to Lennox's clothes.

But how can I not? He could be a model for one of those overpriced clothing companies—the ones you want to buy from if only to make your life as serene and peaceful as all the beautiful lives they depict in their advertisements.

Charlie moseys over and plops down next to the fire, but Toby stays next to Lennox, his tail wagging as he leans his head into Lennox's thigh. It's Toby's way of asking for attention, and something stretches in my heart when Lennox crouches down and gives it to him, talking to him in a ridiculous voice. "That's a good boy, Toby-Tobers. Who's a good boy?"

Everyone says the way to a chef's heart is through a really good knife, and it's true. But more true for me? The way to my heart is through my dog, and seeing Lennox like this is striking all the right chords.

I'm suddenly filled with a desire to stand up and wrap my arms around his waist, press myself against him and feel his arms circle around me. He'd probably run one of those strong hands up and down my back. He might even lift it to my hairline and tangle his fingers in my hair. Or brush his thumb across the edge of my jaw—

"Tatum?" Kate says, her voice slightly louder than normal, like she's trying to get my attention. All at once, my brain catches up with my ears, and it occurs to me that this isn't the first time she's said my name.

"What? Yes? Hi. Sorry."

She eyes me, her expression saying she knows exactly why I was distracted. "I just asked if you were hungry."

"Oh. Sure. Absolutely. Food sounds good."

"And Lennox asked you a question, and you didn't even flinch," she says, laughter dancing in her eyes.

My eyes jump to Lennox, and he lifts his shoulders in a tiny shrug. "I just asked if you've finally warmed up."

"Sorry. I was . . . thinking . . . something. About something. But yes! I'm warm. So warm." And clearly a master with words.

"Okay then," Lennox says on a chuckle, and my cheeks flame. "I have leftover Bolognese from the restaurant, if that sounds good. Brody can boil some water on the camp stove, so we can even have pasta to go with it."

"I'm using my jetboil," Brody says, appearing in the entryway with all the enthusiasm of a boy scout. "Boiling water in one hundred seconds or less."

Kate rolls her eyes. "I think he lives for power outages because he gets to use all his survival gear."

I smile as Brody and Lennox disappear down the hall, their voices fading as the back door opens and closes.

If there is ever a zombie apocalypse, I definitely want the Hawthorne brothers on my survival team—a thought I first had early this morning while I watched the three of them, as well as Olivia's husband Tyler, cut the splintered tree into haulable pieces and stack them on the opposite side of the parking lot. They were too bundled up against the snow for me to see any muscle in action, but it wasn't hard to imagine it with all the heavy lifting and grunting that was happening.

Now, I'm warm and safe even though outside, it is cold and snowy.

I'm about to be fed even though presently, there is no functional kitchen.

And my phone is charging using a portable charging block Brody gave me when I first arrived even though there's no power.

Zombies? Yeah. I'm not worried about them at all.

"I've heard Brody is quite the outdoorsman," I say, turning my attention back to Kate.

She nods. "They all are. They grew up hiking and camping. But forget that." She scoots the ottoman closer so it's just opposite where I'm sitting on the couch and sits down on it, pulling her knees up to sit cross-legged. "I want to talk about what happened to you when Lennox walked in."

My heart starts pounding, and I take a long sip of hot chocolate, hiding behind my mug. "I don't know what you're talking about," I finally say.

"Oh come on. Tatum. You were practically undressing him with your eyes. It was so obvious."

I set the mug down on the small side table next to the couch and cover my face with both palms, still warm from my hot chocolate. It's debatable whether my cheeks or my hands are warmer. "I was not!"

"You totally were," Kate says. "I'm good at reading people, and there is definitely something happening here. It's too late for you to deny it."

I spread two of my fingers, creating a tiny window for one eye to peek out. "Was I really so obvious?"

Kate giggles. "When he said your name, you were staring at him like some kind of starry-eyed middle-schooler. What's going on?" she asks. "You were pretty evasive at lunch the other day. Is this why? Are you actually starting to feel something for him?"

"Maybe? I mean, we were bickering like children when I first got here, but the past couple of weeks, it's been . . . different somehow."

"Good different?"

I sigh. "Definitely good different. He's supposed to make me dinner next Monday. It was the first day we both had a night off."

"Gah. That's forever from now. Chefs and your stupid schedules. But still! It's something. And maybe a little something *else* will happen while you're here." She lifts her hands in a tiny cheer and lets out a squeal.

I shoot Kate a look and glance toward the kitchen, not wanting Lennox, or even Brody, to hear, but she waves away my concern. "They're still outside. I promise they can't hear us. But honey, if you keep staring at him like you just were, it won't matter *what* he hears. You might as well be wearing a sign for how obvious you were."

"Honestly, he's a Hawthorne brother. How can I *not* stare?"

"True," she concedes. "You should have been at the restaurant opening. Flint came, so all four of them were together for the first time in I don't know how long. The sheer magnetism. It was a little overwhelming for all of us."

Lennox's younger brother wasn't famous when we were back in culinary school, so it was a surprise to me when I Googled the farm, found the information about Lennox's restaurant opening, and made the connection to the very famous actor, Flint Hawthorne, who attended the event. Now that I know, it feels obvious because Flint looks as much like his brother as the other ones do.

"I saw pictures," I say. "I can only imagine the impact it had in person."

Kate nudges my knee. "They're all just as good on the inside, Tatum. I mean, I'm obviously biased, but if there's something happening with you and Lennox? I'd hang on to him."

"Do you know anything about Hailey?"

Kate's forehead scrunches up. "Was that the girlfriend he had in college?"

I nod. "I found a box full of pictures and letters and stuff. He left it behind in the apartment."

"I don't know much. I remember liking her, though. She was really sweet."

"Wait, you met her?"

"He brought her home to the farm a couple of times. Brody and I were still in high school then, so we were around."

"So they were pretty serious then." I mean, he saved a box of their memories. Of course they were serious. But bringing her home to meet the family feels even bigger than that.

"Yeah. And he was messed up for months after they broke up. He won't talk about it, but I've always assumed that's why he—" Her words cut off, and she purses her lips like she isn't quite sure how to finish.

"Why he turned into a total womanizer?" I say for her, filling in the gap.

She winces, but she doesn't contradict me. "I swear, he hasn't been like that since he moved home—I don't think it's who he really is."

"He's never been serious with anyone else?"

"Not that any of us have known about." She bites her lip. "Does that scare you?"

I lean back into the sofa cushions and consider her question. It maybe should scare me, but somehow, it doesn't. I don't know what's happening with Lennox, but it doesn't feel like I'm getting played. Maybe because we haven't actually started dating yet. At least not officially. And most of our conversations have involved teasing and good-natured arguing, which makes it seem like whatever is happening is happening *despite* our efforts to irritate each other.

"Honestly, I don't think it does. I mean, there are all kinds of other things that scare me, but not that."

"Because it feels real?"

I shrug. "I don't want to get ahead of myself. We haven't spent a ton of time together outside of work. The dinner really could just be *dinner*."

Kate gives me a knowing smile. "It doesn't feel like it though, does it?"

I bite my lip. "It *maybe* feels like . . . something."

"I like the sound of *something*." Kate winks as she stands. "I'm going to check on the guys. Do you need anything?"

"Nah, I'm good," I say as I reach for my phone, but then I glance at the screen and immediately regret the action.

I have a text from my dad, and right now my world is too perfect and comfortable to ruin it with a message from him. I hate that I feel this way. But with how his messages have sounded lately, it's getting harder and harder to convince myself he has my best interests at heart. Still, if I don't respond now, he'll keep texting, spamming me with a string of messages, each one more antagonistic than the last.

> **Dad:** I hear there's weather where you are. Skies are blue and temps are warm here. I can have a car meet you at the airport whenever you come to your senses.

Another message pops up while I'm reading the first, this one with a winking emoji as if the whole suggestion is just a silly joke.

Dad is definitely not joking.

Tatum: I'm enjoying the weather so much. The snow is beautiful!

I put my phone back on the table, face down, determined not to touch it for the rest of the day. A part of me wishes I didn't even have a portable charger. Then I'd at least have an excuse.

Sorry! Phone died. No power. I'll be off the grid for the next . . . three weeks. Do snowstorms last that long in North Carolina? Can I order one that will?

I drop my head back and breathe out an audible sigh that brings Toby right to my side. He lifts his paws and drops them onto my lap, burrowing his head into my shoulder.

My friend once told me her goldendoodle gave good hugs, and I thought she was just being silly. Dogs don't have arms. They can't give actual hugs. But I ended up eating those words as soon as I had my own doodle because Toby totally gives hugs—especially when he knows I need one.

I scratch his ears and look into his deep brown eyes. "That's a good boy, Tobe. We're going to be okay, yeah? We're going to make it?"

The back door opens, and Kate's laughter rings through the air, then it sounds like they all move back into the kitchen.

Moments later, Lennox leans around the corner. "Food's just about ready if you want to join us."

I nod and smile. "I'll be right there."

A goldendoodle hug can go a long way. But it doesn't quite fill the loneliness I'm feeling right now.

What I'm craving is *human* connection, and not the kind I have with my father, full of judgments and expectations and passive-aggressive criticism.

No, hanging out with the Hawthornes has shown me that I want more.

Acceptance. Love. Support. Kindness for the sake of kindness, even when nothing is received in return.

It all feels incredibly foreign when I compare it to what I'm used to with Dad. I'm sure he loves me in his own way. But our relationship has only ever felt contractual.

I'm not sure I've ever thought about the possibility of it being something different, something more like what the Hawthornes have.

But maybe it's time I start.

I want something better.

I *deserve* something better.

I just have to figure out how to get it.

CHAPTER FIFTEEN
Lennox

"Bacon, right?" Tatum asks as she gathers the plates off of Brody's dining room table. "What else is in it? It tasted too mild to be beef."

I carry the empty saucepan that I used to warm the Bolognese over to Brody's kitchen sink. Tatum steps in beside me and sets the plates on the counter.

"Yes to the bacon," I say. "But no ground beef. I use ground pork loin. The leanest cut I can find. Anything else overpowers the flavor profile of the vegetables, and I wanted them to be the star of the dish."

I reach for the giant pot of water Brody warmed on the camp stove outside. There's running water—Kate and Brody have a well—but it's ice cold, which won't do much good when we're washing dishes. Hopefully, there's enough here for us to get things cleaned up. Brody wouldn't care if we just left everything in the sink, but doing the dishes feels like the least I can do.

Apparently, Tatum agrees because she volunteered to help me the minute the words were out of my mouth. Brody and Kate disappeared into the living room to build up the fire and set up some sort of trivia board game they're very excited about playing with us. Kate and Brody are big board game players, and they seem very enthusiastic about having new people to play against. Normally, I might find this irritating—the two of them are merciless, especially if they're playing on the same team—but they can beat me a dozen times in a row if it means I'm playing with Tatum, too.

"The vegetables," Tatum says, pulling my attention back to the meal we just finished. "Celery, carrots, onions?" She runs her finger along the edge of the mostly empty saucepan and lifts it to her mouth. "No, not onions. Shallots?"

I manage a nod—I'm entirely too distracted by the sight of her lips as she tastes the sauce—but I'm impressed she's able to tell. The difference is subtle enough, not everyone can.

"The sweetness though," she says as she plugs up one half of the sink. She steps back while I pour in half of the boiling water, then turn on the tap to cool it down enough for us to use it without burning our hands.

"It feels like it's something beyond the wine. It feels deeper. Nuttier, maybe?" She adds a little soap to the sink and swirls it around with her fingers before grabbing the first plate and slipping it into the water.

It almost feels like Tatum is having a conversation with herself, walking through the different flavors in the Bolognese, trying to pinpoint what went into it. It's a fun game for any chef—deconstructing, trying to figure out why something works so well, and I'm flattered she's putting so much thought into my dish. It has to mean she likes it—or at least appreciates its complexity.

She holds up the first plate. "I wash, you rinse?"

"So your hands stay warm and mine stay cold?"

She sticks her fingers into the soapy water and flicks a few bubbles my way. "Precisely."

I let out a little grunt as I take the dish, my fingers brushing against hers. When we touch, her eyes dart to mine, fire flashing in their depths.

"Gah, you have to just tell me, Lennox. I can't figure it out." She hands me another dish, her expression open and curious.

"I roast the carrots first," I finally say. "It brings out their natural sweetness more than sautéing them does."

Her face brightens. "Roasting them. That's—" She smiles for the briefest moment before it melts into a frown, her shoulders dropping the tiniest bit. The shift happens so quickly, had I not been watching her closely, I might have missed it. "That's brilliant," she says. "I never would have thought of that."

The comment gives me pause. It's a level of humility I wouldn't have expected from the Tatum Elliott I knew in culinary school.

Back then, she knew all the answers to every question all the time. But she hasn't had that same edge since coming to Stonebrook. She's been openly complimentary of my food, inquisitive about ingredients.

She hands me the last plate and pauses, her hands resting on the side of the sink. "How did you know to do that?" The sincerity in her question catches me off guard. "I've read a hundred different recipes for Bolognese, but I've never seen—" She gives her head a little shake. "But it made a difference. Yours is different. *Better.* How did you do it?"

The compliment sends a burst of warmth racing through me, but I'm not sure how to answer her question. "I don't know, really. Or maybe I just don't know how to put it into words?" I'm silent for a beat while I dry the last plate. "Will you laugh if I tell you I let the ingredients speak to me?"

She tilts her head and studies me closely, but for a moment, it looks like she's somewhere else. Finally, her gaze drops, and she steps away from the sink. She reaches over and steals the dish towel that's draped over my shoulder, using it to dry her hands. "I think this is something that makes us different."

"What do you mean?" I ask.

She shrugs. "I don't think about food like that. I follow recipes. I do what I already know is going to work—what others have already proven works. I don't take risks."

"I'm sure that's not true. I mean, look at you. Look at the career you've had."

She scoffs. "The career I've had was handed to me by my father. I wasn't qualified for it, and the only reason I survived is because I had an amazing sous chef and a staff who probably knew if they didn't tolerate me, they'd lose their jobs."

"Tatum, I've seen you working. You're good at what you do."

"No, I know," she concedes. "But you don't get to be head chef at a restaurant like Le Vin by being *good*. I'm not fishing for compliments here. I'm a good chef. But I don't know how to *innovate*. Not like you do. Not like the sous chef at Le Vin who replaced me when I left—the one who *should* have had the job all along."

"Is that why you left California?" I pick up the pot of hot water and pour it down the sink, then take the towel back from Tatum to dry my hands. As soon as her hands are free, she pushes them into the front pocket of her hoodie.

Tatum knows how to rock her chef's whites, but there's something about this casual version of her that I like even more. Her guard is down, her demeanor open and curious, and she seems happy to just be here. Hanging out. Talking about food, opening up about her life.

Her lips lift into a small smile. "I thought I was getting dinner at your place in exchange for all my secrets."

I step closer, resting my hand on the counter beside her. I lean forward the slightest bit, holding her gaze as I breathe her in. She smells like Carolina jasmine in spring, which is now, officially, my new favorite scent.

"I'll feed you whenever you want, Tatum. With or without the secrets. You just have to ask me."

She bites her lip, her expression coy. "What if I get hungry at two a.m.?"

"I'll send you to bed with snacks just in case."

"What if you just finished the longest shift of your life, and you're bone-deep exhausted, and I feel like eating a steak?"

"If you ask me with the expression you're wearing right now, I'd probably go out and kill the cow myself."

Tatum stills, her eyes widening the slightest bit. The tone of our conversation has been pretty playful, but that last line might have pushed things a little too far. Not that it wasn't true, but still. That doesn't mean I should have said it out loud.

I clear my throat and step backward, running a hand through my hair.

Tatum grabs a dish towel and folds it, then shakes it out and folds it again, a slight tremble in her hands.

The fact that she's as nervous as I am sends a surge of emotion right to my heart.

I'm starting to care about this woman.

Really care.

With anyone else, I would have moved on long before now. Cut ties before anything *real* started to develop.

But Tatum snuck in on the sly. I was so busy pretending to be annoyed by her presence, I missed how quickly that annoyance turned into something else entirely.

And now it's too late to do anything about it because there's no way I'm walking away now.

Brody's words echo in my mind. *She seems different.*

He's right. Tatum *is* different. And I don't want to lose the possibility of whatever this might be.

"Hey," Brody calls from the living room. "Everything's set up. You guys ready to play?"

Tatum meets my gaze, a small smile lifting her lips. So she thinks I'd kill a cow just to get her the steak that she wanted. This is no big deal. We're chill. Everything is *chill.*

"We should probably go," Tatum says softly. "Your brother seems very enthusiastic about this game."

"He's the nerdiest of us all," I say, happy to have something—*anything*—to contribute to the conversation that won't make me look more stupid. "And I'm warning you now, he's hard to beat. Especially if he and Kate are on the same team. She's a travel writer, so she knows everything about everywhere."

Tatum's eyebrows lift. "So that's how we're playing? Us against them?"

I nod. "I'm sure that's what they'll want to do. Are you good with that?"

She props her hands on her hips. "You said they're hard to beat. Has anyone ever done it?"

"We change up teams sometimes to make it more fun, but with the two of them on the same team? They're undefeated."

"Hmm." She smiles playfully. "Good to know." She grabs my hand and tugs me toward the living room. "But just for the record? I play to win, and I have a feeling your luck is about to change."

Tatum *definitely* plays to win.

The woman is a machine. Confident. Bold. A few times, she even tosses out an answer before Brody has even finished reading the question.

I recognize the competitive edge she had back in school, but now instead of finding it irritating, it's sexy as all get out.

At the same time, she's a really good sport. Talking, joking, playing down her success in a way that keeps the game fun and easy.

"Okay, last round," Brody says. "If you guys get three questions correct, you'll win the game, and Lennox will have beaten me for the first time in the history of forever."

"And I bet you aren't bitter about that at all," Kate says easily from her place beside him.

"If you get a question wrong," Brody continues, "we have the chance to steal the win by answering the question you missed, plus two more."

My eyes shift to Tatum who looks relaxed and comfortable, not even a little bit nervous.

Not that she should be. Me? I've been here for moral support. And the odd question about football, golf, or Grand Theft Auto, which I played with religious dedication while I was in school. But even without my help, Tatum would still be winning.

She cracks her knuckles and leans forward. "Okay. Let's do this."

"First category is literature," Kate says, holding one of the trivia cards.

Literature is good. Tatum has gotten every one of the literature questions right so far.

"What nineteenth-century author tried to have his wife committed to an insane asylum so he could live with his eighteen-year-old mistress?" Kate looks up from the card. "Dang. That's cruel."

"If it's any consolation, it didn't work," Tatum says. "The doctor who reviewed the case declared his wife in fine health and refused to send her away. Except, the ending of the story still sucks.

Charles Dickens ended up sending his wife away himself when the doctor wouldn't help. He put her up in a house at the edge of town, kept her from her children, and spent the rest of his life living with his mistress."

"Um, Charles Dickens sounds like a jerk," Kate says. "Also, that's the correct answer."

"How did you even know that?" I nudge Tatum's knee with mine.

She shrugs. "I went through a British lit phase in high school."

"Okay, next question," Brody says. "The category is sports."

Tatum reaches over and squeezes my knee, but then she leaves her hand there, resting it on my leg like it's perfectly normal for us to touch each other, to sit this closely.

I stare at Brody, willing myself to focus on the question and not the warmth of her fingers searing me through my jeans.

"What NFL football team holds the record for most points scored in a Super Bowl match-up?"

Tatum's grip tightens, and I drop my hand to rest on top of hers. "San Francisco Forty-Niners," I say. "In 1990, playing against the Denver Broncos. They won fifty-five to ten."

Brody sighs. "You and your stupid football brain."

"Okay, last one," Kate says. "For the win. The category is science and technology."

This one could go either way. I keep my eyes trained on Kate even as Tatum pulls her hand away. I miss the contact immediately, but then her leg brushes up against mine, and I wonder if she wants the connection as much as I do.

"Okay," Kate says. "What element on the periodic table has an atomic weight of 1.00794?"

Brody grins at his wife as if already anticipating the steal. He's a high school chemistry teacher, so if anyone knows the answer, it's him.

"We can just guess," I say to Tatum, but she shakes her head.

"I think I know it. Is it hydrogen? I think it's hydrogen?"

Brody groans as I shoot my hands up in victory. "We did it! We won!" I stand up and tug Tatum out of her chair, wrapping her in an enormous hug that lifts her feet off the floor. She laughs as I spin her around, her hands sliding down my arms as I lower her back down.

It's just a hug.

But the feel of her against me, the way her hands linger at the top of my biceps, the way she's holding her bottom lip in her teeth as she looks at me.

It feels like so much more.

"Pretty sure *Tatum* won," Brody says. He shoots me a questioning look before his gaze shifts to Tatum. "Great game."

She steps out of my embrace and presses her hands to her stomach, almost like she's trying to calm herself. "Thanks," she says. "As it happens, I was California state quiz bowl champion my senior year of high school. Trivia has always sort of been my thing."

"Seriously?" Brody says, his tone light. "That didn't feel like an important thing to disclose before the game started?"

"What would you have done about it if she had?" Kate asks.

Brody doesn't miss a beat. "I would have put Tatum on my team and made you play with Lennox."

Kate laughs and punches Brody in the shoulder. "Dude. So rude."

"Don't worry," Tatum says to Kate. "I wouldn't have defected. But next time, you and I should absolutely be on the same team."

"Oh, I'm so down for that," Kate says.

As I watch the way Tatum and Kate easily banter, I think about the only other time I've brought a woman home to meet the family. Hailey joined us for Thanksgiving my first year of culinary school.

It was fine. She was nice to everyone, and everyone was nice to her.

But there's a certain rightness about having Tatum here. She fits in like she's one of us. Like she's *always* been one of us.

"How did I not know you were quiz bowl champion?" I ask.

She lifts an eyebrow. "There's a lot you don't know about me, Lennox." She says it like it's a challenge—or maybe an invitation?—and suddenly, I'm all in.

I want to know it all. Everything there is to know about Tatum Elliott. How she works. What she likes. What makes her happy and sad and excited. I want to see the different pieces of her and understand how they all fit together.

A month ago, I was certain I *did* know her. I thought I had her all figured out. But I was wrong—dead wrong—and I've never been so happy to admit it.

Now I just have to figure out what to do about it.

CHAPTER SIXTEEN
Lennox

"How does it feel to officially end your winning streak?" I ask Brody as I gather the trivia cards from around the table.

"I think I'm doomed," he says easily. "With Tatum in the family, I'll probably never win again."

My eyes dart to Tatum, and we both freeze, a very pregnant pause filling the room until Kate says, "Umm, Brody? Did you just say *in the family?*"

Brody's face blanches. If not for my worry over Tatum's discomfort, I might enjoy watching him squirm. But then I look at Tatum, and all she seems is amused. When her gaze meets mine, she almost looks like she *likes* the idea.

"No, that's not—" Brody finally says. "I mean—I only meant *working* for the family." He looks at Kate, his expression desperate, but she seems way too amused by her husband's blunder to offer him any rescue. "I wasn't saying Tatum was going to—with Lennox, but—I mean, she could. That would be great. But she doesn't— you know what? I think I need to walk down the street to check on the Wilsons. Make sure they've got enough wood to keep their fire going." Brody clears his throat and looks at me. "You want to come?"

"Don't take Lennox," Kate says a little too quickly. "I'll come with you. I feel like getting out of the house anyway."

They hurry off, pausing in the entryway long enough to put on coats and hats and boots. Kate shoots a furtive glance over her shoulder, and then they disappear out the door.

"Pretty sure this is her leaving us alone on purpose," Tatum says, humor in her voice.

"I'd put money on it. I used to think having so many brothers was annoying, but it's not near as bad as having so many meddling *sisters*."

She smiles. "They love you."

"They irritate me."

"They just want you to be happy. I'm getting the sense that's the way the Hawthorne family works."

There's a wistfulness to her voice that immediately sobers me. Having so many meddling siblings and now siblings-in-law *can* be irritating, but mostly, it's pretty amazing. Sometimes I forget how lucky I am to be so close to my family.

I fold up the game board and drop it into the box. "Any siblings for you?"

"An older brother, Daniel, and an older sister, Bree. But they're eight and ten years older than me, so we didn't really grow up together. Not like you and your siblings did."

"Do either of them work with your dad?"

"Not even a little bit. Daniel is a doctor in Chicago, and he doesn't get along with Dad at all." She hands me the lid to the game, and I place it on the box. "He and Bree do okay, but I think she keeps stuff surface level on purpose just to make it easier. She runs her own marketing firm in St. Louis."

"What about your mom?"

Tatum is quiet for a long moment. "She died last year," she finally says. "We weren't really close. She and my dad split when I was twelve, and she moved home to France."

I lean forward the slightest bit, one elbow propped on the card table Brody set up for the game, and brush my fingers across her knee. "I'm sorry. That must have been tough."

She lifts her shoulders. "We weren't close. Which makes it easier in some ways, but harder in others. It's like this weird combination of loss and regret, all mixed in with questions I always thought I had time to ask. But now I don't, so I just have to reconcile *not* having answers, and—" She breathes out a sigh. "Yeah. That part's hard."

I nod my understanding, wondering if it would be weird to offer her a hug. Tatum and I are doing this weird dance where we inch closer, leaning into opportunities to touch, then swing apart again. I *think* she'd want a hug, but all of this still feels so new, I can't be sure.

I get up and add a couple of logs to the fire, then move to the couch and sit down, happy that Tatum quickly joins me. She sits sideways and pulls her feet up onto the couch, wrapping her arms around her knees and tucking her feet under my thigh like she's trying to warm her toes. Even if that's all she's trying to do, I'm still happy to have her close enough to touch. The longer we're together, the more I'm feeling the tug to be close to her.

"Did you ever go see your mom in France?"

She nods. "Every summer while I was in high school. She cooked, too. Not like my dad. Just for friends, mostly. But she did a little bit of catering every once in a while."

She sinks back into the cushions, almost like she's falling in on herself, and her eyes turn distant and sad.

I reach down and loosely wrap my hands around her ankles. "Hey. You okay? You want to talk about it?"

"I was just thinking about how Mom was always asking me to cook with her whenever I went to visit, and I never wanted to. I think a part of me was mad at Mom for leaving. Cooking was Dad's thing—something he and I did together. I didn't want it to be something she did, too."

"That's understandable," I say. "Twelve is

a hard age to have to go through a divorce. Especially when one of your parents winds up on the other side of the world."

"Yeah, maybe so," she says, her tone reflective. "But I wonder now what I was missing out on. What could I have learned from her, you know? I don't remember much about why they got divorced, but if my father treated her anything close to how he's been treating me lately, it isn't hard to imagine what they could have been."

"What does that mean? How is he treating you now?"

"Like I'm a business asset," she answers quickly enough that I know she's had this thought before. She frowns. "That sounds bad. Probably worse than it is. But I've only ever worked *with* my father, so he tends to see me for what I can offer as opposed to *who* I am. He's constantly pressuring me, wanting to pull me into branding deals and merchandising—into the fame side of it all."

"And you don't want that? The fame?"

She shrugs. "I don't know. I used to think so. But it's been really nice to be away from it all."

She nestles a little deeper into the couch, and I pick up her feet, dropping them into my lap. "Was it tough growing up with a famous father?"

She scrunches her face like she's considering. "Yes and no. Dad likes to be Christopher Elliott— more than he likes being *Dad*. In retrospect,

I think I tolerated a lot because his life was so glamorous. There were a lot of perks, though it makes me feel shallow to admit it now." She scoops her hair up and lifts it away from her neck for a moment, shaking it out before it falls back into place. "I'm starting to wonder if that actually had something to do with why Mom left. Pretty sure if Dad had to pick between fame and family, he'd pick fame."

"You're making me think working with him wasn't all that it's cracked up to be."

She shrugs. "I mean, I'm living in North Carolina, running a catering kitchen instead of doing what he wants me to do, so take your best guess."

I'm suddenly struck by how different this version of Tatum's life is from the one she projected while we were in culinary school. Back then, she was always talking about the trips she'd taken with her dad, constantly bringing stuff to school—stuff her dad sent—and giving it out to people. New knives, hand mixers, pots and pans. Whatever was the latest and greatest in the Christopher Elliott exclusive line of kitchen tools and cookware.

I never took anything from her because it seemed like she was trying to buy friends. But hearing about her mom, how alone she probably felt, maybe she was just trying to *make* friends.

Our conversation abruptly ends when Brody

and Kate come bustling back through the front door, bringing a blast of cold air with them. "We ran into the power company guys down the road," Brody says. "They're saying they're hoping to have everyone on this side of the valley up and running by tomorrow morning."

"Which means you both have to stay here," Kate says as she unwraps her scarf. "It's still frigid out there. You'll be miserable if you try to go home."

"If you'll have me, I'd love to stay," Tatum says. "Toby is a big wimp when it comes to the cold."

"But you aren't a wimp, Miss I-don't-have-a-coat?" I tease.

She smirks. "Now that I've got yours, I'll never get my own."

"What about you, Lennox?" Kate asks, her eyes darting between Tatum and me like she's *very* happy to see us looking so cozy on the couch.

I look at Tatum. Her expression is open and easy. She isn't communicating with words, but her eyes are telling me she wants me to stay.

"Yeah, I'll stay too," I say, swallowing against the dryness in my throat. "That would be great."

We lounge around for a couple more hours until it starts to get dark, then we eat a cold dinner—crackers, cheese, and whatever snacks we can find in Brody and Kate's pantry. It isn't much, but it feels like plenty after the heavy lunch we had earlier.

After we eat, Brody and Kate bring every pillow and blanket in the house into the living room and pile them up on the floor in front of the fireplace. We all settle in, Brody and Kate in a giant, overstuffed chair that was clearly made for two people while Tatum and I sit on the couch, Toby stretched out on the floor below us. In addition to the fire, Brody sets up a lantern on the coffee table and a couple of lit candles on either end of the mantel.

The room is cozy and comfortable, but I'm still having a hard time relaxing if only for my body's hyperawareness of Tatum's proximity. We're both sitting sideways, our backs against the armrests and our feet extended outward, which means her feet are snuggled up against my thigh, and my feet are snuggled up against hers. It's not particularly sexy, feet touching thighs, but it's still *touch*. It's still her body heat next to mine.

She looks beautiful in the firelight, her face framed by the wild curls that are loose around her shoulders. When she throws her head back and laughs over a story Brody is telling about one of his students, something tightens in my chest, like my heart just grew the tiniest bit and now everything has to shift around to make room.

But just watching her like this—it isn't enough.

I reach my hand under the blanket that's covering us both and wrap it around Tatum's socked foot. Her eyes lift to mine, but she doesn't pull away. Instead, she stretches the tiniest bit, pressing her foot into my hand like she wants the contact as much as I do. I trace my fingers up the bridge of her foot, and she smiles, biting her lip like it tickles, but she doesn't flinch away. I keep moving until my fingers hit the top of her sock. I trace a slow circle on her ankle, and her eyes flutter closed.

"Okay, I'm beat," Brody says, stretching his arms over his head. "What do you think, Kate? Want to sleep upstairs?"

Kate yawns. "I was up there before we ate, and it wasn't that bad. I think a lot of the heat from down here has risen. If we use the down comforter, we should be fine."

I shouldn't be so excited that Brody and Kate won't be crashing on the floor like this is some sort of co-ed slumber party, but I am absolutely excited.

"So, there's an extra bedroom upstairs," Kate says as she lets Brody help her to her feet. "It's in the back of the house though, farther away than our bedroom, so I'm worried it'll be too cold to be comfortable."

"If it's all the same to you, I'm happy to stay down here close to the fire," Tatum says. "Your couch is really comfortable."

"Absolutely," Kate says. "Wherever you want to sleep is totally great. And you know where the bedroom is if you decide you want it, Len."

Brody drops a hand onto my shoulder and gives it a squeeze. "You'll keep the fire going a while longer?" Even though his words ask a very simple question, I feel him saying so much more in the gesture. *Are you okay? Do you need me? I'm here if you do.*

It's funny. I'm the older brother here, but Brody has grown up so much in the last year. It's as though the certainty of his future has grounded him in a way I can't fully understand. It's not that I don't have anything to live for. I have my restaurant. My family. But I don't have *this*. A true home. A relationship.

My eyes flick to Tatum.

"I'll take care of the fire," I say.

Brody nods. "You know where to find me if you need me."

The fire crackles in the hearth as Kate and Brody make their way upstairs. They take the lantern with them, and the candles have burned themselves out, so we're left with nothing but the fire to see by.

My hand is still wrapped around Tatum's ankle, and I tug it toward me, using both hands to press my thumbs into the ball of her foot.

She moans softly and closes her eyes. "Oh man. That feels . . ." Her words trail off and she lets out a little whimper as I move up and down the arch of her foot.

"It's almost like you work on your feet all day," I say.

She chuckles. "Right?" After a beat of silence, she says, "Sometimes, I don't know why I do it."

My hands still. "What, cook?"

She gives the tiniest nod. Her eyes are cast in shadow, and I can't see her expression, so I just wait, my fingers working on her foot, and hope she'll add something to clarify.

"I used to love cooking," she says, her voice soft. "When I was really little. But then when Dad got the cooking show, and everything changed so fast . . ." She shifts, and I give her foot a squeeze before letting it go and reaching for the other one. "I don't know," she continues. "I could be remembering things wrong. But it just feels like once Dad was working with the network, he no longer talked to me about *food*. He only talked to me about my career. And those aren't the same things, are they?"

"No, they definitely aren't," I say softly. "I get what you're saying."

"Lennox, I don't think I ever figured out how to cook just for the sheer joy of it." Her voice sounds farther away, and I think she might be falling asleep. "That's terrible, right? I should love what I do. What if I never love what I do?"

At this point, I'm not even sure she's talking to me. It feels more like I happened to overhear a question she's asking herself.

When her breathing evens out and deepens, I'm even more sure.

I keep my hands cupped around her foot and lean my head back, shifting so I'm more fully reclined on the couch. I can't sleep like this long term, and Tatum won't sleep comfortably with my big body taking up most of the couch, but hopefully, she'll be okay for a few minutes more.

I don't know what to make of Tatum's words.

She doesn't love to cook?

I always imagined growing up with Christopher Elliott had to be such an incredible privilege, but now I'm not so sure. I've had a lot of conversations with Flint about what fame can do, about how hard he has to work to keep himself grounded, to refuse all the fawning and free stuff and catering to his every whim.

But cooking isn't really about fame. For me, it's about love, as cheesy as that sounds. About serving and caring for the people around me and making people happy with something I create. And of course, it's about the food. About recognizing bounty and magnifying it in ways that honor the earth and the many things it gives us. Money, attention, praise in travel magazines or from food critics, those things are like icing. They can help, of course. Make it possible to keep doing what I love doing. But it's never been *why* I do what I do.

My eyes close, and I feel myself drifting off,

but my left leg is fully asleep with the way Tatum is leaning against it, which can't be any more comfortable for her than it is for me. My ankles are bony, and it feels like my left one is currently digging into her ribs.

I shift and pull my legs back, slowly inching away from Tatum without waking her up. It takes some effort, but eventually, I'm on my feet.

Toby lifts his head and looks at me, but he flops back onto the floor with a snuffly breath.

Tatum is curled into a ball at the end of the couch, her head tilted at an awkward angle that she'll regret in the morning.

I move toward her and slip one hand under her back and the other around her shoulders to try and shift her down a little. I lift gently, and suddenly Tatum is moving, her arms lifting and wrapping around my neck. I pause, hovering over her, unsure what to do.

"Where are we going? Are you taking me somewhere?" she asks sleepily.

"Just moving you a little so you can be more comfortable." I shift her down until her head is resting more fully on a pillow. "How's that?" I ask.

"Mmm, that's better," she says.

I have my doubts as to whether Tatum is awake enough that she'll remember this conversation in the morning, and I have half a mind to ask her something ridiculous just to see what she'll say.

Flint used to talk in his sleep all the time, and Brody and I would take turns trying to coax him into saying stupid stuff. We still have an audio recording of him confessing his love to one of Mom's milk goats—with her silky brown fur and soulful eyes.

I don't want to manipulate Tatum, but I also don't want to let her go, which is good because her arms are still wrapped around my neck. I can't stand like this forever though—my quads are already burning from my half-crouched, half-standing position.

I shift one hand out from under her and slide it up her arm. "Hey, are you going to let me go?" I whisper.

She lets out a tiny moan that ignites a pulse of fire deep in my gut. "Mmm, nope," she says a little too sleepily for me to trust her. "You should stay here. You should—"

Before I can fully process what's happening, Tatum slides her hand from behind my neck, tracing my collarbone until her fingers hook over my shirt. She tugs me closer, even as her hand slides up to my cheek, one thumb grazing across my bottom lip. She tilts her head up the tiniest bit, and then her lips are on mine, fire-warm and feather-soft.

Her hand moves into my hair, her fingers pressing into my scalp, and this time, I'm the one that lets out a groan. But I can't do this.

She's too asleep for me to know if *she* knows what she's doing, and I know better than to push when I'm not sure this is actually what she wants.

It takes all of my willpower, but I pull back, grasping her hand with mine and easing it away. "Easy there, tiger," I say. "How about you just get some sleep for now?"

She doesn't answer, which only makes me feel better about my decision to back away. I tuck her hand under the blanket and pull it up to her chin, then move to the other end of the couch and tuck it under her feet.

There's nothing else I can do to make her feel comfortable, and it feels weird to just stand here and stare at her, so I grab a pillow from the pile Brody and Kate left earlier and stretch out on the floor next to Toby. He scoots closer, lifting his head and dropping it on my stomach.

I don't know how to make sense of what just happened.

I kissed Tatum.

Tatum.

Or, Tatum kissed ME.

Sort of kissed me?

Is a sleep kiss the same thing as a drunk kiss? Can I even trust it as something that Tatum wanted, at least subconsciously, or is this more of an impulse thing that, had she been remotely cognizant, Tatum would have overridden and tossed out as a horrible idea? Will she remember and think it was a dream? Or worse—a nightmare?

Tatum shifts the slightest bit. "Lennox?" she says softly.

I push up on my elbows. "Hmm?"

She says my name one more time, except *not* like a question. *"Lennox."*

I smile as I settle back on the floor. So maybe *not* a nightmare.

If she's dreaming, I'm glad it's about me. Because whether she remembers it or not, my first kiss with Tatum Elliott is something I'm never going to forget.

Our *first* kiss. But I'm determined it won't be our last.

And next time, I'll make sure it's one *she'll* remember.

CHAPTER SEVENTEEN
Tatum

The power is back on when I wake up. The lamp in the corner of the living room bathes the room in soft light, and I can hear the refrigerator humming in the kitchen.

Lennox is stretched out on the floor beside the couch sound asleep. He's on his stomach, one arm tucked under his pillow and the other draped over Toby, who is snuggled in beside him. The sight of my dog nestled against a sleeping Lennox Hawthorne does serious things to my heart. I thought it was bad yesterday when Lennox talked to Toby in a silly voice, but this is ten times worse. If yesterday was a gentle nudge to my feelings, this is a seismic shift. Toby has been the sole occupant of my heart for some time now, but apparently, the rebellious organ is more than happy to grow an extra chamber for Lennox.

And that scares me more than I can say.

Toby's head pops up, like he somehow sensed that I'm awake, and when he moves, Lennox moves. I hold my breath, not wanting to intentionally disturb him. It's barely light outside. It can't be much past six a.m., and we were up late. Just because I'm an incurable morning person doesn't mean everyone else has to be too.

Toby settles back down, and I feel around on the couch, knowing my phone is around here somewhere. I find it tucked under my pillow, still connected to the portable power block Brody gave me yesterday. I unplug it and set the charger aside, then snuggle a little deeper into my blankets. Without really thinking about what I'm doing, I pull up Instagram and find Lennox's profile. He doesn't post much—I discovered that when I saw the Stonebrook job posting, impulsively applied, then cyber-stalked his entire family until I got the job. But the Stonebrook Farm Instagram account is full of gorgeous pictures of the farm, including several from the restaurant opening that feature Lennox in all his gorgeous glory.

In my favorite photo, he's standing in his restaurant kitchen, a pan of vibrantly colored vegetables sautéing on the stove in front of him. I can't tell what he's making, but that doesn't matter. The picture isn't about the food. It's about Lennox and the light in his eyes—the sheer joy on his face.

My heart squeezes for the millionth time in the past twenty-four hours.

Lennox loves what he does.

I love that he loves what he does.

But the contrast to how I feel about my work is too blatant to ignore.

I definitely *don't* love what I do. Not like this.

When I ran away from California, I was mostly running away from Dad. But I'm starting to wonder—maybe I was running away from Le Vin, too. From being a chef.

The catering kitchen has been exciting because it's been new, a challenge for me to figure out and problem solve. But now that it's starting to feel easy, or at least *easier*, I'm already feeling . . . I don't know. Itchy, maybe?

I don't know what that means, but I do know I need to figure it out.

I scroll through a few more pictures of Lennox. The man is stupidly photogenic. I'm pretty sure I dreamed about him last night. Which honestly, how could I not? The heat of him next to me on the couch. The press of his thumbs on the sorest parts of my feet, the whisper of his touch across the skin on my ankle.

Every new brush of contact felt like a question. *Do you feel this? Do you want this?*

Yes, yes, and extra yes.

A memory pushes to the surface. Oh. *Oh*, I think I dreamed about *kissing* Lennox last night. I can conjure up exactly what it's like to feel his mouth pressed against mine.

I lift a hand to my lips and close my eyes.

Good job, brain. Excellent, excellent work.

I scroll Instagram for a few more minutes until I can no longer ignore my need to pee. Which is a shame because I am warm and comfortable, and even though the power is back on, the air still feels cool outside the enormous comforter I'm covered up with. I need to get myself one of these. If I'm going to live in the mountains, clearly, I need blankets that provide mountain-level warmth.

The wood floors creak beneath my feet as I make my way down the hallway to the tiny bathroom next to the kitchen. After I finish, I stare at my reflection, wishing I'd grabbed my bag on my way in. I haven't had makeup on since arriving; it was basically the middle of the night when Kate texted and insisted I come back with Brody, so I didn't think to put any on then. And we were all just sitting around in our sweats all day, huddled by the fire.

But now? After how things went with Lennox last night—the camaraderie during the game, the secret, small touches—I feel a sudden need to try a little. To make sure I look my best. I sneak out to the hall and grab my bag, tiptoeing back to the bathroom. So far, it doesn't sound like anyone else is awake.

First priority? The riot of curls on my head. I use a little water and finger comb them as best I can, then tame them into a messy bun. There are still wispy ringlets sticking out around my face, but I need product to control those, and I didn't bring any with me, so this will have to do. I brush my teeth and put on a little bit of tinted lip balm and a light coat of mascara. It isn't much, but it's enough to make me feel slightly better about facing Lennox.

I take a deep breath and press a hand to my stomach. I'm nervous, but it's a good kind of nervous.

When I make it back to the living room, Lennox is nowhere to be found. Someone's making noise in the kitchen though, so I follow the sound, finding Lennox standing at the back door, holding it open for Charlie and Toby.

"You're awake," I say.

He turns. He's wearing the same joggers he had on yesterday and a navy-blue hoodie that looks warm and soft and comfortable. "Your dog woke me up." He lifts his hand and rubs it across his beard. "A tongue bath is a very effective alarm clock."

I wince. "Oh man. Sorry about that."

"He's a dog who knows how to get what he wants. He led me right to the door as soon as I was on my feet. You want some coffee?"

"I'd love some."

He moves to the coffeemaker sitting on the counter. "How did you sleep?"

I lean against the island across from him. "Good, I guess. I was warm, so there's that. How about you? Sorry you had to sleep on the floor."

"Being close to the fire was worth it," he says.

"And Toby seemed like he needed the company."

Or maybe *I* seemed like I needed the company? It's probably too much to hope that he stayed downstairs to be close to me, but a girl can dream.

"I saw you snuggled up together when I woke up." *And it made my heart climb out of my chest to fall on the floor at your feet.*

He turns and folds his arms across his chest, studying me closely. He clears his throat. "So, do you remember anything weird happening last night? Anything . . . different?"

I narrow my eyes. "Should I? Why? What happened?"

He grins. "How about we start with what you *do* remember?"

"Oh no." A beat of panic flits through me. "Lennox, did I talk in my sleep? Please tell me I didn't say anything stupid." I press my hands to my cheeks, feeling them warm against my cool palms. "I used to do it all the time. My college roommates had way too much fun with some of the things I said."

I can see the smile playing on Lennox's lips, but he doesn't cave, just keeps those deep green eyes trained right on me. Finally, he unleashes his smile in all its overwhelming glory. "You talked a little."

I groan. "Was it bad? Tell me it wasn't bad."

He turns around and pulls a couple of mugs out

of the cabinet, setting them on the counter next to the already gurgling coffee maker. "Depends on who you're asking." He lifts his shoulders in a playful shrug. "But I didn't mind it."

I squeeze my eyes closed and move my hands up so they're covering my entire face. "Just tell me," I say. "Can you repeat it? Am I ever going to be able to look at you again?"

He's quiet for a beat, then I feel him move closer. His hands close around my wrists, and he gently tugs them away from my face. He places a warm mug of fresh coffee into my hands. "Stop stressing. All you said was my name."

A surge of relief washes over me. "Oh. That's not too bad, I guess."

"I mean, it definitely sounded like you were trying to seduce me. A little sexy, a little breathy—" He opens the fridge and pulls out the cream, offering it to me.

I swat at his arm before setting my mug on the counter and taking the cream. "I did not sound like I was trying to seduce you."

He smiles. "You kinda did."

Something tugs at the back of my consciousness, and the kissing part of my dream pops into my mind in all its vivid glory. *Was* I trying to seduce him? But I was *SLEEPING*. It couldn't have been that bad.

Either way, Lennox is enjoying this way too much.

"I think you must have mistaken *frustration* for interest." I pour a splash of cream into my coffee and leave it on the counter, turning to face Lennox fully. "I was probably dreaming about you taunting me with dry pastry or expensive cheese."

"Dry pastry?" he says with a smirk. "I wouldn't know where to find any of that." He steps toward me. "Besides, I know what you sound like when you're frustrated. And *this* was not that." Another step. "This was softer." He reaches forward and hooks a finger around my pinky, tugging me toward him. I go willingly, my breath catching when his free hand slips around my waist and pulls me against him, our bodies flush. "You sounded like you wanted me."

Outside the back door, Toby barks, startling us both. I jump away from Lennox, one hand pressed to my heart, and look at Toby who is staring at us through the glass.

Seconds later, Brody and Kate come downstairs, then Lennox is making everyone breakfast, and I'm left to process one of the most emotionally charged moments I've ever experienced while we're all laughing and talking over pancakes.

You sounded like you wanted me.

Well, that's not hard to imagine, because I definitely do.

I did not think about the downside to unexpected days off.

Now that the snow is mostly gone and we're up and running again, I'm playing catch up, and it is *not fun*.

The wedding scheduled for the day after the snowstorm only had to be postponed one day, which, great for the bride and groom, but it means I have to handle a wedding dinner *and* a corporate retreat dinner on the same night. Both events were supposed to happen in the farmhouse dining room, but Lennox has agreed to have the corporate retreat people use a corner of his dining room for one meal, leaving the farmhouse open for the rescheduled wedding. That just means I have to figure out how to have staff in two places—up at the farmhouse serving a wedding, and here, serving thirty corporate attorneys on a week-long restorative mountain getaway. Olivia brought in extra waitstaff, and Lennox offered to let me use a couple of his line cooks, so everything should run smoothly.

But the situation is still less than ideal, and it's made even more complicated by the tree-sized hole in the ceiling of my office. Every time we shuttle food out the back door to the van we use to transport it up to the farmhouse, we're walking through a construction zone which does exactly nothing to soothe my already frazzled nerves.

Meanwhile, whenever I see Lennox, all I want to do is forget I even have a job and run into his arms. What else could I possibly do after that last moment between us?

I can't stop thinking about the way he looked at me, his finger hooked around mine, a fire burning in his eyes. He wanted to kiss me. I'm absolutely positive about that. And had we not been interrupted first, by Toby, then by Brody and Kate, I'm pretty sure he would have.

So that's fun. An unrealized kiss hanging between us, and zero time to actually make it happen. We're both thinking about it though. I can tell every time our eyes meet across a crowded kitchen or our fingers brush, lingering a little longer than necessary whenever we're close enough to touch.

It's just past ten when I finish for the night, but Lennox's kitchen is still hopping. On the one hand, I hate that he's still on his feet. On the other, if his staff is still cooking, I'd do anything for some apple brandy pork tenderloin right about now.

Lennox finally sees me, and motions for Zach to come take his spot as expeditor before he makes his way over. As soon as I see the tired lines etched into the side of his face, I quickly change my mind about asking him for anything. I'm half-tempted to offer to cover for him so he can go home and go to bed.

"You guys are working late."

"About to plate the last orders," he says. "I

guess this big extended family is in town for a funeral, and they all came in together. There's something like twenty of them."

"Do you need any help?"

"Nah, we're through the worst of it. But can I ask your opinion about something else?"

My stomach growls. "Is my opinion worth some apple brandy pork tenderloin?"

He grins. "I'll see what I can do," he says, then he turns and looks over his shoulder while Zach calls an order.

"Plating two tenderloins, one salmon, two filets, one rare, one medium rare, and four southern chickens," Zach says.

The cooks around the room echo back the order, and Lennox nods once before he turns his attention back to me.

"Then you can have all my opinions," I say. "What's up?"

Lennox quickly walks me through what he calls a staffing problem. But to me, it just sounds like a training problem. The hardest part about running a kitchen is how frequently people call out, leaving everyone else to pick up the slack. If there aren't enough people left who can do what needs to be done, the few who can are stressed and stretched too thin. And that creates ripples that eventually hit your dining room.

From what it sounds like, Lennox has enough cooks, he just doesn't have enough cooks who are trained to do more than one thing. Ideally, every station should be at least two deep with people who can handle every single dish on the menu.

"So hiring someone to replace Griffin will probably help, but I still don't feel like it's going to be enough," he says. He pushes his hands into his pockets.

"I heard what happened with Griffin," I say, remembering the conversation I overheard a couple of his waitstaff having. It was more than a little sexy to think of Lennox nearly punching a guy, though I never found out what Griffin actually said to set Lennox off.

"Don't remind me," he says. "Wasn't my finest moment."

"What did Griffin say?" I ask before I can think better of it.

Lennox's jaw tightens. "Don't worry about it."

Oh, now I want to know even more. "That bad, huh?"

One of Lennox's dishwashers crosses behind Lennox, a girl who can't be more than eighteen or so. She looks at me, eyes wide, almost like she's trying to tell me something. I furrow my brow. *Is* she trying to tell me something?

Lennox follows my gaze, making eye contact with her, and she quickly turns away from us, but then she spins back around like she can't help herself. "Griffin said something about you!" she blurts out, then her hand flies to her mouth like she can't believe the words actually escaped. She peels her hand away to reveal an innocent smile. "He was defending your honor," she says, motioning to Lennox, her tone dreamy and sweet. I suddenly feel like I'm in a scene from a Jane Austen novel. Lennox *defended* my honor? *Well, yes please and thank you.*

"Thanks for that, Paige," Lennox says. "Really."

"Sorry," she whispers before scurrying off.

Lennox looks at me, his expression almost bashful. "I'm sorry about that."

"Sorry for nearly punching a guy who said something rude about me?"

"Sorry you found out it happened at all."

I appreciate him wanting to protect me. But does it hurt my opinion of the man to know he nearly lost his cool over me? *Absolutely not.*

Also noteworthy: fancy head chef Lennox Hawthorne knows the name of a random dishwasher.

Every time I think it's impossible for me to like him more, I learn something like this, and my heart stretches a little bigger.

"Listen," I say, stepping closer to Lennox, "I don't think you need to hire someone to replace Griffin. Willow is great, and she's anxious to learn. Train her. And then keep training. Make every station two or three deep so when people call out, you have a backup, and a backup to your backup. If you have a commis chef who's anxious to learn, train them."

He shakes his head. "But I can't pay everyone like they're all chef de partie."

"You won't have to. I'm not saying you have to train everyone down to your dishwashers. But you're covering too much. And Zach is too. Two or three more people who can pinch hit when you have a station chef call out would mean Zach wouldn't have to step in and cover for people, leaving him free to be expeditor, and you free to breathe every once in a while so you can focus on bigger picture stuff."

He nods. "That sounds pretty nice, actually." He props his hands on his hips. "So three people trained at every station."

I nod. "That's what we aimed for at Le Vin. Remember, they won't all work at once. More trained chefs will also give everyone more breathing room in their schedules. That means less burnout."

He finally smiles, and my heart flops into my stomach. "Pretty smart, Elliott. Pretty smart." He holds my gaze, the air crackling between us before his eyes drop to my lips.

Annnd here we are again—the *wanting* almost tangible enough to touch.

"Hey Chef, can I get your thoughts on this?" Zach calls from across the kitchen.

Lennox looks over his shoulder, and he breathes out a sigh before turning back to me.

"Go work," I say, even though it pains me to say it. "I can text you later."

He shakes his head, and his eyes flash with heat. "No, don't leave. I'll be right back."

Well, okay then. I kind of like it when Lennox gets bossy with me.

I watch as he talks to Zach, looking over several plates spread across the counter. He nods once, claps Zach on the back, then he's striding toward me with purpose. He doesn't even pause when he reaches me. He just scoops up my hand and tugs me across his kitchen, then down the hall toward the back door.

At first, I think he must be taking me outside, but then he turns into a little alcove holding a small storage shelf full of to-go coffee cups, prepackaged plastic cutlery, and the cardboard boxes catering uses to make boxed lunches. There's an old chest freezer in the corner I'm pretty sure no one has used in years.

There isn't a door on the space, so technically anyone could walk by at any moment, but this late, with my kitchen already shut down for the night, it's unlikely, making this the closest thing to alone we've been all day.

Lennox stands apart from me, his hands propped on his hips. "I know we're supposed to have dinner next week," he finally says.

I nod. "I'm looking forward to it."

"Me too," he says. "And I thought I could wait—that we could talk and have a nice meal and then . . ." His words trail off, and he takes a step toward me, hunger flashing in his gaze, but then he retreats again, like he's fighting to restrain himself. "I don't think I can wait, Tatum," he says, his voice low. "I know what I'm feeling. Do you—are you feeling it too?"

I nod, barely holding back.

"Good," he says. "Then we understand each other?"

I lick my lips, my heart pounding. "Yes, Chef."

And then he's on me, his strong arms circling my back as he presses his lips to mine. The kiss is frantic, arms and hands scrambling as we practically claw at each other. I cannot get close enough—though part of that problem is that he is tall, and I am short, and I really *can't* get close enough.

But then Lennox reaches down and hoists me up so I'm sitting on the freezer, and he steps into the space between my knees. *Oh my.* He made that look easy, and this definitely improves the height difference.

I tilt my head, deepening the kiss and eliciting a low moan from Lennox that sends a fresh wave of desire coursing through me. I hook a hand around his neck and tug him even closer, suddenly hating that the chef's coats we wear are so thick—so *present*. I want to feel his skin, rub my hands up his arms and feel the steady beat of his heart under my palm.

Eventually, Lennox breaks the kiss, dropping his head on my shoulder as his hands rest on either side of my waist. His chest is still heaving, and we breathe together for several moments.

Finally, he looks up and we make eye contact. "You smell like herbs de Provence," he says as he presses a gentle kiss just in front of my earlobe.

"I was brining chickens in buttermilk," I say, my voice soft and breathy. This is an absolutely ridiculous moment to be talking about chicken, but he's the one who brought it up. "The herbs kick it up a notch."

He chuckles as he trails kisses across my jaw. "Hmm, I bet," he murmurs.

"This—what you're doing," I say, my voice raw with desire, "is entirely unfair." Still, I can't stop myself from arching my neck, exposing more of my skin like an offering. "But also, please don't stop," I whisper.

He seems all too happy to comply, moving down my neck before he shifts and finds my lips one more time. This kiss is more tender, less frenzied than the first, and the heat coursing through me settles to something more like a banked hearth instead of a raging forest fire.

If someone had asked me, the week I started at Stonebrook Farm, if I could ever imagine something like this happening with Lennox Hawthorne, I would have laughed myself sick.

And yet, here I am. Here *we* are. And nothing has ever felt so natural.

I slide my hand over Lennox's beard, cradling his face as we pull apart. "Not bad as far as first kisses go," I say.

Lennox smiles, and my hands fall away. "Technically, that wasn't our first kiss."

My brow furrows. "What do you mean *technically?*"

"The first was at Brody and Kate's house. But we don't have to count it," he says saucily. "Seeing as how you were asleep."

I gasp. "You kissed me while I was *sleeping?*"

"Absolutely not," he says with enough conviction that I immediately believe him. "What do you take me for? But after you fell asleep, I shifted you down so you would be more comfortable, and *you kissed me.*"

"I didn't."

He laughs. "You did. Reached up, tugged me down by the shirt, and planted one right on my lips." He leans a little closer. *"Like you wanted me."*

I gasp. "I did not." My hands fly to my face, fire already pooling in my cheeks.

Lennox grins. "You're blushing, Tatum."

"Seriously, Lennox?" I shift my hands so they're covering my eyes, too. "You aren't supposed to point it out."

"What should I do instead?" he asks, his tone playful.

"You should pretend like you don't notice at all. Celebrate on the inside if you want, but don't make me sit here feeling all embarrassed because now I know that *you* know how much you . . . make me feel," I say softly.

He's quiet for a beat, then he unbuttons the top of his chef's coat and reaches for my free hand. He tugs it toward him and slips it inside the coat, pressing it against his heart. His chest is warm under my palm, and I feel the *thump thump thump* of his racing heart.

"Now we're even," he says softly. "Now you know what *you* do to *me*."

Oh, he's good, I think, but when I look into his eyes, there's a certainty there that makes me think he isn't just feeding me a line. I'm not being played. Whatever this is, it's *real*.

He smiles. "I should go help Zach finish up."

I bite my lip and nod. "You know he's going to guess exactly what you've been doing."

Lennox leans forward and brushes another kiss across my lips. "I hope he does," he says, a hint of possessiveness in his tone. "I want him and everyone else to know that I'm the *only* one around here who gets to think about kissing you."

"Just around here?" I lean up and kiss him again.

His grip on me tightens. "Anywhere. You're mine now, Tatum."

"How very caveman of you," I say, my tone teasing.

He leans back and makes eye contact, his expression giving me the choice his words lacked. "I *want* you to be mine."

"Better," I say. "And there's nothing that I want more."

He helps me off the freezer and walks me to the bottom of the stairs that lead up to my apartment. He touches my elbow, his expression so full of warmth and tenderness, it's all I can do to stay upright. "I'll text you later?" he says.

I nod. "I would love that."

An hour later, after I've showered and put on my pajamas, a knock sounds on my apartment door.

I open it to find one of Lennox's waitstaff holding a to-go container. She holds it out to me. "Compliments of the chef," she says.

I don't even have to open the container to know what it is.

Halfway through my meal, a text message from Lennox pops up.

> **Lennox:** What was the first food eaten in space?

A trivia question?

Before I can type in the answer, another message pops up.

> **Lennox:** Also, hi. 😊
> **Tatum:** Sorry, can't talk right now. I'm eating the best pork tenderloin ever.
> **Tatum:** Also, applesauce.
> **Lennox:** You're eating applesauce?
> **Tatum:** Nope. But that was the first food eaten in space.
> **Lennox:** New goal: stump Tatum with a trivia question.
> **Tatum:** Challenge accepted. Does this mean you're going to text me ALL THE TIME?
> **Lennox:** Definitely.
> **Tatum:** Thank you for dinner. I really didn't expect you to cook for me after the night you've had.
> **Lennox:** What did I tell you about cooking for you?
> **Tatum:** Yes, yes, all I have to do is ask. As a thank you, here's a link to the quiz bowl finals the year I won. You have my permission to laugh at my very bad hair.

I pull up the link on YouTube and send it over. It's five or so minutes before Lennox responds.

Lennox: I approve of this form of payment. I expect baby pictures in exchange for the next meal.
Lennox: Your hair was EPIC.
Lennox: Hey, also, thanks for your thoughts earlier. I talked to Zach, and I'm already excited about what this could mean for us.
Tatum: Of course! I'm so happy to help.
Lennox: Can I see you tomorrow?
Tatum: You see me every day.
Lennox: Maybe I want to do more than see you.

My heart starts pounding, and I let out a little squeal that makes Toby sit up and woof.

Lennox: What time do you work tomorrow? Are you free in the morning?
Tatum: Tomorrow is slammed. But I am not opposed to accidentally on purpose running into you in the pantry a time or two.
Lennox: That is not going to be enough to satisfy me. Meet me in my office for coffee at nine?
Tatum: If you're bringing the coffee, I'm there.
Lennox: Perfect.

I put my phone down and pick up my fork.

The plan does sound perfect. Almost too perfect? Or maybe it's Lennox who seems too perfect.

I want to be an optimist. I really do. But I can't help but worry that when something seems too good to be true, it usually is.

CHAPTER EIGHTEEN
Lennox

Flint: Hey. Anyone have an update on Lennox and his new woman?
Brody: They're definitely a thing. They're almost as bad as Perry and Lila were.
Perry: We weren't bad.
Brody: You were definitely bad.
Perry: We were falling in love. Also, you're one to talk. We watched you pine after Kate for YEARS, Brody. YEARS.
Flint: He's right. It was pretty painful.
Brody: You think it was painful for you? Imagine how I felt.
Flint: So, is Lennox actually serious about this woman? Am I the only one sensing how big of a deal this is?
Brody: Agreed. It's a big deal.
Perry: She seems good for him though. This is a good thing.
Lennox: Should I step out so you guys can talk about my love life more openly?
Flint: YOU SAID LOVE LIFE. DO YOU LOVE HER?

Lennox: Stop. It's a figure of speech. No overreacting.
Lennox: But also, I maybe . . .
Flint: DETAILS, MAN. SPILL THEM.
Brody: WHY ARE YOU YELLING AT US FLINT
Flint: Sorry. Caps lock was on. Didn't realize.
Lennox: I don't know what happened. She annoyed me. I annoyed her. Then all of a sudden, we didn't anymore.
Perry: Does she know how you feel?
Lennox: Pretty sure, but we haven't explicitly said anything or made it official.
Perry: But you think she feels the same way?
Brody: Kate says she thinks the feelings are definitely mutual. Based on her observations and conversations with Tatum.
Flint: DUDE. You know the rules about letting wives read the text thread.
Brody: Sorry, sorry. She was reading over my shoulder. She says she's sorry.
Flint: I can't even with you. Hi, Kate. NOW GO AWAY.
Brody: She says she loves you. And she loved the interview you did with Vanity Fair.

Perry: And by that she means she knows exactly how to stroke your ego so you'll let her off the hook.

Brody: Perry speaks very fluent Kate.

Flint: Tell Kate THANK YOU because the interview WAS amazing. And I'll let her off the hook anyway because she has to share a bed with Brody and we all know how terrible he smells.

Brody: Are we twelve again?

Flint: All I'm saying is the last time I was home and I rode in your truck, it smelled like the river died and rotted in your back seat.

Brody: That was the kayaking gear. Not me.

Perry: Sometimes it's you. Essence of river. Don't worry. We're all used to it.

Brody: Help me out here, Len. Do I smell?

Lennox: Yes. Hazards of the job. I usually smell like onions and garlic, though Tatum seems to like this about me. Not sure Kate is ever going to love river rot.

Perry: I think I win when it comes to smells.

Flint: Wrong, big brother. Because I smell like money, money, money.

Brody: Money . . . and loneliness. How's it working for you, man?
Flint: Shut up.
Flint: Also, point taken.
Perry: Lennox, if you and Tatum care about each other, that's all that matters.
Lennox: I think we do. But everything is still uncertain. I think Tatum likes Silver Creek, and she loves the farm, but I don't think she loves catering. I don't see her doing this long term.
Perry: Um, is that something Olivia needs to be aware of? Tatum might be leaving?
Flint: Perry. Stop being CFO and be a brother for a minute.
Perry: Right. Sorry. That wasn't cool.
Lennox: I'm sure she'll communicate with Olivia when she knows more. But even if she doesn't love the job, she'd never leave us hanging. She'll stay as long as we need her to stay.
Brody: With or without the job though, I don't see the trouble. She could still be with you even if she isn't working for the farm.
Lennox: True. But it's not like Silver Creek is a hotbed of job opportunities. I want her to be happy, to do something she loves, and I'm not sure she can living here.

Perry: So you're worried she might leave.
Lennox: And if she does, I'll be left with all these . . . FEELINGS.
Flint: Awww. Look at our Lennox all sick with love.
Lennox: I seriously hate you so much right now.
Brody: I mean, I hate to state the obvious here, but the damage is already done, right?
Brody: If you've already fallen for her, your feelings are a moot point. You can't change them even if you want to.
Perry: True. Falling backwards is pretty much impossible.
Lennox: So that's it? I'm just doomed?
Flint: Love is pain, man.
Perry: Until it isn't. Then it's amazing. But you never get to the amazing part if you don't take any risks.
Brody: Yes. True.
Flint: Says the man who waited a thousand years to take an actual risk when it comes to love.
Brody: Also true. I have regrets.
Perry: You just have to trust, Len. Something will work out. If you're supposed to be together, you'll figure out a way to be together. Here, or somewhere else.

Brody: Just keep being your charming self. Show her what it feels like to be loved by YOU. You've got this, man. And you know we're here for you if you need us.
Perry: Full stop.
Perry: Also, Lila says I smell like apples. It's part of why she fell in love with me so fast.
Flint: I just threw up a little in my mouth.
Lennox: You guys are idiots.
Lennox: But also. Thanks.

CHAPTER NINETEEN
Tatum

I am in love with Stonebrook Farm.

Spring has finally sprung in the mountains, and I couldn't be happier. Flowers are blooming, trees are greening, temperatures are warming, and I am doing *lots* of kissing.

In the pantry? Check.

The walk-in fridge? Check.

My (finally repaired!) office? Check.

The storage room? The gazebo outside? The outside landing? Check, check, and check.

We finally had the promised dinner at Lennox's place, which was definitely a date since it involved kissing during all stages. Before dinner. During dinner. *After dinner*.

We've also had coffee at my place. Breakfast in the apple orchard. We've even had lunch with his parents.

We've exchanged a billion text messages, including countless trivia questions that I have gotten right at least ninety percent of the time. We've even managed to squeeze in a movie, a scheduling miracle that proved totally pointless because we both fell asleep halfway through.

But my favorite place to be with Lennox is in

his restaurant kitchen after hours. Preferably while he's cooking something.

Tonight, he's working on a new special for Hawthorne's menu, so I've turned cooking into a spectator sport, and taken a seat on the counter to watch while he creates.

We're *weeks* into whatever this thing is between us, and let me tell you, I still haven't gotten tired of the view.

Lennox already lost his chef's coat at the end of his dinner service, so he's cooking in a t-shirt, the sleeves snug around his sculpted biceps, and he's wearing a striped chef's apron around his waist.

"Okay, try it now," Lennox says, lifting his spoon to my lips. He's been trying to perfect a sauce for a new salmon dish for the last half hour, not that I have any complaints. I could watch him do this all night long.

I taste the sauce, the flavor bright and bold as it hits my tongue. "Wait, where's the lemon?" I ask.

"Gone," he says, his eyes sparkling.

"This is sweeter. And better." I lick the last few drops off the spoon, finally catching the full flavor profile. "You went with the mango."

He grins. "It works, right?"

I nod. "It definitely works. So, a creme fraiche sweetened with mango puree? Will that be enough?"

"Not quite, I don't think. I want to use fresh

mango in the dish, too. Maybe a chutney of some kind. Are you hungry? I think I'm ready to put it all together."

I stifle a yawn. "It's after midnight, but sure. I'm hungry."

He immediately stops and spins around. "Wait, no, Tatum, you should totally go to bed. I get like this sometimes, but . . . you don't have to wait up with me." He steps closer, slipping his arms around my waist as I lift my hands to his shoulders.

I smile and shake my head. "I want to wait. I really am hungry. And I'm pretty sure this dish is going to be amazing. Cook. We'll eat. *Then* I'll go to bed." This is my new normal. Pushing aside sleep, chores, anything deemed nonessential to be with Lennox as frequently as possible.

He leans forward and presses a kiss to my lips. "You're good to me."

I catch him before he can retreat, pulling him back for a longer, more intentional kiss. I run my hands down his shoulders and over the curve of his biceps as I arch toward him. He lets out a low moan and deepens the kiss. "Maybe I don't need to cook tonight," he says against my lips.

I nudge him away. "Yes, you do. You know you want to. Also, I really am hungry."

He smirks. "I'm hungry, too."

I laugh as I push him away. "You're shameless. Now, go. Feed me."

He steps away, his grin wide as he heads toward

the fridge. "Feed me?" he says over his shoulder. "And you're calling *me* shameless?"

A bonus to all of the obvious benefits of spending so much time with Lennox: I'm also learning a lot about myself. Observing his process, hearing him deconstruct a dish, talking about what flavors are working and what flavors aren't—I'm recognizing that his brain works in magical and amazing ways that I cannot, in any respect, fully comprehend. It feels a little like watching one of those videos where an artist paints an entire canvas upside down and it looks like a lumpy potato until they flip it over, and suddenly you're looking at a sketch of Harry Styles, a knowing grin on his face.

The point is, Lennox's genius in the kitchen is unparalleled. Maybe it's because I'm finally growing into myself, owning what makes me talented in my own right. Maybe it's because his kisses make everything easier. But the jealousy I used to feel back in culinary school is completely gone.

Now, I just admire him. Respect him. And possibly feel . . . *more* than that. Though I'm not sure I'm ready to admit as much out loud.

"Hey, random question," I ask as he heads back into the kitchen, salmon in hand.

"Shoot," he says.

"What made you want to run your own restaurant?"

His eyebrows go up. "Like, just generally?"

I nod.

He sets the fish on the counter and pulls out his knife, slicing it into two generous portions. "I mean, practically speaking, cooking is what I'm good at, so it makes sense."

"That's it?" I ask when he doesn't say anything else. "It's all very practical and reasonable?"

He turns around and wipes his hands on his apron before folding his arms. "You'll laugh at me."

"I absolutely will not."

He hooks a hand around the back of his neck like he's nervous, which is, not going to lie, absolutely endearing and adorable. "Okay, I guess I just feel this sense of responsibility. Food has always meant a lot to my family because it's the source of our livelihood. The bounty of the earth has given *us* bounty. So cooking feels like a way for me to fuel us and feed us and give us the energy to give back to the earth. It's a relationship—which is why I try to use every part of an ingredient, wasting as little as possible." He drops his hand and turns back to his fish. "That probably sounds really weird."

Oh my word. This man has no idea how sexy he is when he talks about cooking. "I don't think it sounds weird at all," I say, my voice soft. "I think it sounds brilliant."

He walks over to the stove and pours some oil

into a pan. "What about you? What made you want to cook?"

"My father," I answer without hesitation. "But not for the reasons you think."

A lightness fills my chest as I realize I'm going to tell Lennox the truth. Unfiltered. Uninfluenced by what Christopher Elliott or anyone else actually thinks.

"So . . . not because you were inspired by his very impressive career?"

I shake my head. "Nope."

"Then why?"

I shrug. "It was the only option. The only topic of conversation. The only dream I was ever allowed to have."

He lifts the pan, swirling around the oil so it fully coats the bottom. "But was it ever actually *your* dream?"

"Who knows? The lines were always pretty blurry between what *I* wanted and what my father wanted for me. But I will say this. I probably dream about *not cooking* every day a lot more than most chefs."

He lowers the fish into the pan, the familiar hiss and sizzle sounding loud in the otherwise quiet kitchen. Lennox looks over his shoulder and shrugs. "So quit."

I immediately scoff. "I can't *quit*."

"Why not?"

"Because I have a job, first of all, and a very

important one. And I like working at Stonebrook even if I don't love everything about catering. Second of all, I don't know how to do anything else."

"Tatum. You're brilliant. You could do anything you want."

The easy way he's listening, talking to me about options, is a stark contrast to the way these conversations always go with my father. With Dad, there is only *one* path. And it's his.

Still, Lennox is making it sound too easy. I can't just quit something. Until I stormed out of Le Vin in a blaze of fury and indignation, I'd never quit anything in my life.

I wave my hand dismissively. "I don't know. It's probably just the exhaustion talking."

Lennox looks at me again, a flash of worry passing over his features, but then he schools his expression into something more neutral. "Hey, did I tell you I officially promoted Willow to saucier this week?"

"What? That's amazing," I say, happy for the subject change. "I bet she was thrilled."

Lennox nods. "And I've moved two additional cooks over to be commis chefs for sauté and grill, and they both seem really excited. I can already tell it's going to make a difference."

"You're deepening your bench. It's smart, Lennox. I'm so glad."

He drops the fish into the sizzling pan. "Was

that a sports metaphor?" he says, grinning over his shoulder.

I roll my eyes. "What can I say? I know how to make you happy."

The salmon dish is delicious—sweet and light and tropical and perfect for spring.

Lennox declares it an official special for next week's menu, and then it's time to call it a night.

By the time we finish eating and cleaning up, it's almost one in the morning, though that's not so unusual for chefs who start work so late in the day and finish so late at night. Trouble is, my schedule includes breakfast service as frequently as it does dinner, and keeping Lennox's hours is starting to catch up with me.

We walk to the back door together, stopping at the foot of the stairs that lead up to my apartment. I lean into him for a hug, and he tugs me close, resting his cheek on top of my head. I close my eyes and sigh, allowing my body weight to sink into him. "Okay, sleepy head," he says, kissing my forehead. "Off to bed with you."

I yawn as I pull away. "Are we still meeting in the morning?"

"I'd like to, but let's make it ten instead of nine so you can get some sleep."

I lean up on my toes and give him a lingering kiss. "See? You're good to me, too."

I haul myself up the stairs, ready to tumble directly into bed, but I've barely made it inside my apartment when my phone rings. This wouldn't be the first time Lennox has called me seconds after saying goodnight just so he can say it again, so I answer the call without even glancing at the screen.

"Couldn't live without me, huh?"

"Tatum?"

Oh, crap. "Dad?"

"I'm glad you're still up."

I drop onto the edge of my favorite chair, my body tight. Since Lennox and I started seeing each other, I've been ignoring Dad's texts like it's an Olympic sport, so I can't exactly be surprised that he's calling. But I don't like that he caught me by surprise—that I had no time to prepare.

Toby ambles over and drops his head into my lap, and I curl my fingers through his fur, immediately grateful for his comforting presence.

"I just got home, actually. How are you?"

"Good. You know. Busy as always. How's the weather out there?"

I furrow my brow. So we're just going to small talk? A tiny bit of the tension in my shoulders drains away.

"Finally starting to warm up," I cautiously say. "The Hawthornes told me the farm is beautiful in the spring, but it's been amazing seeing it for myself. You wouldn't believe it, Dad. This place looks like it's straight out of a fairy tale."

"Sounds charming," he says, sounding utterly *un*charmed.

Ah. There he is. There's the Dad I expect.

"It *is* charming," I say, the bite in my words surprising even me. Apparently, I'm too tired to be careful. And I'm just . . . really over him making everything so hard.

Dad scoffs, and I brace myself. "Really now, Tatum. Can we please just stop with all this? When are you coming home? I miss you. I *need* you here."

I breathe out a weary sigh. "You don't need me, Dad. Your restaurant is fine. Suki should have had the head chef job a long time ago."

"This isn't about the restaurant," he barks back, his tone harsh. "I don't care about the restaurant."

I sit up a little taller, a sense of unease building in my chest. Dad is often disagreeable, but it's usually in a very passive-aggressive way. He's rarely short-tempered. "Then what is it about?"

He's quiet for a long moment before he lets out a frustrated breath. "Tatum, the network isn't renewing my show. That's the truth of it. If you don't sign on for the show featuring us both, I'm off the air."

I stiffen, a wave of shock moving through me. "Wait, what?"

"They don't want me anymore," he reiterates. "I have no contract unless I sign a new one with you on board."

I sink back into my chair, letting his words percolate in my brain. Suddenly, everything makes so much more sense.

"So me coming back to L.A. has never been about me," I say slowly. "It's always been about you?"

"Tatum, you know that's not true. Of course it's been about you. I want what's best for you. I want what's best for us both."

His words sound sincere, but I know Dad too well not to hear what he isn't saying. He won't tell me I'm throwing away his career along with my own, but he'll think it, and knowing that is as heavy and oppressive as it would be if he simply said the words out loud.

"How can the network do this to you, Dad? After all you've done for them."

"I'm an old man, Tatum. And there are countless younger, better-looking chefs anxious to make their mark on the world. But you—you're young. Beautiful. You have the *something* they're looking for."

"Lucky for you, I happen to be your daughter."

"Lucky for us both. Don't pretend like you haven't enjoyed the perks of growing up with everything my fame has given you."

I run my hand over the butter-soft leather on my chair's armrest.

Dad loves to remind me of this—everything

his career has given me. But all I can think about right now is what it would take away.

Because if I go back to California to do a show with my father, I would have to leave Stonebrook.

Leave Lennox.

Staying together would be impossible. His life is here—his family is here. There wouldn't be any compromise that could possibly work for us both.

Still, if I stay in Silver Creek, what would I do? I've been real with myself the past couple of weeks, and I'm just about ready to admit out loud that catering—or really any kind of full-time cooking—isn't what I want for my future. In that sense, a tv show might be a better fit. It would have better hours, anyway. And there would be a whole team of chefs and consultants available to do the heavy lifting. I've seen the way Dad's show works. He doesn't have to come up with *anything* on his own if he doesn't want to. Everything is scripted, even if it's made to look spontaneous.

But that would land me right back where I was when I fled to North Carolina in the first place. I would be playing a role. Pretending to be someone I'm not.

I may not love being a chef, but at least out here, it's been *me*. It's been real.

And at least out here, I have *Lennox*.

It's not lost on me though that if I stop catering,

if I'm not interested in cooking at all, there isn't much else for me to do in Silver Creek. But that's not a thought I want to dwell on after the euphoria I just experienced in Lennox's kitchen.

"I know I have a lot to be grateful for, Dad. But I've given this a lot of thought, and not just since coming to North Carolina. It's been on my mind a while. I don't *want* to be on television. The fame, the attention—it isn't what I want anymore. I don't want that life."

He scoffs. "You sound just like your mother."

Pain slices into my chest, and unexpected tears pool in my eyes. "Is that such a bad thing?"

His voice is soft, his tone pleading when he says, "Of course not, Tatum. I shouldn't have said that like it was an insult." He sighs, sounding older and more tired than I've ever heard him sound. "Will you just think about this, please? We're family. For so long, it's only been you and me against the world. Think of everything we've done together. The traveling, the cooking. This could be another chapter for us. A *great* chapter for us."

It's my turn to sigh. "Dad, I just . . ."

I don't even know how to finish my sentence.

"I've done a lot for you, Tatum," he says. "Everything you have is yours because I gave it to you. You owe me this much."

An aching hollowness fills my chest. Do I *really* owe him? He's my father. He *has* given me everything I have—worked hard to give me every opportunity. And he's right—for a long time, it was just the two of us, conquering the world together. But love shouldn't feel so contractual. If this isn't an opportunity I want, would he really want me to sacrifice so his career can benefit?

"I'll think about it, all right? But I'm not making any promises."

"You're being foolish," he says sharply.

"I know you think that. But I'm a grown woman. I still get to make my own choices."

"Did you at least look over the contract I sent you? Just read the terms. A couple of years, five max. And branding deals. Tatum Elliott Cookware has a nice ring to it."

"I said I'd think about it," I say, my patience running out. "I have to go. I'm exhausted. I really need to get some sleep."

I hang up the phone before he can say anything else.

Tatum Elliott Cookware?

It's hard to imagine there was ever a time when that might have swayed me.

Still, Dad is family. And family is supposed to stick together. Isn't it?

I stand up and pace around my tiny living room. It isn't fair. Not even a little bit. But . . . could I give him two years? Five years max, he said. Could I give him five? And if I don't, will his career really be over? Do I want that hanging over my head?

I am no closer to an answer when I finally settle into bed, my heart aching with an emptiness I haven't felt in months. It's only when I think of Lennox that I'm able to relax and drift off to sleep, the warmth of his kisses and the strength of his arms carrying me into my dreams.

CHAPTER TWENTY
Lennox

It's 9:53 when Toby comes bounding down the stairs to greet me. I don't see Tatum, but she can't be too far behind.

I crouch down and give Toby a good scratch, his tail thumping against the wall.

"I swear, too much more of this, and Toby's going to love you more than he does me," Tatum says as she reaches the bottom of the stairs.

I stand up and meet her eyes, a pulse of concern immediately seizing my thoughts. Tatum looks exhausted. Still beautiful but *worn* in a way I haven't seen before.

Maybe I'm being too selfish keeping her up late so many nights in a row. It's hard not to want her company every second I can have it. But she has to take care of herself. *I* have to take care of her.

"That works out for me because I'm pretty crazy about Toby's owner." I lean down and place a light kiss on her lips, one hand wrapping around her waist.

She smiles, but it doesn't quite reach her eyes, and I get the sense there's something she isn't telling me. Or maybe she's just tired?

"You ready to get out of here?" I say softly. I heft the small pack at my feet onto my shoulders and hold out my hand.

"Sure. Where are we going?"

I lace her fingers through mine and lead us outside into the warm spring sunshine. "Just on a walk. I want to show you my favorite place on the farm."

A smile blooms across her face, almost pushing away my earlier worry. She would tell me if something was amiss, wouldn't she? "That sounds amazing," she says.

We start off toward the east orchard and the trail that will take us up to the ledge, Toby bounding between us.

"He never got to be outside like this in L.A.," Tatum says. "I think he's ruined for any other kind of life."

"It's a common problem when people come to the mountains. Once you live here, it's hard to want to live anywhere else."

Her eyes dart to mine, but she looks away too quickly for me to read her expression. "Yeah, I can imagine," she says softly.

Crap. That sounded like a loaded statement, and I did *not* mean for it to be a loaded statement.

"Did you do a lot of hiking growing up?" I ask, hoping to steer the conversation to safer territory.

She nods. "Some. In Santa Monica, mostly. And when Dad took me to Palm Springs for

Christmas. Just day hikes, though. Probably nothing like what you've done. Kate made it sound like you guys are all pretty big hikers."

"Perry does more of the long-distance stuff. He hikes a section of the Appalachian Trail every summer and stays out for a week or two. But we've all hiked in most of the national parks and know the trails around here as well as we know the farm. Whenever Brody travels for his kayaking, we try to go with him and hit a few trails wherever he is, too."

"Kate told me about his kayaking." She looks over and smiles. "You Hawthornes are a bunch of overachievers. Must be a family trait."

I grin. "All but Flint, maybe. He's the lazy one."

"Right. Yes. His career definitely indicates he's the lazy one," she jokes.

This is good. *Better.*

"You know, I didn't even know he was your brother until I applied for this job," she says. "It was kind of a crazy thing to discover."

"So you did know *I* would be here?" I ask. "That Stonebrook was my family's farm?"

"When I applied, yes," I say. "But not when I saw the job posting. I did a little digging as soon as I saw it, and that's when I figured it out."

We pass the farmhouse and continue toward the barn, winding down a footpath that skirts the main drive. A row of massive sugar maples, their leaves a vibrant spring green, cast dappled sunlight over us as we walk. "I'm surprised it didn't scare you away—knowing I was here," I say, my tone light.

She huffs out a laugh. "Honestly, it kinda did the opposite."

"I *knew* you'd been harboring a crush all this time."

She rolls her eyes. "Very funny. It definitely wasn't that. Do you remember the peer review you gave me during our last year of school? It was in our sauté class."

"Oh no. I wasn't very nice to you, was I?"

"You were honest, Lennox. My entrée was as bad as your salad dressing."

"Nothing is as bad as that salad dressing," I say, and she grins.

"Fine. It was *almost* as bad as your salad dressing. And yet, no one said anything negative." She meets my eye. "No one but you."

"Okay, and I'm sensing that was a good thing?"

"Of course it's a good thing. You never cared about my father being famous. No one wanted to insult the daughter of the great Christopher Elliott. But if people had been honest with me sooner, maybe I wouldn't have wound up ten years into a career that I'm not even all that great at."

I would argue that she's *definitely* great at being a chef, but I still understand her point.

"In L.A., *everyone* cares who my father is.

About what he might do for them. About how the connection might *serve* them. And I get it. Everyone wants a leg up, and it's hard to make it in this business if you don't know someone who knows someone. But that rat race—it's exhausting. When I left, I think I just wanted to be around people who would shoot straight with me. It was the only way I could think of to clear my head."

We stop at a gate that leads into the orchard, and I unlatch it, holding it open while she passes through, then shut it behind us. "I think I know a little of what fame can do," I say. "Not firsthand, of course. But when Flint's career first took off, he really let it go to his head. We didn't really like him for a couple of years. He's grown up a lot, but he's had to figure out ways to stay grounded, to keep his head clear. I think it's great that you've done the same thing."

"It's hard to imagine any Hawthorne not being grounded, with how close your family is," she says.

"Yeah, that's a big part of it. And Flint stays really involved, even if he's not here in person. He invested in the restaurant, backed Brody's kayaking program at his school. And he covered Dad's medical expenses after his stroke a few years back."

"Has he ever thought about moving home?" Tatum asks.

"Actually, I was just talking to him about that the other night. I never thought it would happen, but he's looking for property, talking about building something out here, so maybe so."

Tatum's quiet for a long moment, her eyes on the ground as we move through the apple trees.

"Lennox, you have a really amazing family," she finally says. "I love the way you show up for each other."

The wistfulness in her voice makes me think she must be thinking about her father, and a pang of sadness pushes through me, followed by an intense longing to give Tatum the kind of family she deserves. Not everything she's told me about her father is negative, so I recognize the man must have some admirable qualities. But I don't like the way he's pressured her since she moved to Silver Creek. And I don't like the idea of her feeling like she's second to his career.

Tatum shouldn't be second to *anything*.

We finally reach the trailhead, and I pause at the bottom. "It's only about a quarter mile up," I say. "But it's pretty steep."

She nods, her eyes dropping to Toby. "Will there be bears?"

"I know better than to promise anything," I say, "but there shouldn't be."

Once we're on the trail, our conversation dwindles, as it takes pretty much all our concentration to watch our feet and not trip on the rocks and roots that litter the trail. Toby does great, leaping over obstacles like he really was born to live in these mountains.

After about ten minutes of hiking, we step into a small clearing.

Tall trees rise up on either side, but in front of us, there's only open air, the ground giving way to an impressive view of the rolling mountains, their hazy blues and greens blending into the morning sky.

Toby tugs toward the dropoff, and Tatum calls him back. "Hey, you stay close to me, boy," she says.

"It looks steeper than it is," I say. "We called this place the ledge growing up, but on the other side of the dropoff, there's plenty of scrubby rhododendrons and an easy enough slope that even if he got away from you, there isn't anywhere for him to fall."

She nods, relaxing her hold on the leash as her eyes scan the expansive view in front of us.

"Look," I say, stepping up behind her. I put my hands on her shoulders and turn her gently, loving the feel of her back against my chest. "If you look down this way, you can see the farmhouse. And the orchards out next to Mom and Dad's house."

"Oh, I see it," she says. "It looks so small from all the way up here."

"Are you hungry?" I move to a smooth stretch

of rock in the middle of the clearing and pull a blanket out of my pack. "Want to sit?"

"I could definitely eat," she says as she lowers herself onto the blanket. "What did you bring us?"

I pull out a couple of breakfast burritos and some bottled orange juice. "It isn't much," I say, handing her one of each. I pull a third burrito out of the bag and toss it over to Tatum. "This one is for Toby. It's just eggs and sausage. I left out the cheese sauce because the internet told me it might make him sick."

Tatum pauses, looking down at the extra burrito, her jaw slack. When she looks up, her eyes are shining. "You made a burrito for my dog."

I shrug. "I thought he might get hungry."

She puts both burritos on the blanket and crawls toward me, shifting onto her knees when she reaches where I'm still leaning over the pack. She cradles my face with her hands and kisses me softly.

She shudders, her breath catching, then a drop of moisture trickles into my beard. *She's crying.*

"Hey," I say gently. I tug her away so I can look into her eyes. I don't care what she says. There's no way she's only crying over an extra burrito. "What's going on? Tell me what's wrong."

She shakes her head, and I shift so I'm sitting on the blanket, pulling her down beside me, my arms wrapped around her shoulders.

But Tatum doesn't want to be held. She tilts her

head, catching my lips with hers, a sudden heated urgency to her movements that almost blocks every one of my rational thoughts. I recognize the impulse to feel *in control* of something, so I let go of the reins and let her set the pace. I yield when she asks me to yield, give when she asks me to give.

I've kissed this woman countless times over the past few weeks, but the sensation never weakens, heat flaring to life between us just as quickly every time.

I am teetering on the brink of losing control, debating whether I want to give in here, on a rocky ledge in the middle of the mountains, when I feel another tear fall down Tatum's cheek.

Okay. Whatever she's feeling, this isn't going to solve the problem.

I ease away, tugging her hand from my face and pressing a kiss to her palm. "Just sit with me a minute," I say gently.

She nods and tucks herself into my side. I don't know what she isn't telling me—what battle is raging in her heart. I can't make her tell me what's going on, but if I can be vulnerable, maybe she will be too. Maybe she'll trade her secrets for mine.

I look out across the valley and take a deep, calming breath, letting the silence settle around us. When Tatum's tears have stopped, I lean down and press a kiss to her temple.

"Tatum, I broke up with Hailey because I caught her cheating on me with my roommate."

Tatum lets out a tiny gasp before she sits up and looks at me. "Why would she do that to you? There is no number of *it's not you, it's me's* that makes that situation okay."

I manage a sad smile. "I recognize now that I was probably more serious about her than she was about me—"

"That doesn't make cheating acceptable," Tatum says, cutting me off, and my heart warms at her defense of me.

"I know. I just mean that because I was *all in,* the breakup really messed me up for a long time. I was scared of getting close to anyone. Because Hailey knew me, and it turned out I wasn't enough. She wanted someone else—someone different. That made me afraid to trust what might happen if I let someone else see the real me."

"So that's why you dated so much."

I nod. "I kept it all surface level. Cut things off as soon as I thought I might start feeling something real. It worked for a long time." I shrug. "And then you showed up."

She gives my hand a squeeze, her thumb tracing slow circles on the back of my wrist.

"You blindsided me, Tatum. I'll be totally honest—I'm scared out of my mind. But I don't want to lose this. I want to be with you. I want us to be something."

Tears well in her eyes, and she shakes her head. "Don't, Lennox."

My gut tightens. "Don't what?"

"Don't give me your heart," she says, her voice shaky. "Because I think I might have to break it."

CHAPTER TWENTY-ONE
Lennox

Okay, so . . . not exactly the words you want to hear after laying your heart on the line. But my brothers said you can't get to the good part of love without taking any risks, so I steel my nerves and place a hand on Tatum's quivering back.

"Gosh, I'm a mess," she says, wiping at her eyes. "This is just so stupid."

"Tatum, just tell me what's going on. Has something happened?"

Toby is standing beside her, looking at her like he can't figure out why she's so upset.

You and me both, man. *You and me both.*

Finally, Tatum takes a stuttering breath. "Lennox, my dad called me last night."

Oh no.

My gut tightens. "Okay."

"His network wants to bring me on for a show—one that would be my dad and me together. They actually pitched the idea to me a long time ago, but I told them I wasn't interested. Only, Dad just told me they aren't renewing his contract for *his* show. So if I don't do this one—the one we're supposed to do together—he's done. Off the network."

A sick feeling spreads through my gut, and I start to understand Tatum's tears. Being on a show with her dad means not being *here*. It means losing her.

"But he's Christopher Elliott," I say, not wanting to understand what she's telling me.

She shrugs. "Who they think is getting old, apparently."

"But you *aren't* old," I say. "They want you to keep the brand alive."

She nods, her eyes sad. "Something like that."

There is a huge part of me that wants to make this conversation about me. About us. But I know enough about Tatum's history with her father to guess the kind of pressure he's putting on her. I also know she feels an incredible amount of loyalty to him which has to make this decision fraught, regardless of what it means for our relationship. I can't make this more complicated for her. And I definitely don't want to say or do anything to drive a wedge between her and her dad.

"Do you want to do it?" I ask, my tone gentle. *Neutral.*

She looks up and meets my eyes, her expression pained. "No. I mean, I don't think so. But Lennox, he's my family. Your family is always showing up for each other, supporting each other. Isn't this the same kind of thing?"

I'm not sure how to answer her. My family *does*

show up for each other. But we also respect each other. Olivia never would have pressured me into opening Hawthorne if it wasn't what I wanted, and I never would have expected my family to back my restaurant if they didn't think it was a good idea.

We sacrifice for each other, sure. But we don't sacrifice who we are.

But Tatum hasn't had those kinds of healthy familial relationships in her life. All she knows is the selfish toxicity her father has conditioned her with.

"Tatum, he shouldn't even ask this of you if it isn't something you want. He shouldn't prioritize his own needs over your happiness."

"Logically, I know that. But he's given me so much. Paid for my education. Given me a career. Don't I owe him this?" She shakes her head, another round of tears welling up. "But I want this, Lennox. I want you. I don't want to leave and lose what we have."

"Hey. You're not going to lose me."

"That's just it. I've been thinking about catering—about being a chef. Lennox, I'm not even sure I want to cook anymore. I love Stonebrook, and I love Silver Creek, but what would I even do if I didn't run the catering kitchen? There's nothing else out here for me, and I hate that because I would love to stay." She presses a hand to her forehead, then shakes her head as she takes a stuttering breath. "I didn't want to have to worry about any of this when we're still trying to figure out what we mean to each other, and I didn't want Olivia to worry because I'm fine running the kitchen for now. But with Dad's job on the line, I feel like I have to think about it. And honestly, it feels kind of foolish to turn down such a lucrative job offer when there's nothing else on the table."

Her chest heaves as she breathes out a sigh, her shoulders falling like she's collapsing in on herself. "I don't know what I'm supposed to do."

She's supposed to do what she wants and not let her idiot father govern her life like some kind of overlord.

But it's not my place to tell her that.

If I pressure her into making the decision I want, then I'm no better than he is.

I'm almost sick with anger that her father would even put her in this position. How can he not see how selfish he's being? How careless it is to put this burden of responsibility on her shoulders?

Has he never asked Tatum what she wants?

Quick on the heels of wanting to pulverize her father is a desperation to grab Tatum and beg her to stay. To just *be* with me. Love me like I'm suddenly realizing I love her.

But deep in my gut, I know loving her means letting her make the choice herself.

I reach out and wipe the tears from Tatum's

cheeks, then tug her forward, placing a gentle kiss on her lips. She's salty with tears, her lips trembling, which only makes me want to kiss her again and again until the tears are gone, along with everything else in the world that might ever hurt her.

I wrap her in my arms, one curving around her back. My butt is numb for how long we've been sitting on this rock, but I don't even care.

"What do I do?" Tatum whispers, her voice as soft as the breeze blowing across the mountain.

"I can't tell you what to do, Tatum."

I *won't* tell her, even if something in me is screaming to do just that—to tell her to stay with me. Here. Forever. *Mine.*

"No, but you can tell me what you want. Your opinion matters to me, Lennox."

I'm quiet for a long moment, torn over how to answer her question. "I already told you what I want."

"I know. But tell me again."

Emotions surge, words tumbling out before I can stop them. "Okay. I want you. I want us. I want you to beat my brother every time we play board games, and I want to feed you your favorite meals, and I want to take your dog for walks around the farm. I want to kiss you before I fall asleep every night and wake up with you in my arms. I want to know everything there is to know about you—learn the person you are so well that I can anticipate how you feel and what makes you happy and what makes you sad." I sigh and shake my head. "But I'm not supposed to tell you any of that, because I also respect you. I want you to be happy. I want you to have a career you love, and I want you to have relationships with the people who are important to you. And I can't decide what those relationships look like. Even if I want to."

She sniffs. "You know, you could have just been a jerk about it. Said something selfish and made my decision easier." I don't tell her that under the surface, I'm feeling pretty jerky—like a raging caveman ready to keep her here by force.

I let out a weary chuckle. "Sorry to disappoint you."

She leans up and looks at me. "I'm not even a little bit disappointed."

We settle into silence then, watching the birds swoop and glide over the trees and the clouds moving across the vibrant blue sky. The view is beautiful, but part of the beauty is having Tatum beside me. What will this place be like if she leaves? I have memories of Tatum all over the farm. Thinking of Stonebrook without her feels like turning down the lights, leeching the color out of the sky and the trees and the mountains in the distance. This place will never be the same.

I will never be the same.

"Lennox, where does this leave us?" Tatum eventually asks.

"What do you mean?"

"I don't know what I'm supposed to do, but I know I want to be with you."

I hold her a little tighter. "Then be with me. Whatever time we have, let's take it. Whatever happens next, we'll figure it out."

She sniffs. "You promise?"

I feel the stupidity in the risk I'm taking, but I can't help it.

I'm so far gone for this woman, there's only one way to answer her question. *"I promise."*

CHAPTER TWENTY-TWO
Tatum

It's late when I find Lennox in his office—late enough that we're pretty much the only two people still around. I've had enough time since I ended my shift to go upstairs and shower and change into leggings and an oversized hoodie, but Lennox is still dressed for work.

"Hey," I say, leaning against the door jamb. "What are you up to?"

He looks up, the smile that spreads across his face warming me from the inside out. "Just finishing the books," he says.

"How are things?"

"Good. Great, actually. The warmer weather must be helping. Revenue is up."

"That's amazing."

"*And* my kitchen is running better than ever." He stands and moves around the desk, approaching me with easy confidence. He slips an arm around my waist and leans down to kiss me. "All thanks to you." He nuzzles my neck. "You smell good."

"Mmm. You smell like kitchen grease and onions."

He chuckles as he steps away and starts to

unbutton his chef's coat. "Okay. Point taken." He sheds it and drops it into the laundry bin in the corner. "What are you up to? I thought you'd be asleep by now." He peels his t-shirt off next, and it follows the chef's coat into the bin before he rummages through a bag sitting by the door, presumably looking for a clean shirt.

My eyes rove over the smooth planes of muscle, the dips and hollows that make up Lennox's body, and my throat goes dry. Whenever I look at him, I feel like I have to memorize him, catalog every inch in case I wind up saying goodbye.

Lennox and I haven't talked about the network's offer since I first brought it up. It's been just shy of two weeks, and I can tell he's avoiding the subject on purpose. I appreciate that he's giving me space, that he isn't trying to pressure me. But a part of me wishes he *would* pressure me—call my father a jerk and beg me to stay with him instead.

Still, I have to respect Lennox for recognizing that this needs to be my choice. He's a good man—possibly the *best* man I've ever known. And that's tricky. Because I aspire to be as selfless and loving as the Hawthornes. And I'm afraid that means stepping up to be there for my dad.

Of course, I also wouldn't mind if Dad happened to call with a good-natured, "Just kidding!" and made this whole nightmare go away. At the very least, that would buy me some time to figure out what I want to do next.

"I was hoping you could help me with something," I say to Lennox.

He stands up, shirt in hand. "Of course. Anything." He pulls the shirt over his head.

I sigh over the loss of the view, but honestly, if we're going to have *any* kind of reasonable conversation tonight, it isn't going to happen as long as Lennox is shirtless. "So, I have this box," I say.

"Mysterious."

Mysterious is an acceptable word, but *haunting* feels more fitting. It's been sitting on my kitchen table for weeks, taunting me, almost like my mother herself is in the room and waiting for me to get over myself and open it already.

I've used work as an excuse. And Lennox as an excuse. And drama with Dad as an excuse. But I don't want to put it off anymore. A part of me hopes that doing this one hard thing will make it easier for me to do another.

"My sister sent it last month, and I've been putting off going through it because it's going to make me feel stuff."

"Even more mysterious," Lennox says.

"It's full of my mom's things."

His eyes soften. "Ahh. Got it."

"Bree mentioned some cooking utensils, some journals and recipe books. I think I'm ready to finally look through it, but I don't really want to do it by myself."

"Let's do it together, then. Where is it? At your place?"

I nod. "If you come up, you can borrow my shower, then we can open the box?"

He props his hands on his hips. "Are you telling me a wardrobe change wasn't enough? I still smell?"

I press my lips together to hide my smile. "So bad."

He lunges forward and envelopes me in an enormous hug, squeezing me until I squeal and burst into laughter. I fake a gagging noise. "I'm dying, Lennox. Can't. Breathe."

"Fine, fine, you win," he says, letting me go. "I'll shower first. Then we can open the mystery box."

He grabs his gym bag from the floor and follows me upstairs. He heads to the bathroom while I take Toby outside for a quick break, then I settle in the living room with the box at my feet. It's still sealed shut with packing tape.

I rest my hands on the top and take a deep, cleansing breath. I can do this.

I *want* to do this.

A thought suddenly occurs to me.

I've been struggling with my definition of family, with my understanding of what it's supposed to look like and feel like. But my mom is my family too. Maybe connecting with her will help me figure out what I'm supposed to do about Dad.

The water in the shower turns on, and I pull out my phone to text Bree while I wait for Lennox. I've done a decent job of keeping my sister in the loop regarding all the current parts of my life. She knows about Lennox, and she knows I've been putting off opening Mom's box. But I haven't told her about the network's offer. That's a secret I'm keeping on purpose because she wouldn't understand why I'm even considering it.

But Bree doesn't have the relationship with Dad that I do. She doesn't feel the same kind of pressure, but she also hasn't enjoyed the same kinds of perks. I can't even get in my car without remembering the conversation Dad had with me when he gave me the keys for my twenty-eighth birthday. "We've worked for it, Tatum," he said. "We deserve to treat ourselves."

I remember feeling thrilled that he'd said *we* had worked for it. But I wonder, now, if it wasn't just a way to make me feel beholden to the Christopher Elliott brand.

> **Tatum:** I am about to commence going through the box.
> **Bree:** You are BRAVE and you can do this.
> **Tatum:** Lennox is with me. Or he will

be momentarily. That's going to make it easier, I think.
Bree: I love that. How are things between the two of you?
Tatum: Too good to be true. I know it's early. That this thing has only just started. But when my mind wanders, it wanders *here.* I can't stop imagining a life with him.
Bree: Then stay, honey. It's obviously what you want.
Tatum: It feels a little early to be shifting my future plans around for him.
Bree: Okay, so take him out of the equation for a sec. Do you like running the catering kitchen enough to keep doing it?
Tatum: That's part of the problem. I don't think I do. I love the farm, but the hours are brutal. And I don't love the cooking enough to make the sacrifice feel worth it. I don't think I can do this for years on end, but Lennox's life is here. It's not like he's moving anywhere else.

Especially not to California.

Bree: Tatum, if he's the right man for you, you'll figure it out. You'll compromise. You'll come up with a

future that works for the both of you. Could you just work with Lennox?
Tatum: He doesn't need me at Hawthorne. Especially not since we worked out his staffing issues. Everything is running smoothly now.
Bree: Uh, yeah. Cause you're brilliant.
Tatum: I was happy to help him. I like to feel useful. And the problem-solving is fun.
Bree: Huh. Can you turn that into a career? Fixing other people's kitchen problems?

Her question gives me pause, a tiny jolt of electricity rushing through me.
Could I?
There are paid consultants in every other area of business. Surely they exist for restaurants, too. It wouldn't matter if I wind up going back to L.A., but if I don't, and I don't want to do catering forever, could I be a restaurant consultant?
When the shower water cuts off, I send Bree one more quick message.

Tatum: Hey, gotta go. Lennox is almost out of the shower. I'll check in later.
Bree: I am going to be the BEST big sister and refrain from making a joke about your man in your shower. Byeeee!!

Lennox emerges looking fresh and clean and smelling like my jasmine body wash. Somehow, it smells different on him, the essence of him still rising through.

He drops onto the floor beside me and leans in for a kiss.

"Better?" he whispers against my lips.

"So much better. I smell good on you."

He chuckles. "Yeah, and I probably won't be able to sleep tonight for the distraction of smelling *you* all over my skin."

The kiss lingers long enough that I'm half-tempted to shove the box aside and pick a different activity for the evening, but I've put this off for too long as it is.

I slide my hand down Lennox's chest. His T-shirt is warm and slightly damp from his shower-fresh skin, which somehow makes this moment feel more intimate. Not just anyone has access to Lennox in this state, and I suddenly feel incredibly overwhelmed with the privilege.

I let him kiss me for five or ten or . . . one hundred more seconds before I break the kiss with a little groan. "Okay, time to do this. Time to be serious."

He nips at my bottom lip. "I am being serious."

I huff out a breath. *"Lennox."*

He grins and sits back, leaning on his hands. "Sorry. Sorry. I'm behaving," he says, then he hops up and retrieves a pocketknife from his bag, opening it and handing it to me hilt first.

Of course he has a knife on him.

"Boy scout," I mumble as I take the knife.

"Eagle scout," he says with a smirk, and I roll my eyes.

When we tease like this, I almost forget that there's a giant question mark hanging between us. But the more time I spend with him, the harder it is to ignore. We can't keep this up forever. We can't keep ignoring the possibility of there being an *end*.

I scoot onto my knees and slice through the tape holding the box closed.

The contents of the box smell a tiny bit musty, but mostly they smell like herbs and spices and olive oil. I pull out the kitchen utensils first. A manual hand mixer with a faded turquoise handle. A set of wooden spoons with leaves and vines carved into the handles. A rolling pin. I hold the rolling pin and close my eyes, a sense of deep loss washing over me.

I didn't know this woman like I should have, and I'll always regret it.

Lennox picks up the spoons. "These are beautiful," he says, running his hands over the intricate carvings.

"I remember those," I say softly. "Her grandfather made them for her."

At the bottom of the box, there's a stack of

notebooks. I pull them out, opening the first one and flipping through the pages. I recognize my mother's slanted handwriting. A lot of what's written is in French, but there's English, too. Notes written in the margins, measurements, conversions. There are also illustrations of food—beautiful drawings.

I run my fingertips over a bunch of strawberries sketched below a recipe for frasier—a traditional French sponge cake. "I had no idea she could draw like this."

Lennox holds out a hand. "May I?" I hand him the book and pick up the next one, and we fall into an easy silence as we flip through the pages.

Half an hour later, we've moved to the couch, Lennox sitting on one end while I lay with my head in his lap, my feet propped up on the armrest on the opposite end.

There are some beautiful recipes in Mom's notebooks, but aside from those, my mother is also an incredible storyteller. My heart is swinging from one emotion to the next, stretching, aching, longing for a relationship I can't have back, and yet somehow still grateful that I at least have this part of her.

"Hey, Tatum?" Lennox shifts, and I look up to see his expression marred with concern.

I sit up. "What is it?"

"Did your parents ever cook together?"

"Yeah. All the time when I was little."

"But your mom was never involved in your dad's show? Or his restaurant?"

"No. The restaurant didn't come until *after* the show. But I don't think she was involved with either. I feel like I remember her not liking the idea of being on camera. Why?"

"Um." Lennox clears his throat awkwardly. "I mean, I could be wrong. But this recipe—it sounds like your dad's bouillabaisse." He holds out the notebook.

I take it, my eyes quickly scanning the recipe. They still serve Dad's bouillabaisse at Le Vin, so I immediately recognize the ingredients and ratios. "I mean, that's not that weird, right? They were married. They probably made it together a hundred times."

Lennox runs a hand across his face. "Okay but turn the page."

On the next page, there's a recipe for sole meunière that's also identical to what we serve at Le Vin.

"There's a few more," he says gently.

I scoff. "What, did you pull up the menu?"

When he doesn't answer, I look up and see his phone sitting on his knee. He *did* pull up the menu.

"Look, it just seems a little coincidental," he says. "You could be right though. They were married. Maybe she shared all her recipes and was totally fine with him taking them on the show and serving them in his restaurant."

"Of course she was okay with it," I say, but doubt is already niggling at the back of my mind. I toss the notebook onto the floor in front of me. "Maybe she wrote the recipes down *after* she and my dad discovered them together."

Even as I make the argument, I know it isn't true. Many of the recipes contain pages and pages of notes—stories about where they came from, who Mom learned them from. The recipes themselves aren't necessarily dated, but the stories are, and they all predate me, even Bree and Daniel.

I do some quick math. They predate my parents' marriage, too.

Lennox watches as I flip through the pages looking for something—anything—that might prove otherwise. But there's nothing.

I sit back with a huff, my heart pounding.

"So she must have been fine with him using them," I finally say.

"That's one possibility," Lennox says.

Something about the tone of his voice sets me on edge. It's kind and gentle—almost too gentle, like he's placating me. I glare at him. "What are you trying to say?"

"Tatum, it wouldn't be the first time a chef has claimed a recipe or an idea that isn't actually theirs."

I stand up, dropping the notebook onto the couch and stalking into the kitchen. "No." I turn around, my hands on my hips. "No. My mom was more French than my dad is, but his grandmother was from Nice. He has just as much right to the recipes in those pages as she did."

I don't really know why I'm arguing the point, except that somehow, it feels like admitting that Dad's career is a sham would, by extension, make *me* a sham.

After all, I am only as good as Dad has made me.

Lennox holds up his hands. "I'm just saying. It seems like there's a pattern here. You, yourself, said you thought your dad would choose fame over family. He did it with your mom, and took her recipes with him—"

"You don't know that's what he did," I say, my voice trembling.

"And now he's willing to do it with you—forcing you into a job you don't want so you can keep his star shining a little longer."

I shake my head. "You can't say that. You don't even know him."

He leans forward, his elbows propped on his knees. "You're right. I don't. But you do."

Tears well in my eyes, his words hitting me like a punch to the gut. "You know what? I think it's time for you to go."

"Tatum—"

"No. I don't need you sitting there judging him. Judging *me*. He's my family, Lennox, and I'm all he has left. It's easy for you—with your picture-perfect family and your passion-filled career. But you don't know him. Maybe you don't even know me. For all you know, I *do* want the job in L.A."

These last words come out like a curse, and Lennox flinches.

Toby hops off my reading chair where he's been lounging this whole time and walks to Lennox, dropping his head on Lennox's knee.

I don't miss that even though we're both clearly upset, Toby doesn't come to *me*.

It only makes me angrier.

I'm self-aware enough to sense that I'm over-reacting, that I'm *really* not being fair to Lennox, but the confusion churning inside me is so sharp, so palpable, it's blinding me to everything else.

Lennox closes his eyes and rubs Toby's head for a moment before slowly getting up. He crosses to where I'm standing in the kitchen, pausing just in front of me. His hands are on his hips as his chest rises and falls with one, then two steady breaths.

"Tatum," he says gently, and he reaches for my hand.

I take it and let him pull me against him. He wraps his arms around my back, and I collapse into his chest, tears pouring down my face.

He holds me while I cry, one hand rubbing up and down my back until the sobs subside. "I do know you, Tatum." He leans down and kisses my temple. "I know you"—he tenses the slightest bit, his hands tightening their grip around my waist—"and I love you."

I suck in a breath, Lennox's words echoing in my mind. *He loves me.*

He loves me.

He loves me.

"That means *all* I want is for you to be happy. If you tell me you want to go to L.A.—that doing the show with your dad will make you happy—I'll believe you, and I'll let you go." He sniffs and he lets out a frustrated groan. "It would kill me. But I would do it. I wouldn't ask you to trade your happiness for mine."

He leans back, his arms moving from the small of my back to my shoulders. He lifts a hand to my cheek, wiping the tears away before cupping my cheek and kissing me. "I'm going to go," he says.

I nod, my eyes on the floor. If I look into those green eyes, shining with unshed tears for more than a second, I'm going to start to ugly cry even worse than I already am.

He steps away and picks up his bag, pausing when he reaches the door. "Tatum, I think I need to keep my distance for a bit."

"Lennox, I don't want you to do that."

"I don't want to either. But you have to figure out what you want, and that's going to be easier for you without me hovering. Plus, now that I know how I feel, I don't think my heart can take the *not knowing* much longer." He opens the door. "You know where to find me though, all right? I'm here. Whenever you need me. I'm here."

He disappears out the door, his footsteps receding down the stairs as I slump to my kitchen floor.

Toby comes to *me* this time, draping himself over my body like a warm blanket, his head leaning into my chest. We sit there for a long time.

Until my tears are dry.

Until my breathing has evened out.

Until logic has finally blown away my storm cloud of emotions.

When my feet are numb, my butt cold from the kitchen tile, I shift and stand up, then move to the stack of notebooks still sitting in the living room.

I give Toby a reassuring pat, then I gather up the books and head downstairs to my kitchen, stopping in the pantry long enough to grab a bottle of wine.

If I can't think myself into an answer, I'm hoping I can cook myself into one.

Not my usual M.O. But if I'm going to make the decision I need to make, I need my mother's strength to do it.

And maybe her recipes will help me find it.

CHAPTER TWENTY-THREE
Lennox

I haven't taken a sick day since opening Hawthorne.

But today, I'm almost tempted.

I'm just not in the mood. I barely slept—worry for Tatum keeping me up most of the night. That, and white-hot rage whenever I thought about her father.

But sitting around doing nothing isn't going to help.

Plus, if I don't show up to work, Tatum will think it's her fault. I told her I'd keep my distance, but I can still work. I can still *see her* at work.

A sharp ache fills my chest. I *want* to see her. I want to make sure she's okay.

I push through the back door of the restaurant, pausing when I see a group of people crowded around the entrance to Tatum's catering kitchen, concerned expressions on their faces.

A surge of panic fills me as I hurry forward. "What happened? What's going on?"

"We don't actually know," Tatum's sous chef says. "It was like this when we got here."

I push past them into the kitchen, willing my heart to slow as I take in the scene before me.

The kitchen is a mess—the countertops covered with what looks like every pot, pan and bowl in the entire place. There are cutting boards, knives, piles of vegetable peelings. Any chef learns how to clean as they cook, and I've seen how efficiently Tatum runs her kitchen, so nothing about this particular situation makes sense. On the counter beside the stove, there are seven different dishes, all perfectly prepared and plated, and an empty wine bottle resting on its side.

My eyes rove over the space one more time. Make that *two* empty wine bottles.

And that's when it hits me.

Tatum made her mother's recipes.

And it must have taken her all night to do it.

Zach comes up beside me and places a steadying hand on my shoulder, then he motions toward Tatum's office.

I find her curled up on the floor in front of her desk, a chef's coat balled up under her head as a makeshift pillow.

I look at Zach who is hovering in her office doorway.

"Get her staff out of here, would you?"

He nods and disappears.

There's a wine glass on the floor next to Tatum, and I pick it up, setting it on the desk behind me. Then I crouch down and shift her into my arms. She groans as I stand up, redistributing her weight, but she doesn't wake up, and she doesn't fight me.

I don't know where Zach took everybody, but I don't see another soul as I carry Tatum down the hall and up the stairs to her apartment. Fortunately, she left the door unlocked, so I'm able to get inside.

Toby stands and woofs—clearly alarmed at the sight of us coming through the door—and follows us into the bedroom. I lower Tatum onto the bed, then tug off her sneakers and shift the covers out from under her so I can cover her up. I grab a glass of water and leave it by her bed, then turn to take Toby outside. It's almost noon, and I'm guessing he hasn't been out since last night, but then Tatum calls my name.

"Lennox?"

I'm back by her side in a second, crouching down beside her. "Hey." I lift a hand and smooth her hair out of her face.

She closes her eyes at the touch. "I drank too much," she says, her voice soft.

"I know, baby. There's water here if you want it. Then you should go back to sleep."

"Nuh-uh, I need to work. I need—" She tries to sit up but only makes it a few inches before she frowns and winces, one hand lifting to her head.

"You aren't working today," I say, easing her back onto her pillow. "We got it covered, all right? I'll send Willow over to help out. You just rest."

She nods, her eyes closing again as she relaxes into her pillow. "I cooked all night."

"I saw."

"I made a mess."

"That's okay. We'll get it cleaned up." I brush my hand down her cheek one more time.

"I'm a mess," she whispers.

My heart shifts and stretches, a sharp ache turning into a sudden heat that spreads through my torso, then out to the tips of my fingers and toes.

So this is what it feels like—this sudden certainty that I would do anything—*anything*—for this woman.

I swear under my breath and let out a chuckle.

Even move to California.

A tightness fills my chest at the thought of leaving Hawthorne—of leaving the farm, my family, the mountains. But one look at Tatum, and I know she's worth it.

I'd do it. I'd leave it all behind.

I lean down and kiss Tatum's cheek just beside her eye. "You're my mess," I whisper.

She reaches up and catches my hand, pulling it to her chest. "Lennox, I love you."

Another wave of warmth washes over me. "I love you, too. Now rest."

I take Toby outside for a quick walk, then return him to Tatum's apartment, pausing inside the open doorway. I crouch down so we're eye to eye, my hands on either side of his fluffy head. "We're in this together now, all right? We've got to take care of her together."

I unhook his leash, and he makes a beeline for the bedroom. The door is open just enough for me to see him jump onto the bed and snuggle in next to Tatum. "Good boy," I say under my breath.

I don't know what's going to happen next. But she loves me, and I love her, and we'll figure it out together.

My confidence lasts until Christopher Elliott shows up at Stonebrook Farm.

"What do you mean, he's outside?" I say as I stalk toward the dining room, buttoning up my chef's coat as I go.

"I mean exactly that. Christopher Elliott is *outside*. Standing in the parking lot, talking on his phone," Zach says. "What else could I mean?"

"But *why* is he outside? Has anybody talked to him?"

"Not so far. He has people with him. Business-y people, but nobody has tried to come in or knocked on the door or anything."

I pause before we reach the front door. Tatum is in no condition to see or interact with her father right now and protecting her is my first concern.

Most of the catering staff should be up at the farmhouse by now, serving hors d'oeuvres at a cocktail party at the farmhouse, but if there's anyone around who might inadvertently reveal that Tatum is sleeping upstairs, I'd prefer they be warned into silence.

I turn to Zach, grateful that he's here, again, willing to help however I need him. "Listen. As far as Christopher Elliott is concerned, Tatum is *not* on the premises. At least not until I can warn her he's here and find out what she wants to do. Can you make sure everyone understands?"

He nods. "Yep. Got it."

I run a hand across my face, wishing I'd taken the time this morning to trim my beard. After last night, I don't particularly care for Christopher Elliott's good opinion as a *chef,* but I am in love with his daughter. And that's a better reason than any to make a good impression on the man.

I take a fortifying breath, then unlock the front door and push it open.

"Mr. Elliott?" I step outside and let the door fall closed behind me. The azaleas beside the entrance are fully in bloom, and the air is warm and comfortable.

Tatum's father turns around. "Ah. Hello." He smiles, his straight, white teeth a nearly blinding contrast to his tan skin. His blue-gray eyes—Tatum's eyes—are warm and friendly as he takes me in.

I extend my hand. "Lennox Hawthorne." He might remember meeting me back in culinary school, but I'd rather not assume.

His eyes lift to the restaurant name stretching across the sign above the door. "Ah. This is your restaurant?"

"It is. We aren't open yet, but I'm guessing you're here to see Tatum?"

"To *surprise* Tatum," he says.

I manage a smile. "Ah, that's great. She's not actually here right now though. She wasn't feeling well this morning and didn't come into work." I move to the restaurant door. "Do you want to come in? Have a drink? I can check in with Tatum and see when she might be well enough to see you."

He smiles tightly, and I get the sense he doesn't like my suggestion, but he follows me inside anyway, his little entourage of people coming in behind us. Mr. Elliott makes no move to introduce the people with him, which strikes me as a bit pretentious. It makes me appreciate Flint. My brother is more famous than this guy, and he always travels with an army of people. But he makes sure we know who they are, where they're from, and why they matter to him.

Mr. Elliott stops by the hostess stand. "I was under the impression that Tatum lives *here*. Upstairs, I believe? Above her kitchen?"

"Yes," I say slowly. "That's true."

He lifts his hands in an expectant gesture. "Maybe I could go see her at home then? You only need to point me in the right direction."

"Sir, I know you're probably very anxious to see her, but she had a long night. She's resting. I don't think she'd want to be disturbed."

He lifts an eyebrow. "You seem awfully familiar with my daughter's well-being, Mr. Hawthorne."

He looks me up and down with a cool, calculating gaze, and every muscle in my body tightens. I don't know exactly what Tatum has or hasn't told her father about our relationship, but instinct is telling me to give this man as little information as possible.

"You know what? What if you text her? Let her know you're here? Then she can come down when she's ready." I glance at the bar where my bartender, Cassandra, is unloading a new shipment of wine. "In the meantime, you're welcome to make yourself at home. Have a drink on me. I could even bring out a few appetizers if you're hungry."

Mr. Elliott's jaw tightens, his gaze growing more shrewd.

I fold my arms over my chest, but I don't break eye contact.

I will not kowtow to this man, not when it feels like doing so would be like throwing Tatum to the wolves.

He finally blinks and offers a thin-lipped smile. "How generous."

I turn and step away, but then Mr. Elliott clears

his throat, and I swing around to face him one more time.

"If it's all right with you," he says, "we do have some business to conduct. Would you mind if we take over one of your tables? It's just some paperwork for Tatum to sign. It shouldn't take long."

I swallow against the knot in my throat, forcing my brain to be reasonable, to focus on the facts.

Number one? Tatum loves me.

Two, her father has a long history of both gaslighting and manipulating Tatum. Showing up with paperwork hoping to pressure her into signing is well within the realm of expected behavior.

Three, if Tatum *does* want to sign on to do a television show with her dad, if she truly believes it will make her happy, I won't stand in her way.

"Absolutely," I say, managing a smile. "Whatever you need."

I push into my kitchen to find my staff hovering around the door, completely oblivious to the storm clouds brewing in my chest. They quickly follow me, crowding around my office and firing off question after question.

"What's he like?"

"Is he going to eat here?"

"Did you shake his hand?"

"Was it so amazing?"

I lift my hands, silencing their many questions.

"That's enough," I say, my voice measured and controlled. "Back to work. That man is not here to see you or meet you or have anything to do with you."

"Yeah but, while he's here, he could probably sign my cookbook," Zach says.

"Or one of the menus," Derek adds.

"Or my chef's coat," Willow says.

I force a smile, even if I don't feel like it. "There will be no signing of anything, at least not while you're on the clock. What you do on your own time is up to you. But let's all remember that Christopher Elliott is here as *Tatum's* father, and first and foremost, our actions should respect her privacy."

"Dude. Tatum's father is Christopher Elliott?" Derek says from the back of the kitchen.

Willow reaches over and hits him on the back of the head. "Honestly, what planet do you live on?"

"The one where dinner service starts in forty-two minutes," I say. "Don't make me ask you again. Back to work."

Zach claps his hand. "You heard him. Clock's ticking. I want to see mise en place in every corner of this kitchen." He looks at me. "Are you good?"

I clasp a hand around the back of my neck. "I uh—yeah, do you think you can send a couple of starters out?"

"Yeah. Absolutely."

I nod. "Also, I think I need to step out for a minute. Can you handle things for a bit?"

He nods. "Of course. Take your time. Take the whole night off if you want. I've got this."

I don't hesitate to leave him because he *does* have it. The last month of training has really elevated the way my kitchen operates, and that's all thanks to Tatum.

When I make it to the back door, Tatum is just coming down the steps. She isn't dressed for work, which makes me grateful, but I still wish she'd stayed upstairs a little longer, if only to make her father squirm for a while. Her eyes widen the second she sees me. "Hey! Are you okay?"

"Um." I shake my head, trying to orient myself to her presence. "Tatum, your father is in the Hawthorne dining room."

Her face blanches. "What?"

I nod. "He came to surprise you."

"He's here," she says softly, her eyes darting in every direction. *"Here."* She presses a hand to her stomach and shakes her head. "Ohh, Lennox, I don't like this surprise."

I reach out and place my hands on her shoulders, squeezing them gently. "He also has some paperwork." I fight to keep my tone neutral. "He said you're ready to sign."

"What? No, that's not—Lennox, I didn't ask

him to come here. I swear I didn't. I don't want to sign *anything*."

A sense of relief pulses through me, but this moment isn't about me. It isn't even about us. "I believe you," I say, my tone as neutral as I can manage.

Tatum's breathing slows and steadies. "I've got to go talk to him, don't I?"

"I think you do."

If she asks me, I'll stay right here beside her. Hold her hand while she faces her father, squeeze her fingers if she starts to waver. But something tells me Tatum needs to fight this battle on her own.

I hope there will be a thousand decisions we make together. A thousand compromises. A thousand sacrifices that I make for her or she makes for me.

But this choice has to be Tatum's and Tatum's alone.

She needs to own it so she knows that she can. She can make choices independent of her father, but she can also make them independent of *me*.

She studies me for a long moment, her brow furrowed. "Are you leaving?"

I look at her, my expression pleading, willing her to understand. "Just taking a walk."

But ask me to stay. Ask me, and I'll be right beside you.

Her eyes are full of questions, and for a brief

moment, I think she might waver, but then she nods and pulls her shoulders back. "I've got this," she says.

I offer her a small smile, pride swelling in my chest. "Atta girl."

I slide my hands down her arms, stopping to give her fingers one more quick squeeze.

Then I let her go.

I push through the back door, my long stride quickly carrying me across the parking lot. I hate that I'm leaving her. But I love that I'm leaving her, too.

"Lennox?"

I turn and see her standing on the loading dock, her expression clear, her eyes blazing. The sight of her takes my breath away. She's so beautiful—so achingly, stunningly beautiful.

"I'll find you," she says.

Warmth spreads across my chest, and I lift a hand, pressing it against my heart.

"I know you will."

CHAPTER TWENTY-FOUR
Tatum

It's all I can do not to run after Lennox, but I understood the words he wasn't saying out loud.

I need to do this on my own.

On my way to the Hawthorne dining room, I take a quick detour into my office to grab Mom's notebook. It'll help for practical reasons during the conversation I need to have with my father, but there's a part of me that just wants to have it with me, too. I look down at the worn cover, my mother's handwriting curling across the top right corner. She only wrote three words, all in French, but they weren't hard to translate. *Recipes. Journeys. Stories.* I press the notebook against my chest, a sense of warmth spreading through me.

You've got this, Tatum.

The words pulse in my brain—Lennox's words—except this time, it's my mother's voice saying them.

I smile. Maybe I don't have to do this *completely* on my own.

Dad isn't alone in the dining room. He has an entire entourage with him, which shouldn't surprise me, but it does take a moment for me to reframe my expectations. I recognize his personal assistant and his manager, but the other three people are strangers.

Being honest with him will be slightly more difficult with an audience, but it's too late to back down now.

"Dad," I say as I cross the dining room.

His eyes brighten when he sees me, and he stands up to pull me into a stiff hug. "Feeling better? Your friend said you were under the weather."

"Much better. Thanks for asking." I step back, my grip on Mom's notebook tightening. "I can't believe you're here."

"Yes, it's a very long way to come," he says pointedly, as if it's my fault he's here. He motions to the table behind him, where there are several stacks of paper and half a dozen pens spread out across the tablecloth. "Care to sit?"

"Actually, can we talk for a second?" I reach out and take his elbow, steering him a few feet away. We still won't be having a private conversation, but it's better than being *at* the table with a bunch of strangers.

Dad clears his throat. "So," he says brightly. "Have you given our situation any more thought?"

Our situation. Six months ago, I wouldn't have flinched at his word choice, but today, it feels fifty shades of wrong.

"*Your* situation, Dad," I amend, my tone cool. "It's your situation."

His lips press into a thin line. "How very generous of you to pin all of this on me."

Ohhh, give me strength, Mom. "It's your career, Dad," I say. "I'm not responsible for your career."

"Tatum," he says, his tone patronizing. "Be reasonable. These people came all this way. They're expecting you to sign."

I take a deep, cleansing breath. "I'm sorry they came all this way, but I didn't ask you to bring them. You asked me to think about the offer, and I did. I don't want it. My answer is no."

He reaches for me, his jaw tightening, and wraps a hand around my arm. "You don't understand what you're throwing away," he says through clenched teeth.

I shrug out of his grasp. "I understand exactly what I'm throwing away. But I don't think you do. If you aren't careful, you're going to lose more than just your working relationship with your daughter. You won't treat me like this, Dad. Not anymore."

He frowns, fire flashing in his eyes. He lifts a warning finger. "You're being unreasonable."

"Like Mom was unreasonable? Is that what you told her after you went on national television and told her stories like they were yours?"

Stories, not just recipes. That's what finally nudged me over the edge. Dad didn't just take

Mom's recipes, in the earliest days of his show, he told her stories. Claimed her ancestors. Talked like he was the one who learned how to make ratatouille in her grandfather's kitchen.

I drop the notebook onto the table beside us. "I have them all, Dad. All her stories. All her recipes. How could you do this to her?"

I expect vitriol. Anger. But Dad's shoulders drop, his face falling, and for a moment, I see a flash of heartache—of anguish—in his eyes. It's the most real I've ever seen my father look, and it hits me all the way to my core.

The emotion in Dad's eyes is gone as quickly as it arrived, masked behind his perfect, tv-ready face. "I didn't do anything to her," he says, but his voice has lost its conviction. He sounds more like he's reciting lines than saying something he actually believes. "Your mother had a gift, yes. But she didn't want to use it. She filled her notebooks, told her stories, but for whom? What was it accomplishing? I refused to let all those recipes go to waste, and she finally agreed to let me use them. That's really all there is to the story. And I'd say it worked out pretty well for all of us."

Mom finally agreed. I at least believe this much of his story. After the months of pressure I've gotten from Dad, it isn't hard to imagine Mom eventually cracking, too.

"You think it worked out well for Mom?" I

say. "You used her, Dad." I square my shoulders. "And she left our family over it. I won't let you do the same thing to me."

Dad is silent for a long time—long enough for me to study his features and recognize how tired he looks. His eyes are rimmed with red, and the creases on either side of his face seem deeper than they did the last time I saw him.

He's desperate. I recognize that much. And he's being irrational.

Hopefully, someday, he'll see it too, and we can come back from this.

I step forward and lift a hand to his arm. "Daddy, you don't have to do this either. So what if they don't sign your show? It was a good run. Maybe it'll give you the chance to slow down a little, relax for once. There's more to it, you know. To life."

His shoulders finally drop, some of the fire leaching out of his voice. "So I came all this way for you to tell me I ought to retire?"

I shrug. "You can see it that way if you want. Or, you could say you came all this way to see your daughter, meet the man she's fallen in love with, and have an incredible dinner at an amazing restaurant."

His eyes lift to mine, a question in their depths. "Love?"

I nod. "I'm living *my* life now, Dad. It's a good life, and I'm happy. I'm going to be angry about what you did to Mom for a while. But we're still family. If you're in town tomorrow night, come back and have dinner with me and Lennox. I'd love for you to get to know him. And I'd like for us to part on good terms."

I squeeze his arm once, then turn and walk out the door, a strange sensation filling me as I go.

I'm all the way out in the parking lot before I figure out what it is.

For the first time, maybe in forever, I feel *free*.

I circle the restaurant and sneak back inside long enough to grab Toby and change my shoes.

I know where Lennox is, and I can't get there fast enough.

I'm halfway to the farmhouse, worrying over whether I remember exactly how to find the trail to the ledge when I see Olivia approaching in a Gator. She stops when she reaches me. "Hey. Just the person I was looking for."

I force myself to smile. To be patient when it's the last thing I'm actually feeling. "Hi. What's up?"

"I didn't see you at the reception earlier. I wanted to make sure you were okay."

"Oh. Right. Sorry. I'm so sorry." Until just now, I'd forgotten I even have a job. "Did everything go okay without me?"

"Tatum, relax," Olivia says. "I'm checking on you as a friend. The party was fine. Your sous chef rocked it."

I nod a little too enthusiastically. "Good. That's good. Great."

She eyes me curiously. "But you are *not* great," she says, and my shoulders fall.

"You're right," I say with a shrug. "I'm not. Actually, are you busy right now? Because Lennox is up at the ledge, and I really need to see him."

Her eyes widen. "Ohhh, so this is a *that* kind of a problem. Get in, girl. I'll get you there in no time."

I help Toby into the back, then slide in next to Olivia, keeping hold of the grab bar. I still remember how Olivia drove this thing the first time I rode with her.

We stay silent for most of the drive, but Olivia's expressive features aren't hiding much. By the time we reach the familiar trailhead, I'm almost laughing for how hard she's fighting to keep her mouth closed.

She shifts into park. "Okay. Here you go. You just follow that trail right there."

I nod. "Lennox brought me here once before. I just wasn't sure if I could find the trailhead."

I climb out of the Gator, pausing with both hands resting on the door. "Thanks, Liv. Your help means a lot."

"Of course."

I only make it half a step away before Olivia finally caves. "Gah, Tatum, I can't not ask."

I turn around and smile, like I fully expected her to ask.

Because I *fully* expected her to ask.

"Please just tell me if this is an *'I'm about to break your heart'* conversation or an *'I'm desperately in love with you'* conversation. I just want to modify my expectations. And also know what kind of support Lennox is going to need after."

I chuckle and shake my head. "Liv!" I say on a groan.

"I know. I'm terrible." She shrugs. "But I'm a Hawthorne. This is what we do."

It's what *family* does.

An ache pierces my chest, and a wave of loneliness washes over me. I'm not sure I'll ever have this kind of relationship with my dad. But I can have it with Bree. Maybe even Daniel if I work on it.

And I can have it with Lennox. And with the rest of his family, too.

I look at Olivia and lift my shoulders. "I am definitely, unbelievably, *desperately* in love with your brother."

She squeals and jumps out of the Gator, then runs around to pull me into a hug. "Does this mean you'll stay? More than just a year or two?"

"Maybe not in the catering kitchen," I say. "But with Lennox? I hope so."

"Who cares about catering?" Olivia says. "Now go find your man."

CHAPTER TWENTY-FIVE
Lennox

Toby finds me first, his wet nose dropping onto my shoulder and nuzzling into my neck.

I scratch his ears and turn to look over my shoulder, knowing I'll see Tatum. But she isn't there. I stand up quickly, panic rising. Why would her dog be here without her?

But then she steps into the clearing, like the sun breaking through the clouds, and my panic shifts into relief. Relief—and *yearning*.

She's walking toward me, and I rush forward to meet her, catching her when she throws herself into my arms. For a split second, we are a tangle of arms and hands seeking, touching, reassuring. Then her lips are on mine, her hands lifting to slide over my beard, then down to my chest.

"I did it," she says in between kisses. "I told him." Another kiss. "And I showed him Mom's notebook, and I said he couldn't use me anymore . . ." *Kiss. Kiss. Kiss.* "And I told him I'm in love with you, and my life is really happy . . ." She pauses, a smile stretching across her face. "I really did it."

I kiss her lips, her cheeks, her forehead, the curve of her neck just below her ear. "You did it,"

I repeat. I lean back and grasp her shoulders so I can look into her gray-blue eyes. "I'm so proud of you."

She nudges me playfully. "You're just happy I'm not going anywhere."

I lift my hands to cradle her face. "I would have gone with you, Tatum. I know it's stupid to think you'll stay here just for me. But if you don't want to keep catering, if there's work somewhere else that you *do* want, I'll go with you. We'll figure something out."

She leans back and looks at me like she can't believe the words coming out of my mouth. "You would have followed me all the way to California? Left your home, your family, your livelihood—just to be with me?"

I nod, not even hesitating. "Absolutely."

"But it's *stupid* to think I'd *stay* in Silver Creek just to be with you?" She lifts an eyebrow. "Are you the only one who gets to be the hero, Lennox?"

"It isn't about being the hero. It's about you being happy."

"*You* make me happy," she says, her saucy tone making me think of the battles we used to have over vegetables. "But also, I love it here, too. I would never ask you to leave this place, Len. This is your home. Your life."

"*You're* my life," I whisper, pressing my forehead to hers.

She kisses me long and slow. "Then I'll be your life right here in Silver Creek," she says. "Besides, I've got an idea about a career I can do from anywhere."

"You do?"

She nods, biting her lip like she's almost nervous to tell me. "What would you say if I wanted to be a restaurant consultant?"

I smile wide. "I'd say you're freaking brilliant. That's perfect, Tatum. You'd be amazing."

"Really?"

"Definitely," I say.

"Really, really?"

I laugh. "Tatum, you saved Hawthorne, remember? Yes. Definitely. It's an incredible idea."

She throws her arms around my neck, her body flush against mine as I pick her up in an enormous hug. "I love you, Lennox," she whispers into my ear.

"I love you, too," I say, my voice catching in my throat.

This woman in my arms—it doesn't feel real. *She* doesn't feel real.

But Tatum *freaking* Elliott is my future.

And I couldn't be happier.

After more kissing, more talking, and then more kissing, we head down the trail. It's fully dusk when we reach the orchard, but it isn't too dark to see my family hanging around the trailhead.

My family?

"What in the world?" Tatum says from beside me.

Several Gators are parked off to the side, and Brody is leaning over his portable fire pit, feeding wood into an already steady flame. Olivia and Tyler are sitting in a couple of camp chairs beside the fire, Asher sitting on Tyler's lap. Perry looks like he's playing a game of tag with Lila's son, Jack, and Lila and Kate are lounging on a blanket nearby.

What in the world is right.

Finally, Brody turns and sees us, then lets out an enormous cheer, alerting the rest of the family to our presence. "You're back!" Brody says.

Olivia jumps up and walks over to Tatum. "I swear, I only sent one text message letting everyone know you were up there declaring your love, and it just kind of happened."

I look at Tatum. "You declared your love to my sister before you declared it to me?"

She grimaces as she shrugs. "I needed a ride. I had to give her *some* reason to drive across the farm like a banshee."

Tyler comes over and drops Asher into Olivia's arms. "Olivia doesn't need an actual *reason* to drive across the farm like a banshee. That's just how she drives."

"Don't you know it," Olivia says before leaning up to kiss Tyler on the cheek.

"So, everyone just came out to meet us?" I reach over and lace Tatum's fingers through mine, suddenly feeling a little overwhelmed. The good kind of overwhelmed.

Perry steps up beside me, Jack on his shoulders, and claps me on the back. "You know Brody will use just about any excuse to use his new fancy fire pit."

"It's called a SOLO stove," Brody calls. "It's smokeless."

"But also, we're really happy for you," Olivia says. "Mom and Dad wanted to come, but Dad wasn't feeling super great. They're hoping we can do a family dinner at the restaurant tomorrow. I already checked the schedule, and Tatum's clear if you can cut out of the kitchen for an hour or two."

I look at Tatum, and she nods her approval. "Sounds good to me."

"Daddy, can I meet the dog?" Jack asks from where he's still sitting on Perry's shoulders.

I'm still not used to hearing him call Perry *Daddy,* but Perry doesn't even flinch. "Sure can, kiddo." He looks at Tatum. "Is that all right?"

"Absolutely," Tatum says. "He's very friendly. You can take him for a little walk if you like." She hands the leash over to Jack, who leads Toby over to where his mom is sitting with Kate. Lila immediately smiles, her gasp of delight loud enough for us to hear it all the way across the clearing.

"Oh no," Perry says. "I'm going to have to get him a dog, aren't I?" He moves off toward his family before either of us can respond.

"Come on," Olivia says to me and Tatum. "I brought stuff for smores, and we need to have a serious conversation about our brother, because I'm pretty sure he just put an offer in on a piece of property on the other side of the river." She doesn't wait for us, and I take advantage of the temporary solitude to drape an arm around Tatum's shoulders and tug her close.

"So Flint's really moving home?" Tatum asks.

"I guess so." I give her shoulders a squeeze. "Tatum, I know they can be a lot."

She slips her arms around my waist. "Are you kidding me? Lennox, I love this. I love *them*." She leans up and presses a kiss to my lips.

"But not as much as you love me?" I turn her so she's flush against me, my hands clasped at the small of her back, and she grins.

"Not even close, Lennox Hawthorne. Not even close."

EPILOGUE
Eighteen Months Later

Lennox wakes me up with a trail of kisses down my spine, his breath warm as it brushes against my skin.

Ninety-nine mornings out of a hundred, I'm the one who wakes up first, so this is an indulgence I've never experienced. But lately, it feels like I've been sleeping longer and harder than ever before. Not that I'm complaining.

"I approve," I say sleepily, as I yawn and roll over. "This is a lovely way to wake up. Ten out of ten, would recommend."

Lennox smiles down at me, the early morning sunlight filtering through the window and casting tiny triangles of light across his bare chest. "Good morning, wife."

I grin. "Think I'll ever get used to the sound of that?"

"I hope so." He leans down to kiss me, but it's much too brief for my liking, then he's out of the bed and walking toward the door.

"Where are you going?" I whine.

"To get you coffee," he calls from the hallway. "We've got places to be."

I grab my phone from the nightstand and

snuggle under the covers, feeling justified in staying in bed at least until Lennox returns with coffee.

I scroll through my notifications. My dad's flight is on time, so that's good. He won't make it by the time the picnic starts, but he should be there well before it's over.

Honestly, I'm just grateful he's making the effort to come at all.

It took Dad a little while to come around. He didn't come to dinner the night after I refused to sign his contract, and he spent many months pouting about his *forced* retirement. But in the end, I think even *he* realizes the change was good for him. He flew out for my wedding and even gave Lennox and me a trip to France for our honeymoon.

I was able to visit with my mom's brother and her father—my grandfather—for the first time in years and explore the country with a mind tuned to experiencing it through my mother's eyes instead of mine.

Don't get me wrong. Dad is still . . . well, *Dad*. A little pompous. A lot arrogant. But in small doses, we're doing okay. As long as we never have to work together again, I think we'll manage just fine.

Speaking of work. I pull up the email that just popped up, glancing quickly through the PDFs my latest client sent over. Kitchen layout, menu, and then, in the body of the email, a breakdown of staff.

I'm less than a year into this new gig of mine, so all of this still feels very new and overwhelming. But it's also challenging in all the ways I want, tapping into my strengths and satisfying me far more than cooking ever did.

Maybe that's something most chefs wouldn't want to admit. But there's something magical about finding exactly what makes me tick and embracing it. I don't have to be what anyone else believes I should be. It only matters what I want to be.

"Your coffee, my very lazy darling," Lennox says, holding out my mug.

I sit up and take it, wrapping my fingers around the warm ceramic. I sigh. "You're my favorite today."

"But not every day?"

As if on cue, Toby jumps onto the bed and flops onto my lap. I lean back onto the headboard, Toby leaning with me, and grin at my husband.

"Okay, I see how it is." He moves into the bathroom and turns on the shower. "Come on. I need to get meat in the smoker by ten if it's going to be ready on time."

"It's always about the food with you, huh?" I joke, following behind him. I take a sip of the coffee and frown. "Did you do something different to the coffee?" I ask. I take another small sip. It doesn't taste *bad,* necessarily. It just tastes different.

"Made it just like normal," Lennox calls. "Are you showering? I don't want to be late."

"The party doesn't start until two," I call, stifling another yawn.

"But the meat!" he calls back.

I smile into my coffee, sensing that Lennox's anxiety has a lot more to do with those *attending* this particular party than it does his responsibility to feed everyone.

Lennox has told me about the occasional opportunity he's had to meet high-profile celebrities through his brother. But the guest list of today's housewarming party for Flint reads like a guide to who's who on Hollywood's A-list. It's a private party. No press, and Flint only expected a handful of his friends and associates to travel across the country to attend. But apparently, nearly every single person whom Flint invited jumped at the chance to come see the secluded house he's built for himself in the mountains of North Carolina.

Even I'm feeling a little star struck, and I grew up in Hollywood Hills.

An hour later, Flint greets us at the door of his stunningly perfect home. Vaulted ceilings, long range view of the mountains, a kitchen that makes me want to weep with envy. It's ridiculously extravagant, but somehow still comes across as understated. Earthy tones, comfortable fabrics. It's the kind of house where you feel like you can rest your feet on the coffee table without offending anyone.

"Tatum!" Flint says, pulling me into a hug. "Good to see you again."

I am fully and completely dedicated to Team Lennox as far as the Hawthorne brothers are concerned. He's definitely the most handsome, the most charming, and he feeds me, which, the discussion can really end right there.

But I'm not blind to the magnetic star power of the youngest Hawthorne brother. With his dark hair and those broody eyes he shares with Perry—I'm just saying. It's not a wonder the world is obsessed with him.

Flint hugs Lennox next. "So glad you guys are here. Also, just a heads up? The Hemsworth brothers are in the kitchen. And Harry Styles is outside in the pool."

"Wait, what? Are you being serious?" I peer over his shoulder toward the large living room windows that look over the pool and the mountains beyond.

"Nah," Flint says with an easy grin. "It's too cold to swim."

He turns and heads toward the kitchen. "Come on back. I've got the smoker warmed up and ready just like you asked."

I grab Lennox's arm. "Wait. Does that mean Harry Styles *isn't* at this party right now?"

Lennox chuckles and leans down for a quick kiss. "Nah," he says, mimicking Flint's tone. "The party hasn't started yet."

"Lennox!" I whisper yell at his retreating form. "That's not even an answer!"

He lifts a hand, waving over his shoulder as he turns the corner and disappears, leaving me in the foyer with exactly zero information about Harry Styles. "I love you when you're flustered!" he calls, and I roll my eyes.

I'm halfway to the living room to look for Harry when Lila and Kate appear in front of me, tugging me around the corner and down the hall to a guest bedroom. They stop outside the closed bedroom door. "Hi. Sorry for the ambush," Lila says. "We have a surprise for you."

"Is it Harry Styles?" I ask.

Kate frowns. "No. But I heard he's out by the pool."

"But it's better than Harry Styles," Lila says. She reaches for my hand. "Come on. You have to close your eyes."

A surge of love fills my chest as I yield control to my sisters-in-law. These women, and Olivia, too, have become my closest friends over the past eighteen months. We've bonded over Kate's struggle with unexplained infertility and her subsequent pregnancy success through intrauterine insemination. She's four months along now and is finally through the worst of her morning sickness.

We rallied around Lila when she lost her grandmother and took turns watching Jack when she and Perry spent a week moving her grandfather into their guest room.

We were all in the delivery room when Olivia had her second baby when Asher was only eighteen months old—way earlier than she and Tyler had originally planned.

But mostly, we just do a lot of laughing. Texting. Joking about small town life in Silver Creek married to men as intense as the Hawthornes. I know these women, and they know me. And that's a pretty amazing feeling.

The door cracks open, and Olivia pops her head out. "Are her eyes closed?"

I lift my hands to my face and cover my eyes all the way. "They're closed! I promise!"

"Okay," Olivia says. "Take four steps forward." One of them—I can't tell who—grips my shoulders and turns me a different direction. "Okay. Now open your eyes," Kate says from directly behind me.

I open my eyes and immediately scream. Bree is standing in front of me.

Here. At Flint's house.

Tears immediately fill my eyes. I haven't seen her since the wedding.

I rush forward and pull her into a hug. "Oh my gosh! What are you doing here?"

"Are you kidding? The Hemsworth brothers are here. I'd have crawled naked to be here if I had to."

"But the twins—where are your girls?"

"With their father. He'll probably be certifiable by the time I make it home, but they'll be fine." She smiles wide. "You've got me for the whole weekend!"

My eyes fall on Olivia, immediately guessing that she's the mastermind behind this particular surprise. "You did this?"

She shrugs. "The party felt like a good excuse."

"But also, we have an ulterior motive," Kate says.

Lila pulls out a little stool sitting in front of a gorgeous vanity and motions for me to come over. "Come sit," she says gently.

"What is this? What's happening? And why do I feel like you're all having a conversation that I'm not a part of?"

"Just sit and we'll explain," Bree says.

"Wait, you're in on this too? Where's Lennox? I feel like I need someone on my team." Despite my protests, I sit on the stool anyway, a part of me enjoying all this if only because these women obviously care about me, and it's fun to bask in their attention.

Once I'm sitting, the four of them sit in a row

along the foot of the bed. "Tatum," Lila says, her soft Southern voice soothing, "this is an intervention."

"What? Why? What am I doing?"

Kate leans forward and squeezes my hand. "Sweetie, we think you're pregnant."

I immediately scoff, tugging my hand back like Kate's is on fire. "What? That's ridiculous."

"You're tired all the time," Olivia says.

"You fell asleep on the phone the other day," Bree says. "Mid-sentence."

"You also threw up the other morning, and you've been complaining about nausea."

"It's because my birth control makes me queasy."

"Does that explain why you haven't had a period?" Olivia says.

"How do you know I missed a period?"

"You told us at lunch the other day," Lila says.

I think back to the conversation. "Right, but that's also my birth control. It's messed up my cycles. I haven't had a period since the wedding."

They glare at me with matching dubious expressions. "It's been three months, Tatum," Bree says. "You've gone *three months* with no period?"

I shake my head, still not ready to cave completely. "*Barely* three months. But the doctor said the birth control might make my periods lighter. I guess I just thought . . . but how could this even happen? I never missed a dose."

"Yeah. It doesn't always work," Bree says.

"Asher was totally a condom baby," Olivia says. "We'd only been married three months."

"*We've* only been married three months," I say, panic edging my voice.

"Hey," Kate says, reaching out to squeeze my knee. "That doesn't matter. You and Lennox are solid. Besides—it might be fun if we have babies at the same time."

"Do your boobs feel heavier?" Lila asks. "That was the first thing I noticed when I was pregnant with Jack."

"Boobs are definitely first," Olivia agrees.

I look down at my boobs. They maybe *have* felt a little heavier lately. "Oh gosh." I press a hand to my midsection, suddenly feeling a little queasy. "I don't feel so good."

"Just breathe," Lila says, her smile wide. "You're fine. It's going to be okay."

"Okay. Time to take the test," Olivia says. "It's on the bathroom counter ready for you."

Bree tugs me to my feet and ushers me toward the bathroom.

I look at my older sister over my shoulder. "Did you seriously fly all the way out here just to make me take a pregnancy test?"

"I flew all the way out here because Olivia said I could meet the Hemsworth brothers." She nudges me into the bathroom. "But making you take a pregnancy test definitely feels like a fun bonus."

I pause in the bathroom doorway. "Okay. I'll be right back, I guess."

Instead of opening the bathroom door as soon as I'm finished, I opt for solitude while I wait for the test to fully process. Of course, I'll tell my sisters either way, but having been blindsided and shepherded into this experience with zero warning, I'm feeling a need to wrench back a little control and handle this part alone.

I lean on the counter, my hands braced against the sink as I watch two tiny pink lines appear on the test.

Pregnant.

I'm truly, actually pregnant.

I slowly open the bathroom door, but the room is empty, the bedroom door open into the hall.

For real? They all abandoned me to process this news on my own?

But then footsteps sound down the hall, and Lennox appears. "Hey," he says, pausing in the bedroom doorway. "Liv said you needed me. You okay?"

I almost start to laugh. They must have been really certain the test would be positive to have already gotten Lennox. Or maybe Bree caught sight of a Hemsworth, and they all bailed for something more entertaining than me. Either way, I'm glad Lennox will be the first person to find out.

I stare at my husband for a long moment.

He's so achingly perfect. Physically beautiful, yes. But also kind and funny and gentle and brilliant and everything I would ever want the father of my children to be.

"I'm okay," I say softly, my lips lifting into a smile. "But you might wanna sit down."

He frowns as he moves into the room and sits down across from me.

"Lennox," I say, a slight tremor in my voice. "We're having a baby."

His face pales. "We?" He clears his throat. "As in you and me?"

I smile and let out a little laugh. "Yeah, baby. You and me."

I suddenly wish I could read the thoughts flashing through my husband's brain. He might be panicking, but knowing him, he could also be coming up with recipes for homemade baby food.

"So your birth control didn't work," he says like he's stating a fact instead of asking a question.

"Nope."

"And now we're having a baby."

I bite my lip. "Yep."

He stands up and takes my face in his hands. "Tatum, are you happy?"

Lennox would ask this question first. He doesn't know how to think about himself if he hasn't made sure I'm happy first.

I nod, finally surrendering to the tears that have been threatening since the test first showed up positive. "I'm happy, Len. I mean, I'm terrified, but I'm definitely happy."

He kisses me soundly, then his face breaks out in the biggest, most beautiful smile. "This is why you've been sleeping so much," he says.

"It totally is. And I'll accept your apology for calling me lazy whenever you're ready to give it."

He tugs me down on the bed beside him, his hand shifting to my stomach. "How are you feeling? Are you tired right now?"

"I'm fine," I say gently, though his concern for me is doing very happy things to my heart. "I'm great, even. A little tired, sure. But I feel good." I take a steadying breath. "Are *you* happy?"

He picks up my hand, squeezing it as he wraps it between his. "To watch you turn into a mother?" He shakes his head. "I'm going to love every minute of this."

He kisses me again, this one touched with fervency and a tiny bit of heat. I lean into it, savoring the feel of him, loving that I belong to him, and he belongs to me. That, alone, is more than I ever dreamed of, but to think of a tiny human who will belong to us both? My heart nearly bursts at the thought.

Lennox breaks the kiss and leans back the slightest bit. "You promise you're okay? You're happy about this?"

I nod, smiling up at him. "The happiest."

"Really? This is it? There are no more levels of happy available to you?"

"Nope. This is the top. I am maxed out happy."

He nods and claps his hands against his thighs. "In that case, let me go tell Harry Styles you don't actually want to meet him."

I gasp. "Lennox Hawthorne, you better not be joking."

He stands and holds out his hand, his eyes bright with love. "Come and find out."

I slip my hand into his, relishing his strong grip, and let him lead me from the room.

Meeting Harry Styles is definitely a memory I'll always cherish.

But at the end of the night, when I climb into bed and settle into Lennox's arms, he's the one I think of as I drift off to sleep.

My maxed out, top level of happy.

Lennox *freaking* Hawthorne.

Thousands of chefs in America, but I fell in love with *him*.

• • •

For access to exclusive bonus content, including Lennox and Tatum's proposal and wedding, visit www.jennyproctor.com.

ACKNOWLEDGMENTS

Thanks for reading, friends. I truly love spending time with the Hawthorne family on Stonebrook Farm, and writing Lennox and Tatum's story was no exception, even if I WAS hungry the entire time I was drafting. I did a lot of research about what it means to be a chef, and about the many challenges of running your own restaurant. I was stressed just doing the research, so I finished this book extra grateful for all the people who make a career out of creating beautiful food. I love to eat, so THANK YOU!

A note about Toby the goldendoodle—Toby was based on MY goldendoodle . . . whose name also happens to be Toby. Okay, fine. Tatum's Toby isn't just based on my dog. He actually IS my dog. Same personality. Same ability to give hugs. I've had a few people mention that they thought goldendoodles had to be golden in color, but that isn't the case! Since a goldendoodle is a cross between a golden retriever and a poodle, there are a lot of color combinations that are possible. Tatum's Toby (and my Toby) is considered a "parti" doodle—meaning he's fifty percent black and fifty percent white. It's one of the rarest color combinations, but it's absolutely possible! I love to post pictures of Toby on my Instagram account, @jennyproctorbooks, if you'd like to get a visual of what Toby looks like in real life!

Kirsten, I needed SO. MUCH. HAND HOLDING with this book, and I'm so grateful that you were willing to slog through so many reads to help me get the story to where it needed to be. Thank you for challenging me to push harder, to dig deeper and to give the story "FREAKING MOE" wherever it needs it. I'm so glad to have you on my team as a critique partner, but even more as an incredible friend!

Becca, THANK YOU for cheering me on, for beta reading in record time and for listening when I needed to talk through questions and concerns. You mean the world to me! Lori, your proofreading prowess and speed is so appreciated! THANK YOU for rising to the challenge and reading for me so quickly! So happy to have you on my team!

And my family . . . especially my ever stalwart and patient husband. This job is hard. The hours are ridiculous. I turn into a functionless ball of stress every time a book releases. I even forget how to eat normal food. Thank you for rolling with it like it's no big deal, for walking the dog when I can't, for letting me sleep when I don't crawl into bed until 7:15 a.m. Josh, I love you. You are the inspiration for every hero I write!

ABOUT THE AUTHOR

Jenny Proctor grew up in the mountains of North Carolina, a place she still believes is one of the loveliest on earth. She lives a few hours south of the mountains now, in the Lowcountry of South Carolina. Mild winters and, of course, the beach, are lovely compromises for having had to leave the mountains.

Ages ago, she studied English at Brigham Young University. She works full-time as an author of sweet romantic comedy.

Jenny and her husband, Josh, have six children, and almost as many pets. They love to hike and camp as a family and take long walks through the neighborhood. But Jenny also loves curling up with a good book, watching movies, and eating food that, when she's lucky, she didn't have to cook herself. You can learn more about Jenny and her books at www.jennyproctor.com.

Center Point Large Print
600 Brooks Road / PO Box 1
Thorndike, ME 04986-0001 USA

(207) 568-3717

US & Canada:
1 800 929-9108
www.centerpointlargeprint.com